RACHAEL'S JOURNEY

RACHAEL'S JOURNEY

CATHERINE ANNE

ISBN: 9798738530098

DEDICATED TO BETH NOTARO...
THE FIRST OF US TO TASTE HEAVEN!

CHARACTERS FROM TARA'S JOURNAL

THE ANGELS

THE ARCHANGEL MICHAEL

This angel is the great Defender of the Father. He is the ArchAngel who threw Satan and all the other fallen angels out of Heaven and into the depths of Hell. There is no stronger angel in all the world. He is the devil's nemesis.

MITKA

He hails from the choir of POWERS. He is the protector of the Holy Land and any other place the Lamb graced with HIS presence. He carries the Sword of Honor. He never loses a battle with the demons. He stands 15 feet tall, has black hair and intense green eyes. He is the leader of the three Angel Generals both in this story and in Tara's Journal.

SYREE

This angel is one of the ten thousand angels that protected the Queen of Heaven, Mary, Jesus' Mother, during HER life. He hails from the choir of VIRTUES, sometimes referred to as the "Shining Ones." He is gentle and kind and his beauty is legendary. He has pure white hair but has the face of a youth. He is a protector to all humans who are consecrated to the Blessed Mother Mary.

TEZRA

This angel is the sole Prince of the entire Animal Kingdom. He hails from the choir of PRINCIPALITIES. He is the most unique angel in appearance of all the angels. He is joyful and child-like but can be fierce in battle. He has been involved with every animal mentioned in the bible. He can enter any animal at any time and control their behavior. He can speak to any animal and direct it.

THE GUARDIAN ANGELS

These angels protect one human from their conception until their death and into their eternity. Every human being has one, but most people spend their lives ignoring their personal Divine being.

THE DEMONS

SATAN, LUCIFER, the BEAST, the TRAITOR

He was the first angel created. He became prideful when God showed the angels the creation of Man. He refused to serve a creature who was not Divine. His biggest enemy is Mary, the Mother of Jesus, and he has hated Her from the moment Her sign appeared in the Heavens. (REVELATIONS chapter 12…The Woman and the Dragon.) He is the Prince of Darkness and the Father of Lies and he rules Hell and Earth and will until Jesus returns.

BENE'T

This demon is a fallen angel. He is the second in command in Hell. He is the brother of the angel Syree and they are both from the choir of VIRTUES. He was the first angel to believe in Satan's rebellion. He is the only demon whose mind Satan can't read. He had a change of heart and wished he hadn't agreed to the rebellion.

RAHOUL

This demon hates humanity almost as much as Satan hates humanity. He rejoices in humans who are in pain. He was one of the demons who possessed the body of one of the six men who scourged Jesus. He is in charge of the "Machine Cavern" in Hell. This is a machine that transforms humans after they go to Hell, if their sin was Vanity. He wants to stay in Hell and doesn't like to go up to the earth.

DEMONS OF EMOTIONS

These are the demons who are their name ie; ANGER, PRIDE, HOPE-LESSNESS, ANXIETY, LUST, JEALOUSY, DESPAIR. FRUSTRATION, DEPRESSION, and SLOTH, to name a few.

THE HUMANS

JACOB

He is a man who started out selfish and had many sinful ways, but had a complete conversion because of his love interest, Madison. He has a gift with animals and can train any kind of animal. He rarely speaks and is intimidating to most men. He has a reputation as a fighter.

MADISON

She is a woman with many gifts of the Holy Spirit, the main one being the Gift of Discernment. This is the ability to see spirits whether they are angels, demons or souls. She is a strong Catholic whose whole life revolves around Jesus. She is the mother of Maria and Rachael.

MARIA

She has the strongest supernatural gifts of anyone. She has no fear of demons and it is impossible to scare her. She is very brave. She was kidnapped by Natash, the head of the satanic cult in Tara's Journal.

RACHAEL

She is the child of Jacob and Madison. She is sick with a mysterious disease. She is in constant pain.

TARA

She was the childhood friend of Madison. She was a reporter for Time Magazine who went undercover to infiltrate a Satanic Cult. She kept a journal where she recorded everything that happened. She did this in the form of letters to her brother, Matthew. She was an atheist who had a conversion before she was murdered.

MATTHEW

He is the brother of Tara. He is a successful business owner in New York City. He is an atheist. He was involved in saving Maria when she was kidnapped by Natash.

FATHER ZACHARY

He is a Holy priest who has taken his vows of the Priesthood seriously. He has taken the vow of poverty and is completely dependent on God. He is Madison's spiritual director. He has many gifts of the Holy Spirit. He is the brother of the satanist, Natash.

NATASH

He was the head of the Satanic cult and the brother of the priest, Father Zachary. He looked forward to reigning with Satan in Hell. He denied Christ his whole life and chose the devil instead. He was killed.

CILLA

She is the sister of Madison and has many spiritual gifts.

MAX

He is a Saint Bernard. He belongs to Jacob and Madison. He can see all the spirits around the humans in his life. He tries to protect them from the demons. He is often instructed by Tezra.

(FROM TARA'S JOURNAL)

.

"Mommy, I know what her name should be!" Maria said, her eyes never leaving Bene't's.

"Tell me baby, what do you think it should be?"

"It's the most perfect name ever Mommy...let's name her Rachael."

"Rachael," Jacob and Madison said in unison. "I love it sweetheart." Jacob said, kissing Maria's head.

"Me too baby, it's the most perfect name for her."

Bene't stared at Maria and wondered why Heaven would allow this incredible little human to be in his life. She never stopped astonishing him. As he began to ponder that very pertinent question, he was interrupted by the youngest soul in the room.

Rachael let out a blood curdling scream that captured the attention of everyone. Jacob thought something was wrong but then she became totally silent as she lay there looking at the many faces around her.

She made eye contact with every single one of them and she seemed to acknowledge their presence. Just before she took her first earthly nap, she rested her eyes on the only one around them that did not belong.

She didn't cry at the sight of him, instead she stared at him intently. After a few moments, her little eyes fluttered to the back of her head and she smiled as she answered the voice of God that only she could hear.

In her soul was posed a question from the Throne of the Trinity and without hesitation she answered silently...

"Yes Father...I accept your Will."   And then she slept...

PROLOGUE 1

"Please Father, shield mine eyes! Close Thy vision to me. Have Mercy I plead."

God looked at the Angel with a burning fire in His terrible, beautiful face.

"It is My Mercy which demands it continue...Behold."

PROLOGUE 2

Tara sat on an enormous mountain of light. From her perch she could see the Earth and all things therein. She was contemplating her existence in Heaven and all she had experienced since her arrival.

There had been many times after her conversion that she had felt great sadness at the thought of leaving her life on Earth. She had even broached the subject with the priest who had walked her through the journey that led her to give her life to Christ. He had assured her that Heaven would bring her more joy than anything she could experience on Earth and she should never be afraid of the day God would call her home. At the time, the well meaning words of the priest did nothing to quell her melancholy. The leaving behind of all she found beautiful and lovely about her life; her brother Matthew, her job, her relationships with friends and even the amazing scenery that the Earth boasted of seemed far too high a price to give up....but that was before. Before she knew what beauty and loveliness were in their truest form.

Heaven was nothing to fear on any level, just one moment of ecstasy after another. Her body was so perfected and altered that only the angels rivaled it. She knew instantly all that had been, all that would be and could know instantly any questions that formed in her now enlightened mind.

On Earth she had visions of doing nothing but remaining on her knees for all eternity praying...and while it was true that she was in a state of constant prayer and praise to the Trinity; for They were always with her as she lived within Them now, fused back into Them where she had begun... Heaven was much more than that. She was ALIVE in a way that paled to being alive on Earth. And she was active and learning and loving and working.

That was one of the million things that had taken her by surprise. She was working to save souls, except now her power to facilitate that far surpassed any she possessed while she lived on Earth. When she prayed, she immediately found herself in front of the throne of the Most High God and her prayers were instantly heard and answered without delay. When her childhood friend, Madison, would ask for her intercession during prayer, the power of that prayer was stronger because Jesus said, "Whenever two or more of you are gathered in My Name, there shall I be." The enlightened souls of the earth who understood this truth, had wonderful allies in the Heavenly realm. When they asked the assistance of loved ones who had passed, to pray with them. Sadly, many souls on earth didn't understand this and they never thought to ask or to talk to their loved ones, thinking all the while that they were "resting in peace" instead of "thriving in peace", and so they didn't disturb them.

Tara was still waiting for her brother Matthew to understand, but so far he had not spoken once to her. Tara was with him constantly, while at the same time being before the Throne of God as well as being other places, learning and working. That was just another miracle of Heaven; a soul could be many places at once and yet be completely present in each place. Pondering this, Tara spontaneously broke out in a canticle of praise for the wealth of gifts the Trinity showered on the souls that lived with Him in Eternity.

As she praised, she looked back at the earth and it disappeared. In its place was a vast field that encompassed all of her vision. The field was rocky with rough terrain. In the distance she saw something coming toward her. "What could this be?" she asked Jesus, for she lived in Him and He in her so she never experienced a moment without Him.

Jesus put His arm on Tara's shoulder and said "Behold, My children approach."

Tara watched as the 'something' she had seen came closer and closer and she realized they were groups of people. There were millions of them split into three distinct groups. Having the gifted eyes of her Heavenly body, she could see each person clearly and distinctly.

They all stopped in a line until Jesus smiled and said, "Come...My good and faithful servants!"

The first group began to move towards Him and when they did, Tara noticed they were in horrible condition. Some had bullet wounds in their heads, hearts and bodies. Some had axes in their heads. Some had been completely stripped of their skin or were burned or decapitated. Each body seemed to be more mutilated than the next and Tara didn't understand what she was seeing.

"The souls that you see here have given their entire earthly existence to Me, without wavering. They offered their hearts and souls to Me in their infancy and I accepted their sacrificial gift."

Tara looked from Jesus back to the first group and waited for her Savior to speak again.

"These souls are My SEED PLANTERS! They have taken My Word to people and places that did not want them. They have taken the hoe of My truth to plow hardened grounds. Never have they been praised nor loved nor honored for speaking My truths...they have only felt the hot wind of hatred and malice for their obedience to Me. Each of these souls was martyred for Me and suffered unspeakable torture and pain because they spoke of Me. Heaven would be empty if not for souls such as these."

Tara looked again at the maimed group of souls as they approached and was filled with such admiration, love and gratitude for them. She thanked them for the sacrifices they had made for the love of Jesus.

She then focused her attention on the next group of people. While they were not maimed like the first, they were all covered in some dark substance that seemed to make their approach 'snail like.' She waited for Jesus to explain.

"These are MY WATERERS! I send them behind the Seed Planters to confirm My Words. I send them into dark, filthy places to reiterate the words I have uttered. The WATERERS stay entrenched in the mud of sin for as long as I need them to. They stay and they pour the fresh clean water of My truth over the souls who are trapped in filth; and who have killed the Seed Planters who came before them. My WATERERS simply clean and cleanse until they help the soul to their feet and bring them forward in their walk toward Me."

The next group was even slower than the Waterers and some of them were crawling towards the Lord. Tara noticed the most peculiar thing about them though and that was that they were all smiling; beautiful, radiant satisfied smiles. Even though they could barely move and were bogged down by some force Tara didn't comprehend, they were all filled with so much delight.

Jesus raised his hand towards them and said "Rise!" and simultaneously they stood up together.

"These souls are MY HARVESTERS! You witnessed them crawling because when I send to them a soul from the Waterers, they are to stay with that soul until they are safely formed in the security of My Church. This requires them to stop their own life plans at My direction. They put the soul they are guiding first, at all times. They have endless debates and answer questions and fears and this takes over their whole lives. My Harvesters are the final step in a soul finding Me. Even though they exhaust themselves and sometimes everyone around them, they find intense exultation in the exhaustion because in the end, they hand each soul over to Me. There is no greater triumph on Earth than doing the very thing their Savior was sent to do."

Tara smiled back at the Harvesters and thanked them for the work they did for Christ and for giving up their lives for this task.

Suddenly, materializing before them and approaching each soul separately, were their Guardian Angels and all of their loved ones who were living in Heaven. Tara watched as wonder filled each face. She remembered with enormous love the moment her angel and loved ones had greeted her as she entered Heaven. She took Jesus' hand and kissed it. She knew what came next for them and she knew He had to go greet each one and that she would be with Him as He did it because she lived in Him.

Just as she was turning to go, excited to see the ArchAngel Michael once again, she noticed that on the horizon of the field there was more movement. She looked up to Jesus as she could not get a clear vision of them and asked, "Who are they, Lord?"

Jesus looked on the horizon and smiled the sweetest most loving smile she had ever seen animate His face and He said,

"Behold my child, these that come now hold the highest place in Heaven among the Saints; only My Mother is above them. Without these no Seed Planter, Waterer or Harvester would ever exist. They have taken My command to heart......"

Tara was mesmerized at what was materializing before her. These souls were the most beautiful of any souls she had seen since her arrival. Each body was a perfect specimen of humanity, so perfect in fact that they seemed unreal. Their hair and skin had a stunning glow. Their eyes sparkled with light and their teeth were a brilliant white. They were the picture of health like it had never been defined.

They looked like they were related, as if they were from the same family, which was strange considering it was obvious they had different nationalities. Black, white, yellow or red, their skin color mattered not. They had a relationship that transcended their race and it may have been due to what each of them carried on their back.

Tara drew a breath of wonderment as thousands upon thousands of Crosses blanketed the horizon.

CHAPTER ONE......THE WHITE BUFFALO

The guards dragged the woman across the floor by her long, black hair. Her skin, or rather the muscles underneath it, were filled with little pebbles, dirt, puss and blood. The only part of her body that hadn't been in some way mutilated was her face; and there proved to be good reason for that. Although the guard's orders had been to torture every inch of her body, none of them could bring themselves to touch her face.

Unparalleled didn't come close to describing anything about her face. Her beauty wasn't in question. Her eyes were a pine colored green, and inside her pupils there was something unique, given just to her at her birth. Her square jaw and high cheek bones displayed her Native American heritage. Her natural golden bronze skin tone boasted a shade any sun worshiper would envy, Her lips were full and her white teeth were perfectly straight. She was 5 feet 11 inches tall and had the stature of an athlete and the grace of a Queen.

There were others just as beautiful as her in the world but with a difference. She exuded a kind of radiance about her that couldn't be explained, almost an aura that misted around her, imperceptible to the human eye. This made her face take on an ethereal appearance. Because of the powerful glow, the guards were ordered not to look upon her face for any reason. It was rumored that she would cast a spell on anyone that dared to defy the order. Just to be on the safe side, they brought her to the new guards with a black cloth tied cruelly around her head. This way no one could get even a glimpse of her face. As they dragged her along the ground, however, the cloth came undone and that's when the trouble began.

When the guards realized what had happened they deliberated over what to do. Patrick O'Dey, the head guard, knew the responsibility of re-covering her face fell on him. But when they stood her up and he reached to put the cloth on her face, he lacked the power to do it.

He thought that her face would emanate pure evil and hatred, after all, she had not uttered a sound during the long hours of her beating and Patrick thought that all that rage and pain would show on her face; he couldn't have been more wrong. She looked at him instead with heartfelt unconditional love and a touch of pity.

Patrick's mouth dropped open in shock. Taken aback, he forced himself to look away; then remembering his position, uttered an unconvincing order.

"No one must look at her face...and be careful because I can't put this cloth back on her."

The other guards looked at each other with bewilderment. This man who had never uttered a kind word to anyone, who tortured people with an almost twisted sense of pleasure, and whose tone of voice had never been under the octave of a roar, seemed to be affected by this woman's face. He walked with his head down and his shoulders slumped in what appeared to be shame, and he acted like a broken man.

"What did he see?" one guard asked in a horrified whisper.

"Shh, I don't want him to hear us," another guard answered, "This woman must be some kind of freak to have gotten to O'Dey; just follow that order and don't look at her face."

"Don't worry," the first guard replied, "I don't want to see whatever it was he saw."

They moved down a long hallway to what they called the "Ditch." This always proved to be an unnerving experience for all the guards because they would come face to face with each and every criminal they had ever bullied, beaten or abused. The criminals were always in a fit of rage whenever any of the guards appeared. Threats of murder and revenge would be thrown at the guards from every direction. The criminals were so graphic in their descriptions that most of the guards suffered anxiety attacks because of them. This was where they were told to place the woman. She would be left in a cell block with the most perverted and insane men in the country.

The Ditch was the only facility of its kind in the world. It did not appear on any official government list. The funds which built this nearly impervious facility came from a budget so black neither the FBI, nor the CIA had an inkling of its existence. There were of course whispers, but trying to catch hold of the truth behind them was like trying to capture a wisp of smoke. Every now and then, an individual came along who represented a threat beyond the capabilities of the justice system. A fair trial by a jury of their peers, or even a military tribunal was deemed too much of a risk to some near or at the highest circles of power. Just who those people were remained a mystery to O'Day, just as this woman's presence here remained a mystery. This weighed heavily on Patrick. One look at her precious face told him she didn't belong here and his guilt over being the one who beat her with so much brutality, caused him more pain than he had ever felt in his life. By the time they reached the entrance to the Ditch, Patrick had had enough.

"Myers, sign her in and get her settled, I'm feeling...sick," Patrick said with a choked sob. He turned and ran back up the hallway. Everyone watched him until he rounded the corner out of their sight. No one said a word as they stood behind the shackled woman waiting for the door to the Ditch to open.

"Whatcha got?" asked the voice of the guard on the other side of the door. Myers pressed the intercom button and spoke.

"We have a Priority One with a Caution Watch, open up already."

This whole situation was making Myers nervous. Something appeared strange about this prisoner and his desire to be as far away from her as possible became foremost in his mind. The guard opened the door and Myers kicked her through it. The woman fell to the ground and lay still, trying to catch her breath.

"It's a bloody woman!" cried the pit guard.

"No kidding, did you figure that out all by yourself you idiot?" Myers replied sarcastically.

"What is a woman doing here?" the pit guard demanded.

Myers was beginning to get impatient.

"How should I know man? I told you she was a Priority One, other than that I don't know nothing."

"Well why isn't O'Dey here, I thought all PO1's had to be accompanied by him?"

Myers looked coldly at the guard. "Stop asking all these stupid questions and take her! Here's her paperwork." Myers slammed the documents into the guard's hands and turned to leave. As an afterthought he took a step back and stared hard at the guard.

"The brass gave one specific order John, do not...under any circumstances...look at her face. O'Dey did and that's why he's not here. There's something bad wrong with her, she is dangerous."

John Waters watched as Myers and the six other guards walked back up the hallway. He noticed them whispering to each other but they spoke so low that he couldn't make out what they said. He shut and locked the door to the Ditch and stared at the heap of the woman on the ground.

He couldn't believe how badly they had beaten her. He'd never seen another prisoner in this bad of shape. With the multiple wounds upon her body he didn't understand how she had survived. She hadn't moved at all and Waters started to think that she might have died. He reached down to touch her and she stirred. He felt sorry for her. He didn't know why but he couldn't imagine her doing anything that warranted her being in this horrendous place.

"Let me help you up ma'am," he said gently as he carefully touched her arm.

"Thank you," she said in the sweetest voice he had ever heard. He lifted her up as if he were holding a china doll, ever mindful of the enormous pain he knew she must be experiencing.

She made no sound other than some labored breathing. Standing fully erect she stood with her head hanging down and her long black hair covered her face. Waters did not take her into the Ditch. All of his senses screamed that it would be a great injustice if he did. He picked up the phone and called O'Dey's office.

"Get me O'Dey now!" he demanded.

"Mr. O'Dey isn't available Mr. Waters, can anyone else assist you?" The secretary sounded as if she worked in a Four Star hotel instead of in this Hell hole they all called "work."

"Yes you can assist me," he said sarcastically, "You can tell whoever the idiot was that sent this PO down here that he can come place her himself cause I ain't doing it!" The secretary was flustered and told him to hang on. When the hold button was released Waters didn't hear the secretary's voice, instead he heard the voice of Tim Nethers.

"Waters, am I to understand that you are refusing to do your job?"

Waters swallowed hard. He'd only met Tim Nethers once and he didn't want to repeat the experience. Nethers turned out to be the most evil person he had ever laid eyes on. His huge frame, over 6 feet 6 inches and built like a mountain, intimidated all of them in the Ditch. He had black hair which he wore slicked back and he had a goatee. His mouth was set in a cruel line and he filed his teeth to look as if they were pointed, all to add to his daunting appearance. Known to have a very short temper, he killed prisoners without provocation and laughed at anyone in pain. Waters didn't want to be on the receiving end of his anger but after taking another look at the woman, all fear left him.

"That's right Nethers, I ain't doing it. We ain't never had a woman here and I won't be the one to break tradition. If you want her in, you can come down here and do it yourself!"

The phone slammed down and a great crash could be heard several floors above them. Waters knew it was all over. Nethers killed anyone who defied authority and Waters knew he wouldn't be spared. He broke out in a cold sweat. That's when the woman brushed her hair from her face and looked upon him.

"Thank you," she said.

Water's heart began beating wildly. He didn't understand what he was seeing. His eyes locked with hers and he could not look away. Her eyes were a beautiful green. They reminded him of the color of a mossy green pasture. But as brilliant green as they were, that was not the unique feature that had him stunned. In each one, there was a dazzling white shape and as he stepped closer to her to investigate, she lowered her gaze so he couldn't identify the shape. While hoping she would look at him again, he noticed that the glow around the woman seemed palpable. He felt peace surround him. He knew without doubt that when he suffered the wrath of Nethers, it would all be worth it; he had done the right thing. For the first time in his life...he knew he'd done something right.

"You're welcome ma'am," he said as he reached out his hand. She took it into hers and the warmth that filled him felt like a healing balm. He was still holding it when Nethers stormed into the Ditch.

"I hope you're prepared to die!" he spat as he advanced on Waters.

"I am," Waters replied bravely. The woman took a step so that she stood in front of Waters. Nethers lost his composure for a moment and stopped in his tracks.

After a few seconds he recovered and glared at the woman with intense hatred.

"Malaya...so nice to see you again. I see my guards didn't do their job very well, you seem to have some fight left in you," he said with mock politeness.

"It looks like you worked your magic again; I see the hood has been removed. How very clever of you."

Nethers was getting angrier by the moment. Malaya was making him look like a complete fool with her silence. He turned his attention to Waters.

"You made a fatal mistake boy!" he sneered.

Still engulfed in the peace that being around Malaya had given him, Waters also remained silent. This further enraged Nethers. Malaya could feel the demonic power starting to build around him. He was calling on all of his resources to fight her, just as she was doing to fight him.

Nethers reached out to shove Malaya away so he could reach Waters but his hand snapped back to him as if he had touched a flame.

"You will not hurt him, Timothy, not now or ever. My Father forbids it. You will let him leave and it would be to your advantage not to stop him. I think you remember what happens when you try to interfere with the army of my Father." Malaya finished with a bright, victorious smile.

Nether roared out a string of obscenities and then told Waters he could go. Waters couldn't believe what he was hearing. No one had ever challenged Nethers before and lived, but this woman, Malaya, he had called her, had some kind of power that Nethers clearly feared. He couldn't fathom that he would follow her orders and release him.

"Your Father must be a very powerful man," he thought as he looked at Malaya one more time. As he thought this, Malaya turned her head towards him and answered his thought.

"There is none more powerful. He is the only true power. Jesus loves you John, go now and serve him."

She smiled and reached for his hand again. Waters had tears in his eyes as she answered his silent question. Emotions coursing through him, he could only manage a nod as a goodbye.

Malaya turned her attention to Nethers. He stood furiously. Had it been within his power, he would have killed her then and there. The hatred he felt radiated from him even as he tried to hold his body rigidly, his fight for control seemed a losing battle.

Malaya rolled her eyes at his behavior and looking at him with great pity she said, "It's okay Timothy, I'll go with you now. It is the Father's Will that you and you alone bring me in. Show me the way."

Nethers fumed, feeding off the evil hosts surrounding him who willed it; he pulled his fist back and punched her with enough force to kill her. Malaya again found herself on the ground. She could have asked her angels to protect her from the blow, much like she did when she was protecting Waters. Instead, she took the opportunity to grow in grace and offer up the pain for those in worse situations than hers.

Nethers grabbed her by the hair and began pulling her along through the Ditch. The prisoners started making noisy threats as soon as the inner door was opened.

They realized Nethers was dragging a woman and immediately their usual threats turned to vulgar pleas; each begging Nethers to put the woman in their cell. Nethers stopped and looked at each set of prisoners.

"Let's see, where should I put her?" he said in a sing- song voice.

All the prisoners tried to get his attention. "Give her to me, Nethers, I know how to treat a lady."

Nethers laughed out loud. "This is no lady and I don't want her with someone who KNOWS how to treat her. I want to make sure she gets what she deserves."

The prisoners were even more stirred up now; some of the rapists professed that they would give her what she deserved and so did the murderers. They were all doing their best to give him a reason to put her with them. Every man on the cell block pleaded, every man but one, and this man would be who Nethers deemed the best choice.

His name was Carl and he earned the award for being the most vile and despicable of the lot; a serial killer, who raped, mutilated and then ate his victims. There were others in the block with the same M.O. but Carl was unique. He never used a weapon. Each time he killed, he used his bare hands. Everyone said that a demon possessed him and Nethers knew this to be true because he'd seen it.

Carl felt no remorse for any of his crimes and he had no impulse control. No one could be left alone with him because the person wouldn't survive the first minute. Nethers had watched him tear the head off of a guard once while the prisoners were being transferred to the Ditch.

Because of the danger, Carl was the last one to be brought into the cell block. There had been eight guards moving the shackled Carl along at gunpoint. All the other prisoners were locked up tight. The last man had just been put in his cell and the guard who put him there was walking back towards Carl and his entourage. Just as he was getting ready to pass Carl, he dropped his gun. He reached down to get it and when he came back up he was looking right into Carl's eyes. Carl reached out and put his huge hands on the guard's neck. Before anyone could stop him, Carl broke the guard's neck and then with his bare hands he ripped his head off. Everyone was so stunned by the unnatural speed of Carl's action that no one moved. Carl carried the head with him to the last open cell, stepped inside and then closed the door himself. There was no way of getting the head away from him, so Nethers let him keep it.

From that day on, every guard knew that Carl was not just criminally insane but that Satan possessed him. Even the other prisoners were stunned by such a diabolical display. Nethers decided that Carl would be the perfect candidate to give Malaya her due.

"It looks like you're the winner, Carl." Nethers said as he put the key in his cell door. Sitting on the floor in a corner at the back of his cell, Carl looked at him with saliva foaming from his mouth. Nethers threw Malaya into the cell and shut the door.

"As much as I'd like to stay and watch, my dinner is waiting for me. Save me some bones, Carl. Goodbye Malaya."

Nethers turned and walked down the corridor of the Ditch. When he reached the door, he turned around and laughed.

"Enjoy your dinner, Carl." His laughing could be heard even after the inner door was shut.

CHAPTER TWO....THE PAIN

Madison had never been so tired in all of her life. Every part of her body ached and the migraine she'd had for more than a week would not subside. It took every ounce of strength she had to keep moving. It even hurt to blink as her eyes pleaded with her to be allowed to close.

She's known "tired" in her lifetime. She had been "tired" when she'd stayed up all night with a girlfriend or from reading a book for too long. She had been "tired" after training in the gym for several hours, or running around chasing Maria at a park from morning till night. But what she felt now WASN'T that.

She had even known "exhaustion." When Maria was born and she got up like clockwork every three hours to nurse for six straight weeks. She would have just fallen asleep and it seemed she'd be awakened almost instantly by Maria's cry to be fed again. Every new mother knew that kind of exhaustion, but this was not THAT.

The only thing she could compare it to was what happens to prisoners when they are being sleep deprived as a form of torture. This had to be what that was like, but Madison thought even the prisoners got a few minutes to sleep in a twenty-four hour period; in that moment she both envied and hated them for that luxury.

She also knew that in order for them to be on the same playing field with her, they would have had to have a child in their arms who would never stop crying. They would need to be overwhelmed with anxiety, fear and worry, over someone they loved beyond distraction. Their arms would have to shake continually because it was impossible to put this child down; because to do so would deprive her of the small amount of comfort Madison could offer her by holding her. And Madison would rather die than deprive her.

Something was wrong with her baby! Something was terribly wrong with Rachael! Madison didn't know what was wrong, she just knew with every fiber of her being that something was. Both of Rachael's doctors had told her that it was just "colic" and that it would pass, but when they explained that colic only lasted for a few hours a day and then there was a reprieve, Madison knew they were wrong. On her second "well baby" visit with the doctors, one of them actually had the audacity to snidely remark, "If you had a tight diaper on all day you would be screaming as well." The remark was so ludicrous all Madison could do was stare at the man.

This wasn't her first go around at having a baby. She knew the difference between a tight diaper that might make a baby cry or whine, and the blood curdling screams that were continually coming out of her beautiful child. Rachael had agonizing pain and it never, ever went away.

The only time Rachael didn't cry happened when she was nursing and even that was short lived. The poor baby would nurse like it was the last bit of milk she would ever receive and then she would fall into a momentary deep sleep. Every time this happened Madison began to pray.

"Thank you God…thank you. Please let her rest…let me rest."

Madison spent more time in prayer now than she ever had before because every other moment, she was pleading with God for some relief for both the baby and herself.

She prayed during the night the most, because she knew that both Maria and Jacob needed to sleep. Rachael's screams made that almost impossible in the tiny 856 square foot house they all shared.

"Lord, I need your help. Can you send angels to protect Jacob and Maria from this? Can you have angels keep them from hearing her? Jacob has work and Maria has school and they need their rest. I trust you Father but I'm losing it here. I don't want to let you down...or Jacob or Maria or Rachael but I feel so useless." Madison finished her prayer by telling God she loved Him and made the Sign of the Cross.

All during the pregnancy Madison felt safe and happy in their little house but now there was nowhere to go to get away from the noise. The wood floors and wood walls became an echo chamber and the cries bounced in every crevice of the house. Even though it was dangerous, she sometimes put Rachael in the car in the middle of the night. She would drive for hours so that Maria and Jacob could sleep. Usually just as she would get close to the house, Rachael would fall asleep and Madison would start to pray again.

"Please God, please...let her sleep just for a few hours...help me God.... help me."

If God was listening, Madison saw no proof of it. Her exhaustion wouldn't allow her to discern if there were any demons in the house. She couldn't discern anything spiritual. Even so, she thought she should be safe more than sorry, so she constantly rebuked the demons that she couldn't see or feel; to no avail, Rachael's agony continued.

Poor Jacob! Madison had assured him that having a baby would be a wonderful experience and he would be overjoyed. That joy lasted only until Rachael woke up from her first nap and that joy turned to concern. Jacob did not know what to do for the baby or his new bride. The only way he offered any kind of assistance to Madison was helping Maria with her home-work or taking her out for ice cream. But as far as helping with Rachael, he was paralyzed. He had tried many different times to hold her but the baby felt no comfort in his arms and her cries became so intense that he imme-diately gave her back to Madison. No one could comfort her, but Madison seemed to be at least a little effective.

Maria would help when they had to go somewhere like church or to a family gathering and they were stuck in the car where the noise became excruciatingly loud. She would rub Rachael's little tummy and coo,

"It's alright baby...I know, I know...it's going to be alright."

Silently, Madison would say to herself that nothing could ever be alright again if she and Rachael didn't sleep soon. It had been three weeks since Rachael's birth and Madison had not slept more than an hour, and only in ten minute intervals.

She felt like she could collapse at any time. One day slipped into the next, as a never ending span of time without rest stretched in front of her. She didn't have the time or energy to clean her house, and cooking was out of the question. She would open the fridge to see what she could prepare, and couldn't even remember how to plan a meal. Sometimes she would just stand there staring until her brain would become so confused she would start to cry and just give up. The control that marked much of her personality, began to rapidly slip away. Something had to change and it needed to change soon because Madison didn't know how much more either of them could take.

Anxiety, Despair, Hatred, and Envy watched as Madison sat staring straight ahead with a blank tortured look in her eyes. They spoke to each other only in hushed tones for fear the human would sense them and rebuke them once more. Hatred had assured the other demons that that was beyond her capability at the moment, and that they had nothing to fear, but they proceeded cautiously nonetheless.

The only resistance they had at all was from the two Guardian Angels that never left the human woman and her putrid child. Although the angels were allowing the attack, for reasons unknown to the demons; which was always the case because demons were never privy to why they were allowed to attack some humans with such viciousness and others hardly at all. The angels still would not permit the humans to be touched.

This angered Hatred because he wanted to inflict bodily harm on this woman who had so wounded his master and who had been such a part of destroying the Satanist, Natash. Hatred had spent nearly 45 years fostering the poison inside of that man and all of Hell had plans for him which were beyond human comprehension.

Between this woman and the woman Tara, the men; Matthew and Jacob and especially Zachary the priest, years of important planning had come undone and because of that, Lucifer was in a fury. He had called a meeting in Hell with his main advisers after Natash's death to formulate a plan to annihilate each of the humans involved.

Lucifer's anger intensified towards all of them but the one who he hated beyond measure was the little girl, Maria. He hated all children because in them, the light of the Trinity shone brightest, and each of them held a secret destiny that he would struggle to decipher. The worst part was that the Father kept sending them in droves and like ants coming to a picnic, they were being born in enormous numbers.

Lucifer explained to his Hellish court that not only were they being born in great numbers, but more and more of them were being born with the "Mark of the Kingdom." This mystery consumed him and annoyed him because he would have to exert extra effort to monitor and plot the destruction of these chosen souls.

Maria had been born with that mark, but he had not known about it until after Natash died when the satanist gave an account of why he failed in completing his earthly mission. Natash explained, like a whimpering dog, that the blame for everything that had gone wrong should be placed on Maria. He said she possessed some exceptional supernatural powers that he couldn't defeat, and even when he called on the forces of Hell, nothing could harm her.

Enraged, Satan needed to see this child for himself. When he arrived he found her alone in her room playing with a baby doll. On first inspection he noticed nothing unusual about the child and made a mental note to increase Natash's punishment for making this 'nothing of a being' his scapegoat.

Maria was singing a song about being a big sister as she wrapped a blanket around her little doll. That's when Lucifer smelled it…roses…the sickening smell of his greatest enemy; the Queen of Heaven and Earth, the Mother of the Savior and the one who scriptures foretold would crush his head.

He withdrew into a position of submission, as the decree of Heaven dictated when the Woman was present. Since the great sacrifice of Jesus and the victory of Heaven over Hell, Satan received a new insult over his great injury; he was bound to submit to this mere mortal's authority. The Heavenly Father knew that no punishment could be more painful for Satan than to have to bow down and honor Mary, a human being, the very thing he despised with indescribable hatred.

As by his custom, Lucifer raised his eyes ever so slightly to acknowledge Her authority over him, and became stunned to see that She wasn't there. He scanned the room both in the physical realm and the spiritual and saw no trace of Her.

He sniffed the air again and realized the smell was coming from the child herself. He moved in closer to her and the smell intensified as another human approached. Lucifer began to squirm because as Madison walked into the room the odor became stronger, and although it was causing him agony to remain there, he knew he would endure it until he had all the information he craved.

The human woman was carrying a child and though it repulsed Satan to be in such close proximity to the Father's handiwork, he peered inside her womb and almost instantly regretted it.

The reason the smell had intensified was not because of the woman, but instead because of the life forming inside of her. Satan knew instantly that both of these children were protected by the Queen and his hatred for them multiplied immensely.

He made a decision then and there that he would make them all suffer for Her favor. He'd decided he'd seen enough and began to descend back to Hell. He took one last involuntary glance at Maria and became astounded to see the child staring at him. He immediately tried to approach her but found it impossible because The Blessed Mother appeared in front of them. She simply pointed towards the floor and Lucifer found himself thrown violently into Hell.

His counsel in Hell was instantaneous and he let it be known that the woman and Maria and the unborn child were to be the target of his wrath because he felt Heaven would use them to save many souls. He also wanted to punish them because the Queen had humiliated him and the mortal child had dared, not only to notice him, but to meet his gaze.

After the meeting he set off to see Natash. He thought of new ways he could torture him; not because he'd been wrong about the child's uniqueness but because he'd been correct. Lucifer sneered at his perverse sentencing. In Hell, a distinction did not exist between a decision that would honor Satan or dishonor God, the reward was always the same…pain!

CHAPTER THREE...RAISING THE BANNER

Father Zachary knew why he was dying. He'd known it the moment he saw the headlights flashing under the train that passed in front of him. Everything began to move in slow motion as he stared blankly into the pulsing beams, waiting for the caboose to pass.

Once it did, he heard the car approach him before he was aware of its movement towards him. It sounded like what you hear when two teenagers are sitting at a red traffic light waiting for it to turn green; each egging the other on by revving their motors; making it known that each thought they would be the victor of a race if it were to occur, except this was louder.

Once the motor revved, it didn't stop and it became louder as it sailed over the now empty tracks. It became airborne for a moment as it jumped the track and when it settled back down on the road it was already almost nose to nose with the priest's car.

He couldn't tell who was driving the vehicle, it all simply happened too fast to register that kind of information, but he clearly remembered what he'd been thinking...he had finally crossed a line. But it was their line, not his.

In the next moment he couldn't see anything and he didn't understand why. He thought his eyes were still working but all he saw was blackness. He tried to move his body but it felt like he was made of bricks and it was much too difficult a task to accomplish. He tried to speak, but his lips would not open so he tried to groan. His vocal cords produced no sound.

He couldn't see, couldn't move and couldn't speak, as he tried to take a breath to see if he had the ability to smell, he realized one of his senses was working perfectly, he could still hear. And almost as quickly as he realized he could, he suddenly wished he couldn't.

"Oh man, have you ever seen anything like that? This one's a goner for sure." One voice said in horror.

"Diego, get over here now and bring a body bag, We gotta cover this guy up."

Diego ran over the little hill towards the second victim in this horrendous accident. The first one had been burned beyond recognition and the only way you could tell it was a human was because of the hands. They had been handcuffed together and then handcuffed to the steering wheel. When the impact happened, the body flew through the windshield and the person's hands had been ripped off of the body. The steering wheel came off of its base at some point and also exited the car. When they came upon the accident, the car was on fire next to the body, which was also on fire. The steering wheel lay ten feet away with the handcuffed hands dangling from it.

Diego knew this had to be a hit from the Mexican mafia because he'd seen it before; trap a 'Mark' in a car and put him in the path of an oncoming train. But someone must have screwed up and timed this one wrong because the car missed the train, jumped the tracks and hit another car by mistake. The other car was also on fire with a broken windshield so the victim was thrown out as well. Diego hoped this guy fared better than the other one but all hope for that was lost when he topped the hill and saw something he had never seen in his thirty years of being a cop.

"Dios Mio, what happened to him?"

Father Zachary didn't think they were referring to him, he thought they were talking about the other driver so he did what his vocation required and said a prayer that the man would be ok. He didn't hear anything for a few minutes from the men. He assumed they were paramedics or policemen, so he reached back in his memory and replayed what he thought led up to this tragedy.

After he left Indiana, following Jacob and Madison's wedding, the bishop in his diocese reassigned him to a small barrio in Mexico to pastor a parish. This would be yet another new experience for him and he always marveled at the adventures and challenges God presented him with since becoming a priest. Each new place and experience brought him in contact with new souls and new opportunities to serve God and nothing made him happier. So, as his custom demanded, he embraced this new assignment with all the love and faith he could muster.

The little barrio had 540 parishioners at the church site and another 15,500 that were spread out in little villages spanning about 120 miles. The "church" was really nothing more than a small little hovel, in major disrepair and in need of just about everything. The humble parish was extremely poor so funds for repairs were non-existent, but that didn't deter the little priest. He knew he had all of the resources of Heaven at his disposal if God so ordained, so he worried over nothing.

His first task had been to take the list of addresses of everyone involved in the parish and start making visits to each and every one of their homes. This proved to be a very lucrative move in the spiritual sense, because word spread quickly about the friendly new priest who took the time to get to know everyone in the parish.

Although funds were limited, his second order of business was to go to the closest markets in each village and buy goods. His purpose in this endeavor provided relief for each family he'd met whose needs were dire. He spent the first few months walking from village to village taking care of his flock.

At each village he would say Mass. Sometimes he would say 3 to 4 Masses in one day before he'd sleep and then he'd wake up to start the process over again. His happiness escalated during this time. He enjoyed serving God's children. One of the things that pleased him was the way he traveled.

He walked everywhere because there wasn't any other transportation, except for donkeys. Even if he wanted to, he didn't have the money to buy one.

There were cars, but only the very rich owned those and they were usually members of the drug cartels. His congregation was very simple and humble and walking to and fro made him feel so close to Jesus. Even in the monastery in Israel transportation existed in some form. Other than the time he walked through the desert with his friend Matthew, on the way to find his brother, Father Zachary had never walked so much in the name of his ministry.

He had never met such a generous group of people. As poor as they were, they never let a week go by when they didn't bring him some kind of tithe. Sometimes it was money from their meager paychecks. Sometimes they gave him a chicken or some eggs or some kind of produce for the priest to pass along to people who were in even greater need than they were. They gave out of their need, then they gave some more and Zachary was humbled by their alms. He was also stunned as week by week, in each village, his congregation began to grow.

One day a bunch of people came to him with money they had collected from all of the parishioners and asked him to build them a real church and whatever else he needed to house their growing numbers. He began in earnest and within the year had built them not only a beautiful church but a rectory for himself and another priest, the bishop had sent to help him. He also built a community building, a food pantry and finally a school. With all of the construction happening at lightning speed, he had little time for himself. If he wasn't working with the contractors, he was saying Mass, hearing Confessions, taking young couples through marriage preparation, Baptizing, Confirming and then seeing to the needs of the very poor.

Many times during this time he had nothing to eat, but there was a reason for this. Father Zachary had taken a special vow of poverty. All priests take a vow of poverty; this means that they will not covet material things and they live off of the miniscule check that they get from their dioceses.

But Zachary took a special kind of vow and this meant that he would not receive a check from the church but he would daily live off of the Divine Will of God; and like a holy beggar, would wait for people to give to him at the Holy Spirit's direction.

He credited a lot of his spiritual growth to this vow. Even though he lost weight and appeared to be sickly, he was never stronger. It was an amazing sustainment from God and he never took it for granted.

Although things for the most part were going well, there was a darkness in his new world and it came in the form of drugs. He and his growing band of followers lived in one of the most dangerous places on earth. The drug cartels ran everything in the area. They were involved with all of the financial institutions. Most retail shops were fronts for their drugs or human trafficking operations. To make matters worse, he had been told that many in the police department were corrupt. He'd even been threatened by some of them. First, it started with parking tickets for a car he didn't even own. Then there were the endless building code violations to try and keep the church's property from expanding. But the priest took each new obstacle in stride and fought it with prayer and always won whatever battle he was fighting. Then one day a new danger presented itself. To deal with this problem, he knew he needed a much stronger weapon.

By this time, his congregation numbered 40 thousand and counting. That's when the cartel started blatantly targeting his sheep. They would harass them, physically attack them, abduct them and even rape and murder some of them. The reports flooded in like raindrops in a summer storm and Father Zachary knew drastic measures were needed.

He spent one whole twenty-four hour period fasting and praying, asking for the direction God wanted him to take. During the night, exactly at 3 am he was visited by a host of demons. He completely ignored them, as he had been taught to do at the direction of the Blessed Mother. He had learned that the more attention you pay them, the more energy they draw from you and the more damage they can cause. Since he had been bothered by them since infancy and really all through his life, he was used to their tactics. They never startled or disturbed him when they made their appearances, in fact, when they were waging war on him, it just verified that he was doing God's Will. As the battle raged and their attack became physical, he asked his angel to intervene. Without hesitation his angel manifested and bound them and sent them back to the Hellfire from where they'd come.

When all was peaceful again, he closed his eyes and the answer came. In his mind's eye he saw Mary, Jesus' Mother approach him. In Her right hand She carried a crucifix, and a rosary in Her left. She appeared to him as Our Lady of Guadalupe, which was the way she appeared to Juan Diego, the young Mexican Indian, who helped to bring Christianity to Mexico. She handed Zachary both objects and then pointed to Her right. When he looked in that direction, the priest saw a street he had never seen before. The buildings were ransacked and the streets were filthy. On every corner stood prostitutes and pimps and he could see drug deals taking place everywhere he looked.

There were people with guns and knives, and fights were breaking out all over. People were yelling and screaming and the cursing was appalling. He saw women and children hiding in their houses behind curtains. Then he looked deeper.

Beyond the physical and into the spiritual, he penetrated the veil and saw them. Each form hideous and petrifying and their evil permeated the air. Around each person swarmed a multitude of demons. These were even worse than the ones that were bothering him earlier because they were gaining power and strength through the actions and attitudes of the humans they attacked.

The priest became righteously angry as he surveyed the scene. "Sweet Jesus, show me what to do to lead your people back to the safety of your almighty arms. I offer myself as a holocaust for these children who were made in Your image and whom You cherish with love unimaginable. Defend us in battle against Your enemy and cover us in Your sanctified blood. Oh sweet Victim, let not Your perfect sacrifice be in vain in regards to these poor sinners. I ask for the counsel of Your Holy Mother and the protection of Your warring Angels as I willingly battle for these souls. In Your Most Holy Name, Jesus, I pray. Amen."

As soon as the prayer was answered he knew what to do and so he went to prepare his flock.

At Mass, that Sunday, he asked them to trust God in what He would ask of them, because it would require their bravery. He told them that they were going to march down the streets of the drug infested parts of their city saying the Rosary. He promised them that they would have the protection of God and that none of them should fear, for this was indeed what God wanted them to do.

And so, word spread like lightning from burrio to burrio asking for parishioners who could join him, to march through one of the most dangerous places in the world. Father Zachary led them in great numbers, carrying a huge banner of Our Lady of Guadalupe and saying the prayers with a booming strong voice and a peaceful smile on his face.

The reaction was one of shock from every direction. The prostitutes and pimps had never seen people of the cloth in this part of the city. The women and children hiding behind the curtains were stunned that there existed people this brave in the world. The rapists and murderers ran from the holiness that was advancing on them. Like roaches in the daylight, they scattered back into the darkness of their houses.

The leaders of the Cartel were beyond dismayed. They were seething and they weren't going anywhere. Their evil ran so deep, and the demonic forces influencing them were so mighty, that they were not affected by the power of God coming towards them. And all of their hatred was directed at the little priest. No one touched them, or unbelievably, said a word to them as they proceeded. But after they had gone up and down all the streets in the area and were leaving the neighborhood, the noise began.

Threats from every direction were being hurled at Father Zachary, most all of them promising death. Completely undeterred, he kept marching joyfully until all of his flock were safely back at the church. He wouldn't know the repercussions of the march until the next day, when he was sitting at the railroad tracks waiting on a train.

Sargent Diego walked over to the second victim and in a stunned whisper he said, "I can't believe what I'm seeing, he's as flat as a pancake. How did that happen?"

Diego's partner answered, "I don't know hermano, but I'm wondering why he isn't burnt like the other one."

Diego moved in for a closer inspection. "Wow you're right, not a burn in sight! And look he doesn't even have a cut on him, but how in God's name did he get like this?"

Father Zachary heard what they said and now realized they were talking about him. Was he really dead? It was odd because he didn't feel dead, just heavy…very very heavy. He tried once more to move to no avail. He heard the sirens approaching. The two men must have gotten up to go meet them, because he didn't hear them anymore.

It was surreal because all things considered, he felt fine. He may not have control of his body, but he still had charge of his mind; so he began to compose a prayer to Jesus for God's Will to be done.

Without warning he suddenly could see again and came face to face with his heart's desire…a visitation from the Queen of Heaven, Mary. He could only muster one thought, "MOTHER!"

Mary faced him with her arms down at her side and her palms turned outward. She was smiling at him with more love than he thought possible to express. He heard Her voice in his heart as She spoke but this,

"God has more for you to do yet my son. Be at peace."

She raised Her eyes to Heaven and then returned Her gaze to him. She reached her right hand to her lips and then released it towards him. As the kiss She blew came towards him, he had the strangest sensation. He felt like a deflated balloon being blown up, as life returned to his limbs and torso. And in less than a second he was restored to his former self. He whispered his thanks and eternal gratitude to his Mother as the vision of Her faded away.

He took a deep breath and stood up just as the two men came running over with the paramedics carrying a stretcher and a body bag. All four men stopped in their tracks and stared at the priest.

"No way! You were dead, I saw you... you... you were flattened and now you're... you're not!" Diego put his hand over his mouth, made the Sign of the Cross, and shook his head in disbelief.

One of the paramedics spoke next, "Wait aren't you the new priest in the barrio, Father Zachary, right?"

Zachary stuck out his hand to shake and replied, "I am he. It's nice to make your acquaintance."

No one could get over the miraculous recovery the priest made. In spite of it, they insisted he lay on the stretcher and go by ambulance to the hospital to be checked out. Father Zachary was compliant just to sooth the shocked men's nerves, but he knew his health had been perfectly restored.

As he lay in the ambulance on the ride to the hospital he spoke to his true Mother, "I have raised the banner...so now it begins."

CHAPTER FOUR...
SUFFER THE LITTLE CHILDREN

From his hidden place, Mitka watched as Lucifer again approached Jacob's house. He had not left his post since the birth of the child Rachael. The ArchAngel Michael had once again assigned the three generals, Mitka, Syree and Tezra, to work together to protect this family. Michael told them that they would be together for many years, in human terms, as directed by Divine Providence.

This brought all the angels great jubilation, for many reasons. Firstly, guarding the child Maria proved to be an honor. An exceptional child, she possessed spiritual gifts far superior to her human counterparts. But more than that, her bravery drew all three Heavenly beings towards her. She fought without fear. She always knew which beings were present, even when they were cloaked with invisibility. Syree had told Mitka that the Mother of God was the only human he had known to be able to do this.

Syree was one of the Ten Thousand Angelic Chorus who had the privilege and prestige of protecting Mary from in utero to Her Assumption. He had an intimate relationship with the Queen that very few other angels could boast. So when he told Mitka and Tezra that Maria's gift of being able to see any being, at any time, came from the Blessed Mother, it could be nothing but truth.

It was apparent in many other ways that Maria imitated graces from the

Queen of Heaven. She had an unshakeable calmness that mirrored Mary's, especially when the enemy of God came personally to attack. No one watching would ever know that a demon was engaging in battle with her. She kept her sweet countenance, didn't change the inflection or tone of her voice, nor did she seem rattled in any way. Syree had told the other angels a story of when Mary was attacked by all Seven Legions of Demons.

This occurred very early in the Her holy pregnancy. From the instant of the Incarnation, our Lord Jesus began communication with His most Holy Mother in an audible way. Mary could hear Jesus' voice as she heard the voices of other mortals. This was just one of the gifts of Grace that the Heavenly Father decided to bestow on His Daughter. For all intent and purposes, Mary became a student of Her Holy Son from the moment that the Holy Spirit came upon Her and became Her Spouse. Divine Providence deigned that no other human would receive the extensive education that Mary received. This was one of the privileges of being HIS Mother.

It began when Jesus said, (1) "My Spouse and My Dove, the infernal dragon thirsts with such wrath against My Holy Name and all those that adore it, that he wishes to drag toward him all without exception and with daring presumption he tries to blot out My name from the land of the living. I wish thee, My Beloved, to come to the defense of My cause and of My Holy Name, by giving battle to the cruel enemy: and I will be with thee in battle, since I am in thy virginal womb. I wish that thou confound and destroy the enemies before I appear in the world: for   they are convinced the Redemption of the world is nigh and therefore they desire to gain over and ruin all souls without exception, before the world is redeemed. I trust this victory to thy fidelity and love. Do thou battle in My Name, just as I in thee, against this dragon and ancient serpent."

Syree explained that The Blessed Mother's heart was so moved by the plea of the Most High God that She was inflamed with Divine love and filled with invincible fortitude.

As Mitka recalled the battle Syree described to them, he could see the correlation between the Queen and this special little child.

The second reason all the angels rejoiced at their assignment over Jacob's family had to do with the other members in it. Jacob was a 'lost' soul when their previous assignment began, but he had become a 'found' one. In his life, before Madison, he thought only of himself and engaged in sinful worldly activities. But as soon as he "knew" the truth about God, he changed his life completely. He became what a man walking with God should be and each day he surprised and delighted the Angels with each new growth of his soul. Tezra, along with Serena; Jacob's Guardian angel, were his constant companions.

Since one of Jacob's gifts was connecting with animals, this made Tezra; the Guardian of the entire Animal Kingdom, ecstatic. Nothing brings an angel more happiness than watching a soul turn his life over to God and journey towards Heaven. This man was on that path and had a huge responsibility because of the spiritual gifts of his family.

Madison's gifts of Discerning spirits and Prophetic dreams were passed on to both of her daughters, although only Maria knew that Rachael had these gifts and more.

All the angels were enamored with the sweet little baby from the moment of her birth. And so, Mitka thought, was one demon. The General prayed for clarity, as he always did whenever Bene't entered his mind or his atmosphere...but again the Throne of the Trinity remained silent on the behavior of the demon. Mitka did not need an explanation from the Trinity, he simply trusted as he obediently protected Jacob's house.

Not two seconds passed as Mitka considered these things. Still hidden, he watched Lucifer's measured approach, he would wait for a Divine Order before he became visible. Lucifer, for his part, took his time to proceed. He stood and glared at the tiny house as if he wasn't sure what it was.

All of the guardian angels were on alert. Mitka had spoken with each of them, except for Maria's. Maria's angel was another strange mystery to all of the generals. This angel's countenance was a brilliant white...whiter than any angel they had ever seen. He was so white in fact that there was nothing to see BUT light. He never spoke to any of them and when Mitka tried to speak to him he disappeared. When they asked Michael to explain it to them he said,

"The Father's ways are above our ways...trust and believe." and so without question, and out of love and obedience for the Trinity, they did.

Mitka could see the light of Maria's angel becoming brighter as Lucifer finally approached the house.

Lucifer's pride was utterly wounded that he had any trepidation approaching these wretched humans. He had been so confounded by the appearance of the Queen the last time he had come and also the stare of the bold child Maria. After observing the house, he was certain the Queen was not present, but he could smell the putrid smell of roses coming from both of the children. He had sent Bene't, his second in command to witness the birth and to relay any information about her dignity. The report he received was benign in nature, but because Bene't was the only demon whose mind Satan couldn't penetrate, he decided to come for himself and see the truth of the situation.

He did not, could not, trust the mind of a demon he couldn't control and Bene't was the one demon who eluded Lucifer's power. Even after all the beatings and torture, to throwing him into the Machine Cavern, still something defiant remained in Bene't, something he couldn't quite comprehend. Lucifer hated things he didn't understand, and in his battle with Heaven he seemed to always misunderstand things. His pride would never let him admit it, so he attributed everything he failed to understand as being a trick of the Father. To credit any fault to himself would lessen his greatness in the eyes of the other demons, and he could not allow that.

Through all these centuries he had his sycophants adoring him, out of fear if nothing else, nonetheless they believed in Satan's superiority over themselves and over the Father as well. They always believed in his cause and supported his hatred of this inferior race called Humanity. They all most definitely loathed Mary, the biggest insult to them all. Lucifer knew he had complete loyalty among the fallen angels, every single one, except Bene't. It wasn't that Bene't had betrayed Lucifer in any way, and Bene't did, with one exception, always know his place. It was something else; something Lucifer couldn't comprehend, that made him hate Bene't almost as much as he hated Heaven.

During his approach, Satan noticed the crying baby. As he listened to the child, he reveled in the sound of her pain, it was like a balm to him. Anytime a human experienced pain, Lucifer gained enormous pleasure from it. The only time he wanted to be near the lesser creatures occurred when they suffered. It utterly delighted him to be in the company of helpless victims and tortured souls.

As he entered the house he saw the woman Madison. He immediately felt repulsion for her but was very pleased to see that her spiritual state had weakened considerably since his last visit.

Sitting at the kitchen table with her elbows on the table and her head resting in her hands, her distress and exhaustion were apparent. Satan ascribed it to the four demons, Hatred, Anxiety, Anger and Envy that were surrounding her. They all bowed dramatically when they saw Satan and then, as if to impress him, they hurled even more of an attack on the already weakened woman. Believing she was being properly attended to, he went towards the source of the crying.

Rachael lay on the couch in the living room, swaddled in a soft white blanket. She looked as if she had been placed against the back cushion carefully, so that there would be no danger of her falling off. For such a tiny little thing, her crying was very loud. As Lucifer approached her, her guardian angel sent a mental message to Mitka asking for permission to materialize. After an answer to "wait", the angel just continued to hold his little charge invisibly on the couch. Sensing Heavenly beings were present, Lucifer became bolder. In his insolence, he believed that all the Heavenly beings were terrified of him. He believed he had free reign around them, with the exception of Michael that is, but Lucifer would not give thought to his Nemesis here.

As he moved closer, he put his hideous face next to Rachael's beautiful one and took a long deep breath. He was sniffing like an animal to see if he could smell a sickness inside of her body. He was trying to identify the source of her pain but instead of being able to name it, like he could in any other human, he just got a nose full of the scent of roses.

He reeled backwards as his senses were assailed but only for a fraction of an instant, because it would not do to let the Heavenly beings see him affected in any way that made him appear weak.

He put his face next to hers again and this time she opened her eyes. It was only for a fraction of a second and then she cried out again in pain. Lucifer defiantly smelled her again and began to laugh at the fear he'd instilled in the child. He touched her cheek with his sharp pointed talon and cut it. The cut was extremely small and only a tiny single drop of blood came out of it. Lucifer was just about to touch it when he heard Madison's prayer.

"Please Father, I don't know what to do for her now. I'm so weak and tired. My arms can no longer hold her and that's the only thing that brings her comfort. Please Father help me, help her, I'm begging you. Show me what to do!"

Madison was sobbing on the table now, uncontrollably and without reserve when she heard it. It was loud and it came from everywhere at once. It was as if an earthquake was happening inside of her body because she was shaking when she heard the words.

"My daughter, you prayed for a saint, now serve her!" Madison knew she had just heard the voice of God the Father, and without delay she got up and ran to the living room. She knelt in front of her baby girl, gently picked her up and kissed her cheek. Then she stared at her baby in awe.

As soon as the voice of God began speaking, the four demons and Lucifer were violently hurled into Hell.

CHAPTER FIVE...CRADLE AND ALL

Bene't heard Satan and the four demons coming into Hell long before he saw them. The noise preceding their entrance was deafening. It began at the entrance of the abyss with the wailings of the damned intensifying as Satan and the demons flew by them. He had no control of how he was traveling through each cavern of Hell, nor did he have any management of the speed of the travel. The demon's couldn't control their movements either. To say they were spinning would be an understatement, as the maneuver was much more violent. Their bodies weren't just moving, they were distorting, as if they were bread dough being kneaded by giant hands. They were clearly in torment and so that torment passed to the damned and also to all the demons in the abyss. This was yet another horror of Hell. There was never a reprieve from the suffering and if Satan was wounded in any way, the torments increased a thousand fold for all the inhabitants.

Bene't waited for the wave of torture to hit him and when it did his shrieks joined the symphony of agony serenading the dark caverns.

When it was over, it was only over for the demons. The Damned would have to suffer it until Satan's pride was appeased and his humiliation averted.

Bene't tried to leave the Abyss as soon as his torment abated but was stopped by the ferocious summoning of his "Master". He knew there was nothing to do but to go. He knew that whatever had happened wasn't good. There were just a few times in the history of the world when Satan himself was hurled into Hell. The demons had some form of this experience many times over when some Saint understood the power of Christ and rebuked them, but for the Dragon to be thrown with such force, could only mean that a powerful Heavenly being was to blame.

Satan hadn't even completely composed himself before he began to speak to Bene't. Although Bene't tried to avert his eyes, because to do the opposite would be considered an affront to Lucifer's greatness, he did notice that the hideous shape had not quite returned to normal. This was significant because there had only been three other times he'd seen him in such a state:

The SECOND time occurred right after he had tempted Adam and Eve in the Garden. After the Father had pronounced that "The Woman will crush your head", Lucifer was violently cast into the Lake of Fire and did not have time to return to normal before he was seen by the other demons. It would have been much more of a main event if all of Hell wasn't in such an utter state of confusion because they had just witnessed what they had all believed impossible. All the time they had spent in their Hellish counsels planning the demise of the human race and especially the ruin of Christ and His Mother, were brought to naught in one moment.

When Adam and Eve fell, all of their interior beauty and grace and original justice were changed into the ugliness of sin. The devil was triumphant and celebrated with glee with his demons but it was very short-lived. He stopped his proud boasting when he saw how kindly the merciful love of God dealt with the delinquents, and how He offered them a chance of doing penance by giving them hope of pardon and return to grace. He watched in confusion as the two humans were sorrowful and contrite and was horrified as the beauty of grace was restored to them. And then his terror increased as God pronounced again the same threat He had given to Lucifer when he saw the sign of Mary in Heaven and was told he would serve Her. When Lucifer refused, he heard,

"THE WOMAN WILL CRUSH YOUR HEAD," for the first time.

The THIRD time that his entrance into Hell was so violent happened at the culmination of the Great Sacrifice of Jesus on the Cross. That time, every single demon in Hell was with him and they all experienced the violence together; like the very FIRST time, when the ArchAngel Michael had thrown them out of Heaven. They became the hideous unrecognizable entities that they were now; full of gnashing of teeth and wailing.

They had been so deceived in the life of Jesus and His most Holy Mother. They had been the losers in the battle they had been fighting since they left Heaven. The pain of Lucifer's injured pride, because of his ignorance, was the tool that inflicted even more pain and torture on the Damned that unfortunate day. So Bene't knew historically that this violent entrance had great significance too.

"Why were you not guarding your post at Jacob's house. Bene't?" As soon as Lucifer asked the question, Bene't began bawling as fire began to consume him.

"Master, you forbade me to go back. You told me to wait here, that you would do the deed yourself as I had failed you in prior attempts. You chained me cruelly to the spiked wheel that removed my skin and every part of my body, only to regenerate so the process could begin again. You told me more "appropriate" punishments were coming." but Bene't said none of this aloud, the thoughts only chased their way through his head. He knew that it was a lesson in futility. Satan would justify his actions if he didn't heap more cruelties on Bene't first for daring to confront him. Instead Bene't lowered his giant head and said, "Forgive me Master, I have failed you again."

Lucifer allowed the fire to continue to consume Bene't and every other demon in sight until he was restored to the hideous form he had been before he was thrust into Hell. Once composed, he spoke again,

"Because I am a merciful father, I will allow your suffering to cease for now. Once again my greatness has been offended by my Father through this child Maria and now the 'Mark' is also on the hideous newborn…"

"Rachael!" Bene't interjected; surprising both himself and Satan.

Satan's eyes narrowed and his wrath was once again turned toward Bene't as he spat,

"What did you say?"

Bene't hesitated just a moment, he didn't realize he had spoken her name out loud and thought that maybe something had happened that Satan now had the ability to read his mind. After that initial panic he had a secondary one. What possessed him to make such a critical mistake in front of Satan, especially considering the deadly mood he was experiencing?

Locking his features, even as panic set in, he tried in every way to hide the depths of his feelings and look and sound benign. "My Lord, I was repeating the name I heard the humans give the child, in case you weren't aware."

Satan's next words were liquid hate, "In case I wasn't aware? I'm aware of everything in the Universe. Everything that has been, is and will be. Nothing escapes my magnificent eyes. Now bow down and praise and honor my greatness, Bene't. Show me the adoration I deserve as your master, my warrior. Let me see your love."

Bene't was going to refuse, if he could, but before the thought was completed in his mind he was pulled by an invisible force onto his knees directly in front of Satan. The position he found himself in was awkward, as he was almost in the shape of a ball. His head was pushed into the floor so hard and with such force that it made speaking impossible. His arms were cruelly tied behind his back with chains of molten lava which burned as he tried to raise his head to speak. Satan ordered the other demons present to inflict every form of torture upon him as Satan insisted Bene't praise him. In a climax of wicked laughter it ended as quickly as it had begun and Bene't was able to rise.

Bene't stood slowly, and in the moments it took him to do so, decided that he would never praise Satan, even if he were made to experience that torture for all of his eternity. He rose to his full height and leveled his eyes with Satan's. He was prepared for the fight, but no fight came. Instead

Lucifer was staring off into the distance...listening to something...or some-one. He leaned forward and a wicked smile began to form on his awful mouth.

"Guess who's awake? Baby Rachael." He immediately sneered at Bene't.

"I guess I'll go pay another visit. Or should I send my greatest warrior? Hmm, I haven't yet decided on the best course of action... but I will, in due time...in due time. But know this, the moment that either you or I is afforded an opportunity by My Father, we will slaughter both of those wretched children and bring them here so I may use and abuse them for all of eternity."

With that, Satan moved beyond the pit. Bene't staring after him, col-lapsed onto the floor in utter despair.

CHAPTER SIX... ROUND TWO

Matthew sat on the bar stool glaring at the bartender. The stupid man was taking way too long to come over and take his order. He looked around the bar at all the people. There were people talking and laughing. Some people were dancing and gazing deeply into each other's eyes. Some were watching the television as they drank their beer and ate pretzels. He looked up on the small stage at the back of the room and noticed all the people in line to sing karaoke. Everyone seemed so happy...so normal. Even the people who came in alone, like him, seemed content. But Matthew wasn't content. Matthew wasn't happy. Matthew wasn't normal. Matthew didn't know what he was. He only knew that he hated every single person in that bar. He hated them because they all seemed to be able to feel something that he couldn't...joy.

"What is wrong with people?" he said. "All I want is a drink! Is that so hard to get?"

He thought he was speaking in a normal voice and was completely insulted as the other customers all turned in unison to stare at him?

"WHAT?" he yelled at them. "What's your problem? Am I bugging you? Am I ruining your PERFECT... BEAUTIFUL..LOVELY evening?" The other patrons looked at him pitifully and most of them turned away and continued with their previous conversations.

"IDIOTS!!!!!" he spat, and pointed his index finger at the people sitting around the bar.

By this time the bartender had returned with his drink. "Here you go sir," he said as he eyed Matthew.

"I need to get another job," the bartender said beneath his breath. He walked over to the sink to clean some glasses when the new bartender, a girl named Lilly asked him,

"Hey Rick, don't you think you need to cut him off now?" she whispered.

Rick looked down and shook his head no.

"I can't!"

"What do you mean you can't? Why not? This guy's sloppy drunk and we could be liable if we keep serving him!"

"He owns the place, Lilly!"

Lilly's facial expression showed that this information was indeed a hurdle, but still she persisted.

"But Rick, he could go out and get in his car and end up killing himself and maybe others." she said a little too loudly.

"He won't," Rick replied quietly, as he continued washing the bar glasses.

Lilly followed suit and lowered her voice.

"How do you know that?"

Rick stopped washing the glasses. He let his eyes scan each of his customers to make sure they had what they needed then, motioned for Lilly to follow him to the other side of the bar. When he was safely out of earshot of the other customers he explained.

"He won't because as soon as he's finished, I'll ring the bell and his doorman will come take him upstairs to the Penthouse. This is his building...his hotel!"

"Oh wow, ok well that's good then." Lilly glanced again at Matthew. He was awfully drunk. She also noticed that he was quite handsome and he seemed pretty put together in his appearance. "It's a shame," she thought, "if he wasn't so plowed, I would've tried to talk to him." She continued to look at Matthew as she asked, "So what's his story anyway?"

Rick did another quick check of his customers and decided everyone was fine for now.

"His name is Matthew Bradley. He owns a bunch of stuff in Manhattan. I think he owns a television network and some other business and he owns this hotel and one up off of Broadway. Anyway the guy is filthy rich. I used to like it when he came in here because he was always nice and was a huge tipper. It was nothing for him to slap down several hundred bucks just to make someone's life better. He used to just order one, maybe two drinks and then he was gone. But something happened to him several months ago and no one really knows what. But after that, he changed. He started coming to the bar every day. As soon as he had a couple drinks in him he'd start getting loud. He'd tell anyone who would listen about all his accomplishments and about all the important and famous people he knew. He became a real narcissist and it became harder to be around him. He'd give hundred dollar bills to every person he talked to and tell them "Go treat yourself or, Enjoy this." It seemed really generous, but there was something kind of dark about it too. If anyone stopped paying attention to him he'd get verbally abusive and turn down right nasty. Suddenly, they were enemy number one to him. I've watched him tear into people for getting up and going to the bathroom. When the person came back, he would tell them how worthless they were. He would say they were losers and they didn't deserve to be alive. I've watched him make several women cry. He's gotten in lots of fights too and when the customer's complained, they were banned from the bar for life."

"Oh my gosh, what a jerk," Lilly said as she peeked at Matthew.

"That's the sad part, he really isn't, or rather he didn't use to be. Before whatever happened to him, he was well liked and well respected. Anyway, the more he drinks, the weirder he gets."

"What do you mean?"

"Well I can't really explain it, except to say he really freaks out."

"Oh come on, you gotta give me more than that. You can't just.."

As if on cue, Matthew started to scream.

"Nooooooo, get away from me! Stop! Go away!!!!!!!!!"

Matthew's hands were in front of his body in a defensive position. One hand was in a fist, poised and ready to strike and the other was shielding his eyes as if he couldn't bear to see whom he was fighting. All of the other patrons stopped and stared at him.

"And the show begins," Rick whispered to Lilly as he walked over and picked up the phone. Matthew continued to fall apart as Rick spoke into the phone.

"Mr. Peter? It's happening again. Time to come get him."

Peter hung up the phone and hurriedly made his way through the penthouse.

"Not again!," he said. "When will this stop?" Peter grabbed the keys and walked out the door through the long corridor. Once again he was baffled by this behavior of Mr. Bradley. Nothing was making sense. How could this wonderful man turn into this? What happened to him when he was gone for all those months?

Peter would never forget giving the package to him on the last day he'd seen him before he left. When Mr. Bradley opened that package, all color left his face. He looked as if he had seen a ghost. Peter was walking back to the front desk when he saw him. He had intended to ask him if he was alright or needed a drink of water but before he had a chance to do anything Mr. Bradley disappeared.

Over the next couple of months no one knew what had happened to him. Peter wondered why the police weren't called in to search for him but then it occurred to him that maybe his office knew where he went and they just weren't telling anyone.

When Mr. Bradley returned, he was a shadow of the man he had been. He was underweight and looked exhausted. He didn't smile anymore and seemed to be looking over his shoulder all the time as if he were being followed. He began to go down to the bar daily and he would stay until closing most nights. He became extremely paranoid and began working from home.

He stopped going out to Opera's or the Theater. He no longer went on dates or out to dinner at all. Most evenings, if he ate, he did so in the bar. He no longer hosted any parties at the Penthouse and he spent every day alone. Peter was the only interaction he had with someone from his "old" life.

It bothered Peter that Mr. Bradley had become this. He was such a special person and to be reduced to this kind of man was sad.

As Peter entered the elevator, he sighed deeply. If this was any other person he would've refused to work for them anymore. Many times he thought about quitting but each time he couldn't bring himself to do it. He loved Mr. Bradley and he kept hoping against hope that this nightmare would end.

The elevator opened and he could hear Matthew's voice from the bar. It sounded bad tonight. Peter was glad that he was a big man because when Matthew got like this he was a handful.

When he reached the bar Matthew was in a crouching position on top of the bar. There were three men, including the bartender around him trying to deal with the situation.

"LEAVE ME ALONE!!!!! STAY AWAY!!! I'LL KILL YOU!" Matthew shrieked at the men.

Peter rushed over to the bar. He directed the men to move back away from Matthew. This seemed to calm him a little bit because he became silent. He just squatted there breathing in and out through his mouth, sounding like a woman in labor. He was breathing rapidly and very loudly. His eyes were huge, round and bloodshot. He was moving them slowly around the room looking at all the horrified customers. No one moved or talked, everyone just stared at Matthew.

By now he had his eyes downcast and he kept breathing rapidly. He was looking at the floor as if he saw something no one else did. Peter approached him cautiously, which he knew from experience was the only way this worked.

"Mr. Bradley," Peter said gently. Matthew shut his eyes for a moment and then continued to look at the floor.

"Mr. Bradley, I could use your help upstairs sir...if you're finished here that is."

Peter touched his arm as he spoke, but Matthew jerked his arm away. He looked up at Peter and he had a wild look in his eyes. The same look he got every time this happened. Peter told his wife that Matthew looked like a caged animal ready to pounce.

One time Peter's wife saw it for herself. Peter's car was in the shop so she came to pick him up. He told her he would be down shortly but he was taking a very long time. After an hour, she walked in the building just in time to see the elevator doors close. As it was closing she saw her husband with his arm around Mr. Bradley. She took the next elevator up to the Penthouse, thinking she might help in some way, after all they owed him so much. He had always been so generous with her family. He gave huge bonuses to Peter. He set up a trust for each of their children so they could afford to go to college. He even sent a maid service over to clean her house twice a week, which to this day was hard for her to get used to, but she so appreciated it. On their 15th wedding anniversary he sent them on a cruise, even paying for the babysitter to take care of their children during the week they were gone. He was a wonderful man.

When she reached the Penthouse she entered carefully. Peter was taking Matthew to his bedroom. As soon as they entered the room Matthew stopped hard and dug in his heels, refusing to go one step farther. His eyes were fixed on the giant open window that looked out over the city.

"They're here!" he said, his voice quivering.

Peter looked at the window but saw nothing. His wife however saw plenty. Because the window took up the whole wall, it acted like a giant mirror and she could see Matthew's face clearly. She watched his eyes widen and his mouth open wide as if he was trying to yell, except no sound came out. He looked like a character in a horror movie, his expressions were so exaggerated. She looked all over the window and could not see whatever

Matthew saw, but she felt something. She looked back at the window and saw a black shadowy form moving. It started on the left hand side of the window in the corner closest to the floor. It started to move up to the top of the window and continued to travel to the right. She looked at Matthew again and this time he put his hands over his eyes.

"No no no no...please no." Matthew whimpered.

"It's okay Mr. Bradley," Peter tried to console him.

"It's not okay..it will never be okay again," Matthew said. He raised his eyes Heavenward and spoke in frustration. "WHERE ARE YOU? WHY WON'T YOU HELP ME?"

Peter noticed his wife for the first time in the window and noticed the expression on her face. She kept watching the window and as soon as the words were out of Matthew's mouth, she saw a bunch of little tiny sparkles in the air, almost like the dust you see in a sunbeam. They multiplied quickly and overtook the black shadow on the window. As they moved, the black just dissipated. She looked to see if Matthew was reacting to the little sparkles but he wasn't. When all the black was gone Matthew collapsed in a heap on the floor and passed out.

"Finally!" Peter said. "Joy, can you help me get him to the bed, please?"

Joy lept into action and helped her husband move Mr. Bradley to his bed. They took off his shoes and removed his tie. They each grabbed an end of the blanket and covered him. Peter ran to the kitchen and grabbed a glass of water and placed it on his bedside table.

"I do this in case he wakes up in the middle of the night and needs it," Peter said as an explanation as he and Joy walked out of the room.

When they got to the front door Peter looked once more at the Penthouse to make sure he didn't forget anything. He shut off the lights and locked the door behind them. He looked at Joy to see how she was doing.

"See, I told you the truth, he's gone crazy!"

The elevator doors were closing as Joy looked at her husband severely and said,

"He's not crazy Peter...he's being haunted!"

The next morning Matthew was awakened by the bright sunlight shining through his window. He looked at the clothes he was wearing and once again he had no idea what had happened the night before. He just knew one thing...he needed a drink.

CHAPTER SEVEN....LET THE GAMES BEGIN

Rachael lay in her mother's arms. She had just finished nursing and she took a deep breath before the pain in her body began. It didn't take very long at all for the comfort and peace she felt while nursing to go away and the now predictable pain in her stomach to take its place. She started to whimper as it began and Madison immediately stood up and placed the baby on her shoulder to burp her. As soon as Rachael had burped she began to cry again.

Madison placed her on her belly. Rachael was now facing the floor but suspended in the air on Madison's arm. She began to rock the baby back and forth. This was what her mother called the "football hold" and it seemed to be the only thing that helped Rachael at all.

Before Madison had heard God's voice telling her who Rachael was, this rocking and standing had become so hard on Madison's body that she couldn't do it for more than a few minutes before she had to sit down again. Each time she sat, Rachael would start to cry in agony. But now, with her new found knowledge that she was the "mother of a saint", she would suffer anything to comfort her.

As she swayed back and forth she sang to Rachael. She sang every lullaby she knew and hoped that Rachael would fall asleep. Her poor baby hadn't slept more than twenty minutes a day since she'd been born. Madison wondered what kind of effect this was having on her. She wondered for the millionth time what the source of her pain was.

After she ran out of songs to sing she started to sing a prayer to God. None of it rhymed or had any of the normal structure of a song she would normally compose. It was merely comprised of thoughts she was having, linked together with a melody.

"SHOW ME LORD...SHOW ME. WHAT'S WRONG WITH MY BABY GIRL. NOT SLEEPING CAN'T BE GOOD FOR HER AND I'M SO CONCERNED. CAN'T YOU SEND ME AN ANGEL TO WHISPER IN MY EAR. SO I CAN HELP THIS BABY SAINT...SO I CAN HELP MY BABY GIRL."

When she was finished singing she looked up to the Heavens and sighed. Then she remembered that she had extra help up there and began to pray.

"Tara...Tara are you here? Please show me how to help Rachael. I know from your perspective you know everything now. Will you approach the Throne of God for me and ask God to lead me? Thank you! I miss you my friend and I love you."

Just as she finished the prayer, Maria came home from school. She opened the door a bit too loudly and once she saw Rachael asleep in her mother's arms she looked apologetically at Madison.

"She's sleeping Momma? She's really sleeping?" Maria whispered as she approached them with a huge smile on her face.

Madison smiled at her oldest daughter. "At least for the moment."

"Are you tired Mommy? Have you been standing long?" Maria said as she placed her hand on Madison's arm.

"I'm okay honey," Madison smiled. "How in the world did I ever get so lucky to have you, baby?" Maria smiled back at her mother. Then she bent down and took a little peek at Rachael.

"She's so cute, Mommy. I love her so much!"

"I know you do. And I know she loves you 'so much' too."

"She does Mommy. She told me she did." Maria said as she looked at

Rachael again.

Madison continued to sway back and forth in a slow rhythm.

"Hey Mommy, why is there a little cut on her cheek?" Maria asked.

"I didn't know there was a cut on her cheek honey. Can you see it? Is it bad?" Madison asked.

Maria got down on her knees and looked closely at the cut. It was very tiny but very red. Maria looked at her mom and put her thumb and index finger together indicating to Madison that it was small.

"Oh okay then," Madison said.

Maria reached out to touch it, but Madison stopped her.

"Let her sleep for now honey. She'll be awake soon enough and I'll look at it then."

Maria shook her head yes.

"Mommy, can I babysit her while you take a break?"

Madison smiled at the thoughtfulness of her daughter. Not even eight years old and always trying to take care of everybody. So young, yet an old soul in many ways.

"Well I do need to start dinner before daddy gets home. If I lay her on the couch will you sit with her and make sure she doesn't fall?"

Maria answered by running to the couch and jumping on it. Very carefully Madison walked over and laid Rachael on the couch next to Maria. The baby didn't stir at all and Madison gave a sigh of relief and tiptoed from the room into the kitchen.

Maria looked at her baby sister with great love. This was HER baby, her mommy had told her so. It was her responsibility to teach her and help her and love and protect her and Maria was the happiest she'd ever been. She couldn't wait for the day when Rachael wasn't in pain any more so they could talk longer. But for now she HAD to be in pain and only Maria knew that...and only Maria and Rachael knew why.

Just as Maria began to watch Rachael, Lucifer once more approached the house of Jacob. He decided to leave Bene't behind. The demon needed to be punished a bit more for calling him out on the child's name. This time he sent all the minor demons from the house. He didn't want any witnesses if things went wrong... like the last time.

Mitka and the Guardian Angels once again disappeared and were silent as the greatest evil known to man approached. All of them were poised and ready for whatever the battle would entail. They had been summoned back to the tower earlier in the morning and yet another wonderful experience awaited them. They had been privileged over the last two years with the extraordinary interaction they had with the Great ArchAngel Michael. They had been given all of their orders personally from the Great Defender of the Father and all of them were immensely honored.

As they were summoned to the Tower all of them were looking forward once again to being in Micheal's chamber. But as they entered, it wasn't Michael who awaited them. In his place were two more ArchAngels. The first was the beautiful ArchAngel Gabriel...the Great Messenger of the Father. This extraordinary Angel was the Father's mouthpiece. "The appearance of this great prince was that of a most handsome youth of rarest beauty; his face emitted resplendent rays of light, his bearing was grave and majestic, his motions composed, his words weighty and powerful, his whole presence displayed a pleasing, kindly gravity and more of godlike qualities than most other angels. He wore a diadem of exquisite splendor and his vestments glowed in various colors full of refulgent beauty. Encased on his breast, he bore a most beautiful cross, disclosing the mystery of the Incarnation."

It was Gabriel who spoke with Abraham and told him to sacrifice his son, then it was he who stopped Abraham from completing the deed. He appeared to Zechariah telling him that his prayers had been answered and that his wife would bear him a son that he was to name John. He was referring to John the Baptist. Zechariah had insulted God by questioning him because of his and Elizabeth's advanced age. To this the angel responded. "I am Gabriel who stands in God's presence and I have been sent to speak with you and bring you this good news. Look! Since you did not believe my words which will come true at their appointed time, you will be silenced and have no power of speech until this happens."

He was also the Archangel who appeared to the Most Pure Mary and said, "Hail Mary, Full of Grace, the Lord is with thee." He also appeared to Joseph in his dreams, both about not divorcing Mary and also to tell him to leave Bethlehem and flee to Egypt

This Angel was critical to all of human history and precious to the Trinity and here the Generals were standing in front of him!

Next to him was another ArchAngel, Raphael. This angel is the Healer of the Father; his name literally means GOD HEALS. He is very tall and elegant, with long flowing light brown hair. He emits peace and calmness. He is soft spoken and gentle and very beautiful. He is sent to heal, in miraculous ways, any human that calls on him. He is a healer of infirmities, a protector for those that travel and a terror to demons who dare to encounter him. He is one of the seven ArchAngels "who stand before the Lord." The glory of God that sprang from these two Angels was overwhelming for Mitka, Syree and Tezra.

Syree had encountered Gabriel before, because he had been with the Queen of Heaven and Earth from Her conception to Her Assumption into Heaven. But never had the angel spoken to him and all three of the Protectors fell to their knees to worship the Trinity and the glory produced in creating these two Beings.

At this meeting only Gabriel spoke to them. He warned them that they were to be constantly battling their greatest enemy in Jacob's house. He told Mitka he was to stay at Jacob's house at all times with the Guardians. He told them they would be hidden by a special grace from His Majesty, God the Father, whenever the deceiver came into their midst. He gave them specific instructions on how they were to behave and that through Mitka, each Guardian angel would know when to intervene. He told them that he would need to use Syree and Tezra in other places. He let them know that all the power of God would be at their disposal in their battle. He assured them that this was the Divine Order from the Throne and that it's end would be for God's greater Glory. All the Angels broke out in canticles of Praise for the Divine Providence of the Lord. Now as their enemy approached all the angels were on alert.

Satan entered the house. The smell that accompanied him was abominable. Madison was cooking with onions and was lost in thought, so the smell escaped her senses.

It did not, however, escape Maria's. She was on her knees on the floor in front of Rachael. She wanted to get another look at the cut on her face. She had decided that if she touched it ever so softly that she could keep from waking Rachael. She held her breath and carefully allowed her index finger to touch the cut. When she touched it, several things happened at once. Her finger began to burn violently and she saw a hideous face in her mind's eye. She also looked and saw the light of her Guardian Angel become brighter, this was a vision only and not something in the physical world. She instantly knew what the cut was and who had given it to her.

Description of Gabriel taken from the book, Mystical City of God by Mary of Agreda.

Satan stopped and stood behind Maria. He stared hatred at the two little girls. He wondered if he could reach out and touch the older one and kill her on the spot. He surmised that the Heavenly Beings, that he couldn't sense or feel but were assuredly around, would not allow it to happen without a fight. And he wasn't looking for a fight today. This was an information gathering mission only. He wanted to know as much about these abominations of his Father as he could. He especially wanted to tempt the older child to hurt the newborn. So, to that end, he implanted in her mind a strong image of Maria picking up a heavy lamp and crushing Rachael's head with it. As soon as he did this, he saw Maria take a deep breath.

Children were always so easy to persuade to follow his directions. Especially when he exerted his full force upon them with the suggestions he made to them, or when he made them repeatedly until the child felt compelled to act on them. This was getting easier and easier to do too in this century that belonged to him. Lucifer had been so successful in breaking the family" apart.

His first order of business had been to cause great conflict and strife between husbands and wives. He and his demons were relentless to this end. He would continually attack them with the demons of Misunderstanding, Anger, Hatred, Envy, Selfishness, Confusion, Pride and a host of others. His goal was to never relent so that both of the spouses would grow to hate each other so much that they first; desired a life without the other, second; wished harm on the other partner and filled them with bitterness and rage; thirdly; he never allowed them to resolve their differences until the only thing left, as a way out, was to divorce. Once he broke up marriages and made the excuse of "not being happy;" a norm in society, he turned his attention to the children.

He tried in each marriage to have one or both parents in some way abuse their children. If it didn't happen in the marriage, then he tried to make it happen with the new spouses of the parents. He implanted the demon of Jealousy in every step-parent's heart so that it became a competition between the parent's love for their spouse against the parent's love of the child. This never ended well. Usually it ended with the children being physically, emotionally or sexually abused. Then that marriage would end and he would continue to place people in their lives who would harm the children. This played very well into the hands of his next plan which was to cause such hatred and fear into the hearts of the children that they would learn to perpetuate the cycle on their own children. Lucifer needed the children to be abused for the next part of his plan.

If a boy was abused by his father or another male, then he sought, for the rest of his life, male approval. He did the same thing with the females and their mothers. Then he would implant inappropriate, inordinate desire into their hearts and minds toward their same sex. He loved it that society had accepted so readily, that people who called themselves homosexuals, had been that way from birth. Although this had no basis in fact, it did in only one way.

Satan knew what kind of people a child would be around and could surmise, and in a lot of cases inspire, their abuse. So in these cases he would begin attacking the child in-utero. He would continue the abuse by placing people who were possessed with the demon of Perversion to attack and abuse these innocents. In this way, they WERE that way from birth, because he mounted his plan of attack since their birth. But not because his Father would create them that way... because HE would not. Satan did this to torment these poor souls their whole lives. They were so busy trying to figure out how they felt and who they were, that they wasted their life and never completed the destiny they were created by God to complete.

The only possible escape from his attacks were the true Christian families in the world. If they understood what the Church taught and had a personal relationship with the Christ, then none of his attacks worked.

Even now, in Jacob's house, he watched his suggestion being carried out by Maria. She slowly stood up, with her back to Satan, and walked over to the table. He watched her hesitate for a moment so he once again implanted the suggestion into her mind. This time he included a mental image of what the newborn would look like afterward; this was to adapt her mind to the gruesome image so she wasn't later shocked by it. In this way he could desensitize her, then continue to use her for the rest of her putrid existence to carry out even more heinous crimes against humanity.

Maria reached for the lamp, and although it was heavy, she picked it up with one hand. Once she had a grip on it she moved back over in front of Rachael. Lucifer began foaming at the mouth, as he always did, right before he destroyed a human soul. He couldn't wait for this child to act so he could groom her for the rest of her life to come dwell in Hell with him. He knew that Bene't would love torturing her. He knew right where he'd put her.. next to the satanist, Natash. He would establish an order that when he or his demons weren't tormenting her, that Natash could.

He shut his eyes and imagined the worst punishments for this little human who had foiled his plans. She single-handedly stopped Natash from completing the assignments that would have hastened the growth of his Satanic church and brought about his prize pupil sooner. She set back that plan by two years. Yes, he couldn't wait to watch this child suffer.

As he was thinking, he watched as Maria raised the lamp in the air above Rachael. His thirst for blood was increasing. He sent the image of killing Rachael repeatedly in blasts to Maria's brain, not allowing any time to pass between each vision. He increased the force of it too, just for good measure. He saw her lift the lamp up but instead of hitting the newborn she turned around and faced him.

"I will NEVER hurt my baby sister," Maria said in a strong steady voice. She was making direct eye contact with him and there wasn't a trace of fear in her gaze.

"Don't you put thoughts in my mind ever again and don't you ever touch Rachael! You go back to Hell, right now devil!"

Maria didn't budge, still holding the lamp in the air threatening to throw it at Satan.

Lucifer was rarely surprised but he was more than that, he was astounded. He recoiled just an inch but it was enough that every being in the room noticed, including Maria.

"That's right..you better be scared. Why are you still here? In the name of Jesus Christ, ONLY begotten Son of the Father, I rebuke you to Hell... be gone!"

At her rebuke, every angel materialized. Maria's Guardian, became so bright and moved with such force towards Lucifer that it was like Satan was falling down a giant hole; all the while the light of Maria's angel chased him.

As soon as he was gone, the angels gathered around the two children and encased them in their wings of protection.

Madison had been beating the mashed potatoes with the electric beaters, so she didn't hear any of the commotion. But then something occurred to her; something Maria had said earlier that she had totally dismissed. She leaned out of the doorway and said,

"Maria, did you say Rachael TOLD you she loved you?" She didn't get an answer because the ringing phone distracted her.

CHAPTER EIGHT...FATHER KNOWS BEST

Jacob pulled into the driveway and looked at the clock. It was 7:30 pm. And once again, he was late. It really couldn't be helped, the boss needed him and he needed the overtime.

He felt badly leaving Madison and the girls alone so much, but he had to get them out of this house. He and Madison had decided to start looking to buy a new house right before Rachael was born. That was before they were in this terrible situation with the baby. The house was becoming smaller daily.

"Suffocating" may be a better word, he thought. He sighed deeply and opened his door. As soon as he did he could hear Rachael crying inside of the house. He pulled the door shut and stayed in the truck.

"Oh God, help our baby! Help Madison care for her and keep us all from going crazy."

Jacob placed his hands on the steering wheel and laid his head down. He felt so helpless, so useless. He held Rachael exactly twice before this nightmare began. She had been sleeping both times so he had no real bonding time with her at all. Every time he tried to hold her she would start to cry immediately. Then it turned from a cry into a wail and then into an ear piercing scream that no one in the house could get away from.

He could do nothing to comfort her. So he would give her right back to Madison and would immediately regret it. His wife was so exhausted and was not herself in any way. She rarely talked or laughed and they literally had no time together. It made Jacob sad because he missed her.

Even though they shared the same house, it was like she was never really there. All of her energy went into the girls, and he knew he shouldn't feel resentment, but he did.

They had just celebrated their first year anniversary and it was like he was a ghost in the house. To be fair, he knew she tried. She smiled when she saw him and she had a longing in her eyes that he took to mean that she missed him too. But truth be told it could've been a longing for a nap. She hadn't slept in the five months since Rachael's birth. Every time she tried, Rachael would cry within five minutes and she'd jump out of the bed and run to her.

She tried to make dinner while she was holding Rachael but most days her arms were too tired to hold her, so she would put her in her crib and try to throw something together in the short time she had before Rachael's tears demanded she pick her up again. Jacob would go in and finish whatever she had started, but he and Maria ate alone together every night.

Maria, the only bright spot in his day, tried to comfort him in his frustration. This daughter he had inherited was a very special little girl. He was constantly amazed at her ability to read a situation and know just the right thing to say or do. She always had a smile on her face and a sweet disposition. She was doing everything she could to help Madison, although in truth, there wasn't a lot she could do.

When they were at the ice cream shop she tried to get Jacob out of his black moods by telling him jokes and stories. It seemed to bring her a lot of happiness to make Jacob laugh or smile. She would tell him to be patient, that everything would be okay and he should just pray more. She told him if he did that he would feel so much better. She was right, of course, and Jacob knew it. Before these two amazing people shared his life, he never prayed; he never even thought about God or angels or demons for that matter. He lived only for himself and his needs and his wants.

He had been a very self-centered man and looking back, all the alcohol and drugs never brought him the happiness that his new life brought him. But on the other hand, he never thought that their life would have so much turmoil in it. It wasn't even anyone's fault...it just was. He knew that he and Madison were still madly in love and that he loved both of the girls with all his heart, it was just that he felt so... useless. There wasn't anything he could do to help the situation and the failure of that weighed on him. But Maria was right, he did need to pray more because that was the one thing he hadn't tried.

He looked at his house once more and said, "Father, give me strength to help my family. I know this will last as long as You WILL it and I'm fine with that. Just please make me a better husband and a better father and do whatever needs to be done to me to make that happen. Amen."

He got out of the truck and walked towards the house. He saw Madison through the window rocking Rachael in her "football hold." She was rocking back and forth with her eyes closed. Every time Rachael began to whimper Madison would shift her to the other arm and resume her rocking. The silence never lasted more than a few minutes before she'd shift her again. Madison bit the corner of her lip and Jacob knew, from the short time as her husband, that it wouldn't be very long before she began to cry.

He walked in and saw Maria sitting on the floor doing her homework. When they made eye contact he saw the anguish in her eyes that said "Help her, daddy". He looked at Madison and she had opened her eyes to look at him. She gave him a small smile and said "Hi honey, how was your day?" It was a crazy question because there was no way he could answer over all the noise Rachael was making. He walked over and tousled Maria's hair and then went and kissed Madison's cheek.

"I think it was better than yours," he said sweetly. "Listen, I'm gonna finish dinner and..."

"I already finished it. It's just spaghetti. Maria watched Rachael while I cooked."

Jacob looked back at Maria and she was beaming and nodding her head. "I babysat, Daddy!"

"Really! Well that's something. How did it go?" he asked moving closer to her so he could hear her over Rachael's cries.

"It went really well. I'm good at it," she said proudly.

"I bet you are. Did she misbehave at all? Did you have to put her in time-out?"

Maria knew he was joking and said, "No, she was acting like an angel... she wasn't the bad one."

Jacob completely misunderstood what she said but Madison caught it. She wanted to ask her about it. She wanted to continue their earlier conversation but her body was so weak that her mind couldn't even formulate a question.

A thought occurred to Jacob. If Maria could "babysit" Rachael, then surely he could. Just the thought of it filled him with fear. He knew he couldn't comfort her and that she didn't want him, but one more look at Madison told him he had to try. He walked over and gently put his arms around Rachael and tried to take her from Madison. Madison's eyes flew open,

"What are you doing?" she said, a little panicked.

Jacob looked at his wife lovingly and replied, "I'm going to take care of my daughter while you go take a nap."

"But, but, you can't...she will cry the whole time Jacob and I.."

That was all she could manage before he put his finger to her lips to quiet her.

"Maddie, I've got this! Go lay down right now. If I need you I'll call you."

"Thank you honey, I just need twenty minutes...twenty minutes that's all, then come get me, okay?"

"Okay, I will, now go!" Jacob said sternly.

Madison put down her head and walked to her room like an obedient child. She literally collapsed on the bed and immediately fell asleep.

Jacob was holding Rachael and he picked her up and held her up so her face was even with his. Her tiny eyes were squinted and tears were pouring from them. Her face was so red and her crying was so loud.

"What's the matter, Rachael, what's the matter baby girl?" he asked soothingly.

Rachael opened her eyes and looked at him. She seemed surprised to be in his arms and not her Mother's.

"Oh! Your eyes are really blue aren't they?" Jacob realized he'd never had a chance to see her eyes up close. They were an ice blue color and stunning.

She stared at him and just for a moment she stopped crying. She opened her eyes wider and looked around the room until she found what she was looking for. As soon as she saw Maria she made a sobbing sound and stuck out her bottom lip.

Maria got up and ran to them. She put her hand on Rachael's arm and said, "It's okay baby, Daddy's got you. Daddy is very very good."

Rachael looked immediately at Jacob and stared into his eyes. Jacob felt a wave of electricity go through his body. His body tingled and he felt a warmth that started at the top of his head and traveled through his entire body.

"See baby, Daddy IS good," Maria said knowingly.

Rachael stared for a fraction of a second longer and then a tiny smile formed on her face. It was very quick though, so quick in fact that Jacob thought he'd imagined it. Then he saw it...the pain welling up in her eyes. She went from calm to full out agonizing wailing in less than a second. His first reaction was nervousness but Maria came to the rescue.

"It's okay Daddy, just turn her upside down on her belly and swing like mommy does."

Without hesitating Jacob turned Rachael over and began to swing her. Almost immediately she stopped crying. Jacob looked at Maria and raised an eyebrow.

"That feels good to her Daddy..she likes it."

Jacob was so shocked that she'd stopped crying. He analyzed the position of her body and wondered if maybe the muscles in his arm were putting pressure on her stomach and that's why her pain was relieved. He furrowed his brow and looked at Maria as if she had the answer.

"I don't know Daddy, but it's working, look, she's falling asleep."

Jacob felt Rachael's body lighten and he knew she was right. He stayed standing for a few more minutes and then thought he'd risk it and try sitting in the rocking chair. He didn't want to wake her or take her comfort away but he'd been on his feet all day and NEEDED to sit down.

He carefully sat in his recliner and tried to keep a rocking motion during the transition. It worked. He turned Rachael over on her back and moved his hand so that it covered her entire stomach and applied some pressure. It worked! He smiled at Maria.

"Good job, Daddy!"

Jacob began to leisurely rock and let his body relax. This was a special moment for him to be able to hold his first born child, and to help relieve her pain as well, was an enormous accomplishment.

He looked closely at her little face. She had dark black hair and she had a lot of it. It was fine in texture but it was curly and unruly and the amount of it was more than any baby he'd ever seen. She had her mother's face structure but he was sure she had his nose and her chin boasted a dimple much like his own. Her eyelashes were very long and thick and her skin was velvety soft. He took his finger and began to trace each part of her face and that's when he saw it.

"How did she get this little red mark on her face? Do you know, Maria?"

Maria stared at the mark and felt protective of her sister all over again.

"Is it okay if I tell you later Daddy, I need to eat and go to bed."

Jacob thought the remark was a little strange but he said that was fine and then it dawned on him that neither of them had eaten.

"Baby girl do you think you can get the spaghetti yourself, or would that be too hard for you to reach?" Maria considered the question and replied,

"I can get it Daddy, don't worry." She made her way to the kitchen.

Jacob continued to rock and turned his attention back to the little cut on Rachael's cheek. He couldn't imagine what would've caused it. Maybe it was from a bracelet Madison was wearing or a watch, but then he remembered he hadn't seen his wife wear jewelry in months. Madison had literally devoted all of her time to Rachael's care and she didn't have any time for herself at all. Since she was home constantly, she wouldn't have dressed up to go anywhere which would require jewelry.

He put his finger on the cut and because the baby didn't stir he kept it there, as if doing so would tell him the source of it. As he was contemplating that, the wave of electricity he had felt earlier began again as well as the tingling and the warmth. He lifted his finger from her face and it stopped and when he touched her again, it began again. He sat there and played this little game until he noticed Maria coming out of the kitchen with a plate of spaghetti. He was about to tell her that she knew she needed to eat at the table but then he realized she was bringing it for him.

"Oh honey, thank you but I can't eat and hold the baby."

Maria didn't glance up as she answered him, she was trying to be very careful not to spill his dinner. When she put the plate down she ran off to the kitchen and grabbed his iced tea and a napkin with silverware in it.

"I think that if you lay her on her tummy on the couch she will be fine until you finish supper, Daddy. You have to eat too and anyway I want to babysit her again." Maria said with complete authority, as if the matter no longer needed to be discussed.

Although Jacob didn't think that the baby would stay asleep, he couldn't deny that he was hungry and needed to eat. He also didn't want to disappoint Maria. He carefully moved Rachael to the couch and laid her on her stomach. Maria sat right next to her on the couch and assured Jacob that she wouldn't let the infant fall.

Jacob ate all that Maria had put on his plate and then went to make himself another plate. He noticed that Maria's plate had been rinsed and was in the sink along with her fork and her glass. He couldn't believe she had fed herself and brought him dinner then cleaned up after too. He was reminded that she was growing up and a part of him saddened.

On his way back he went to check on Madison. She had not moved from the spot where she had landed. He felt her arm and it was cold so he grabbed a blanket out of the linen closet and covered her lovingly.

"You poor thing," he whispered. "I don't know how you've done this for five months."

He bent down and kissed her cheek. He felt so lucky to be her husband. She would laugh if she heard him use the word lucky. She would say luck had nothing to do with it, God did. He was getting ready to turn off the light and shut the door when he heard her talking in her sleep.

"No! No please, help her...help her. Malaya!" She stopped speaking and returned to the dream she was having. 'Who was Malaya?' Jacob thought. He shut off the light and shut the door but not all the way. He wanted to be able to watch her from his chair.

When he walked in the room Maria was examining Rachael closely. She turned around brightly and said, "You erased it Daddy...it's gone!"

"What's gone, honey?"

"The cut on her face. You erased it."

Jacob knelt down next to her and looked at the place the little cut had been and she was right, it was no longer there.

"Well that's weird, where did it go?" Jacob asked confusedly.

As he searched the baby's face he found no trace of the cut. Bewildered, he kept trying to solve the mystery.

"Your gift found you Daddy!" Maria said excitedly.

Jacob had intended to respond, but he was interrupted by a blood curdling scream coming from Madison. She continued and kept repeating one word over and over, MALAYA!!!!!!!!!!!!!!!!!!!!!!!

He ran into their room and Madison was sitting upright in bed with her eyes shut continuing to yell "Malaya!!"

Jacob wrapped his arms around her and repeated,

"It's okay Maddie, it's okay...shh..it's okay."

In the living room, Maria looked at Rachael and Rachael opened her eyes and was staring at Maria.

"Yes, I think you're right. I think Mommy knows now too!"

CHAPTER NINE....VENGEANCE IS MINE

Bene't was not in Hell when Satan was thrust back to the fiery cavern. He left shortly after Lucifer did. He couldn't bear to have Satan in such close proximity to Maria and not witness what was happening. He knew he would pay for it later but he was beyond caring. He had to see what the dragon did to the children, he had to try and stop him from hurting them, if that's what Lucifer tried to do. Bene't didn't even know if this was possible. Never in his existence in Hell did any demon try to battle with Satan. Bene't doubted it had ever even been considered by another demon.

When they were cast into Hell the first time, it was made instantly clear that all the demons would be subject to Satan. He was truly the Prince of the Darkness they had all chosen over the Light of Heaven.

In the beginning Satan spoke to them as if they were equals, brothers in arms. They all shared the common denominator that God had betrayed them by abandoning them to this place of fire and despair. Satan would ask for their counsel and they would have planning sessions to bring human nature to ruin. Their first goal was to find and destroy the "Woman" they had seen in the sky. The one the book of Revelation chapter 12 describes, "And a great sign appeared in the Heavens: a woman clothed with the sun, with the moon under her feet and a crown of twelve stars on her head..."

They had been informed by the Divinity that this 'Woman' was to be the Mother of the second person of the Trinity, the Christ, the Messiah.

She was going to be held in the greatest regard in the Kingdom. They all were informed that because She would be the only human in the history of humanity to hold the title of" Mother of God", that all the Heavenly and Earthly beings would be under Her in the Hierarchy of Heaven. They would all be subject to Her Will.

This would not be tolerated by Lucifer. It was already a grave insult that the Father did not choose him, the "first born, the "light bearer", to be named the King of the Earth and the head of this inferior race called Man. But to force him to be subject to, not a man, but a woman, whom they were informed was inferior to man in the hierarchy, was far too much to ask him to bear. The Father made His greatest error in judgment to attempt this atrocity. This became the reason he challenged the Trinity and ultimately fell from Grace. This Woman!

Satan's second goal was to seek out and find the Christ so that he could destroy Him and stop His Kingdom from coming. And finally his last goal was to kill each and every human ever created and bring them to Hell to be tortured for eternity.

In those days Satan pretended that what the demons said, held weight. He asked for their counsel and ideas. He took their suggestions and thanked them for participating. Now though, Lucifer didn't even pretend to value their opinions..they had none.

Bene't made his way to Jacob's house right as Satan entered. He knew that if he got too close, Satan would sense him and he would be in for a severe punishment. But it was important to him to be as close as possible to hear all that transpired, even if that meant harm for him later.

He hadn't been able to speak to Maria since the birth of Rachael. He had not been allowed to ascend to the Earth's surface until now because of the punishment he'd endured for failing Satan on his last assignment.

He perched himself in a tree just across the street from Jacob's house and turned all of his senses in that direction. He sensed that there were at least four Heavenly beings inside of the house, but they were hiding from Lucifer. He knew Maria's Guardian angel was strong by the bright white light it emitted and also because he could never see any features of it, it was ONLY light. Every time he'd been around Maria he'd been far too occupied with circumstances to try to look into the light and see who her Guardian was. If he got close to her today, he would try to see her angel's face, as long as the situation was conducive to it.

He watched Satan approach both of the little girls and he strained to hear Satan's voice so he would know what was happening. What he picked up on was the vision the devil kept sending into Maria's mind of her killing Rachael. Bene't jumped out of the tree and went right over to the front window where he could watch and try to stop this nightmare from happening. He was filled with trepidation for Maria and now for Rachael as well. He didn't even worry about the fact that Satan would surely detect his presence and he would be in grave danger. He only wanted to protect the children from the attack Lucifer was trying to inflict.

When Maria turned around and faced Satan, Bene't saw the look in her eyes and all the fear he had for her multiplied. He'd seen that look in her eyes before and it confirmed for him that whatever she was ready to speak would be profound...and there was no way Satan would tolerate anything like that from a human and especially not from her.

He listened to the words she spoke and watched her offensive posture against the devil and once again, couldn't help being impressed with this very unique human. He then watched Lucifer's surprise as he was cast into Hell by this tiny child. Then it struck him that by Divine law he would've also been cast into the abyss along with Satan, but he was not...he was still there.

He stared at Maria as she kissed Rachael and then put her arms protectively around the infant. Then the angels that were in the house surrounded them with their wings to comfort them.

When Maria's Angel returned from chasing Lucifer into Hell, Bene't took that time to try to get a better look at it, but again couldn't penetrate it's light. It reminded Bene't of an exploding star. Its light was so intense and such a bright white that you would think it would hurt the eyes to look upon it, but that was not the case, in fact the opposite was true. It was soothing to the eye to look at it and it also made Bene't feel a calming warmth. He tried again to penetrate the light and this time something did happen. He couldn't discern any features but there was something oddly familiar about her angel. Bene't searched his memory of Heaven so that he could place the angel, and how he knew him, but he wasn't successful. Giving up, he turned his attention to Maria. It had been so long since he'd seen her or talked to her and he was feeling a deep sense of sadness. He tried to sit with that emotion and hoped his intellect would clarify it, but he had no luck.

All Bene't wanted to do was go into the house and comfort her like the angels were doing. He wanted to tell her how sorry he was that Satan had put those awful pictures in her pure, innocent, perfect mind. He wanted to tell her how proud he was of how she stood up to Lucifer and let her know how brave she had been. But once again he knew he did not belong where she was and it would not be good for her to speak to him again. It would be extremely disrespectful to the Heavenly Beings if he were to materialize in their presence. He knew what an abomination he was in their eyes and just being in the same place with them had to repulse their Divine nature. He knew he should leave soon and go back to the abyss. Lucifer would be enraged by being rebuked again and he would want to take his anger out on Bene't, no doubt.

As he turned to leave, Bene't took one last look at Maria. His heart swelled. He had a strong feeling that she was in terrible danger now. Satan had made her a target and when that had happened all throughout eternity, it usually hadn't ended well for the human involved. He wanted to protect her from all of this and to keep Lucifer far away from her and Jacob's family. But as he was suddenly pulled violently into Hell it reminded him that he couldn't even protect himself.

His entrance into Hell was swift and he landed at the foot of the fiery throne of Satan. All the demons in Hell were there, all seven legions. He thought that Satan would be focused directly on him because of the manner that he returned to Hell, but as he watched other demons being thrust into the pit, he realized this was a mandatory general summons.

Lucifer didn't wait for everyone to arrive before he began to rage. His voice was furious and booming. He was ranting about the unfairness of the Father distributing Heavenly gifts to mere humans...gifts that belonged only to the divine creatures. He sent an image, or memory into the minds of all the demons there. It showed Satan arriving at Jacob's house and all that transpired between him and Maria. It was exactly the truth until the part when Maria rebuked Satan. Lucifer changed the image to show that when she rebuked him he wasn't affected by her at all. Bene't did everything he could not to laugh.

"The deceiver, deceives even himself," he thought.

Satan then went on to rant that this mere child should not be able to stand against his greatness and that she was being unfairly assisted by the Trinity and the Queen. He showed all of the demons her entire life in a vision, being careful to change anything that made Satan look weak. He didn't, however, change the parts where Rahoul and Bene't were bested by her and made to look foolish. To this end he criticized both demons and encouraged all other demons to inflict punishment on them both for their weakness and because they failed their father, Lucifer. Almost immediately they obeyed and thrust themselves like a pack of hungry wolves upon the two demons. They were burned, tortured, mutilated, stabbed and ripped apart. It all happened so quickly that they couldn't defend themselves in any way. Lucifer watched with pleasure as the two demons who had failed him, were rightly punished. He quickly tired of their bellows and waved his hand to end the assault.

All the demons were panting heavily, exhausted from the lashing they delivered. It had happened before when they were ordered to beat another demon or a damned soul. If they didn't do it with all their strength and ability, Satan would single them out as disobeying him; then they would become the object of the beating. For their parts, Rahoul and Bene't were using all of their energy to recover as quickly as possible because if they didn't pull themselves together fast enough, Satan would say they were ignoring him. He would then have another reason to torture them.

The Damned were not excluded from this punishment. Anytime the demons suffered Satan's wrath, the Damned did too. Only their pain and torture came from the hands of the demons themselves as a way for the demons to relieve whatever pain they suffered at the hands of Satan. This was yet another law of Hell. Sometimes Satan himself would single out a soul to torture himself, although these times were rare and it was done for a singular purpose. Mostly though, after their initial entrance into Hell, Satan left punishing the Damned to his demons so that he could concentrate all his efforts on tempting and deceiving the living.

Today however was one of those "singular purposes days" because Bene't noticed that Natash had been brought to this party of pain.

He was inside of a clear box and flames were shooting up from the bottom of it and he was being continually consumed by the flames. Bene't could hear his agony but to say he was screaming wasn't really correct. Bene't thought there were no words to describe the sound someone makes when they are in that kind of anguish.

Natash couldn't concentrate on any of the things Satan was saying, he was just surviving from one second to the next. Realizing that the weak human couldn't listen to him and be tortured, Satan stopped the flames in the box and gave Natash a reprieve.

"Ah Natash, my good and faithful servant. How are you enjoying your 'reward' so far? I hope the accommodations are to your liking?" he said, dripping with sarcasm.

Natash dared not utter any response. He learned immediately after meeting Lucifer for the first time that every word he uttered would bring him torture. He learned that nothing would be what he'd imagined it would be. That his life long devotion to this Demon would bring an eternity of torment that nothing could have prepared him for. Even all the thousands of warnings his brother Zachary, the priest, had given him didn't come close to describing the reality. He thought about every decision he'd ever made against God every second of his time in Hell. He relived all the opportunities he had to do good and be who he was created to be.

This same process happened to every one of the damned. They relived it all and instead of filling them with feelings of regret or remorse, it filled them with hatred, anger and bitterness towards God and Humanity. This happened because there was an absence of God in Hell, so no such feeling of goodness could live in that environment. The Damned hated all living beings because they still had the chance to choose rightly and live for God. And unlike a movie Natash once saw where a man from Hell came back to warn another man on Christmas Eve to change his ways, the reality was that the Damned souls wanted only to lash out and hurt the living. Their sole desire was to wreak as much havoc as possible on them because they didn't want them to acquire eternity in Heaven since they themselves could not.

Satan didn't wait for Natash to respond because he didn't care what the vile human thought of his eternal condition. He just wanted to torment him further with the question. So he continued as if he had never addressed him at all.

"Brothers, as you may recall, my servant Natash had his own encounters with the putrid human, Maria, during his wasted life on earth. Let me remind you of his interactions with her."

Satan then sent more memories through the demon's minds showing each time Maria had bested all of them. He would reach inside the demons' minds and pull the memory of interacting with her out and replay it for the other demons. He would add, subtract or embellish them in any way he wished and no demon would dare correct the memory. While recalling

Rahoul's interaction with her and showing how he had been rebuked by her while praying the Hail Mary, Satan forced Rahoul to his knees and ordered magma to be poured over him as an additional punishment for his failure with the child.

Satan did this with all of them, exposing each demon's failure to all the other demons. He stopped though when he came to Bene't. He could not transmit his memories, because he could not read Bene't's mind. Once again Lucifer became enraged with the Father for closing this demon's mind to his.

Every memory he sent about Bene't to the other demons came from either the mind of another demon who had been present or from the mind of a human who had been with him during his times of failure. He pulled all of his memories with Maria from the child herself. He looked into her memories for the purpose of finding Bene't's defeats. The child didn't give much information about him though, only other demons. Lucifer did this because he had found it to be true throughout history that any human whose special graces and gifts were undetected by him usually were undetected because a demon left out certain details of their encounter with the human when they gave a report to him. It was only when he searched the demons' memories that he got the complete truth of the interaction.

The problem he faced with Bene't...had always faced with Bene't, was whether or not he was getting a completely accurate version of anything.

He first realized he couldn't penetrate Bene't's mind when they still resided in the Kingdom. He, as the first born, was able to meet each angel after it's creation. He was not privy to the HOW or WHY of the creation itself, but after each angel was "born" they were placed in the same space that Lucifer occupied.

Because of their Divine Nature there was a "knowing" that took place upon introduction. It was a joining of their minds and intellects, as well as a joining of their actual essences.

As the Father placed each new angel in his space, Lucifer joined with them. In less than an instant he knew the thoughts of each of them. He knew how much they loved their Creator and how each one was capable of loving all of the other angels. He could not see any of their futures because time was a concept yet to be created, but he had a sense of what their strengths might be and a small inkling of the distinction between each of their intellects.

They were separated into nine distinct "choirs". Each choir of angels had a similar purpose and a similar outward appearance. The purposes were not shown to them in those early moments, other than the fact that they were different. The reasons hardly mattered to any of them in the beginning because they were nothing but love, peace and joy. They all were perfect and without defect. All of them were in harmony and none of them questioned anything.

The Angels were formed from lightning and water that became fire. Not the fire of the earth that is hot, red and dangerous. They burned a brilliant white fire that was pure spirit and only existed in Heaven. This is not to say that they didn't have form, because they could. They were not in any way bound by the laws of humanity. They were able to take any form they desired and were never limited. They could become very large or very small. They could be everywhere at once. They could split themselves into a million pieces and go forth in space. Never would any piece of them become disconnected intellectually from their original form, even if they were just briefly physically separated. They had but one desire, which was to praise their Creator. It was a beautiful, joyous existence and none of them knew anything other than Love.

Only Lucifer, the Light Bearer, the most Beautiful of all of them, had questions. He wanted to know why these choirs had differences..to what end? He very easily could have just asked the Trinity this question but because none of the other angels seemed concerned with these answers, he concealed his thoughts. He didn't want any of the other angels to know he had questions. He wanted to ascertain if they themselves were questioning. He didn't want the Father to know that he had questions, if he were the only one. At this point, he wasn't being evil or sinning in any way. His first great mistake was not running to the Father for the answers he sought. This was the beginning of the formation of the trait he would become most known for, the one that would cause the greatest schism in the whole of creation... his Pride.

One of the first things Satan did was a variation of the "knowing" that he had done in the beginning. But instead of joining with the angels, he secretly invaded their minds to see what they were thinking and how they were feeling. He was in no way capable of inciting any of them to change a thought or action but it was a lesson in reconnoitering. As he gathered his information, he could more fully understand the degrees of strength of each angel. He was very pleased that none of the angels seemed to know when he was penetrating their minds.

He began to practice and learned very quickly that he was able to send messages to their minds, and to his astonishment, none of them seemed to attribute any of the messages as coming from him. The first time he tried it, he simply sent an image of the Trinity into an angel's mind. He watched as the angel reacted to it with an even greater posture of praise and adoration towards the Trinity.

It fascinated Lucifer that he was able to accomplish this. It never occurred to him to mention this new found skill to any other angel. This time it wasn't because he was afraid of being different...it was because he WANTED to be different. He did not want to reveal this skill or bring attention to it in any way, lest the other angels also learn it and take away something he intended to be just for himself.

Shortly after this, the Father made known to all of the angels that He was now going to create another Being. This race would be made in the image of the Father, Son and Holy Spirit. He would be, "Small in his Greatness and Great in his Smallness." He would not be of the same Divine nature as the angels and would be inferior to them in intellect and most every other way. God showed them the sign of Mary in Heaven and THIS was how they saw human nature first, in the form of this Woman. The Lord infused the angels with the knowledge that the Second person of the Trinity would descend to be a part of this race and that because of that fact, all of Humanity would forever be lifted on high and placed above the Angelic nature.

He showed them that this Woman would be the Mother of the Son and because of that all important fact, She would be inferior only to the Trinity. The Lord further explained that He was now decreeing that both races and all of His Creation would now be given a great gift....Free Will. This meant that the choice to love and serve the Creator would now be a choice that each and every creature would make. He showed them what would happen if they freely chose Him. They saw the very vision of the best that they could be in the Kingdom. He also showed them that if any of them did NOT choose Him that He would not be with them for Eternity.

He let them know that He would not force any of them to choose Him, that He desired that they choose to make their home with Him by their own volition.

He showed them Earth and he showed them Man. He showed each of them the center of the earth and that this would be the place designated for anyone that chose to be apart from Him. They were made to understand that because His light would not shine there, that it would be absent of any and all love..because HE was love. Where HE was not...love COULD NOT exist. He showed them that this place called Hell, would have inhabitants and this was the greatest shock to their sensibilities. Many of them murmured that no one would consciously make the choice to be absent from the Trinity's beautiful light and love.

"Whom, my greatest Love, wouldest not choose Thee? Whom would run to darkness and ruin? Whom wouldst douse the Fire of Love you formest in your creatures by choice? We adore thee Most High and Indisputable Father as our only source of Life! We, whom Thou created out of nothing will serve thee throughout eternity and beyond!"

It was MICHAEL who had spoken these words and all the Heavenly

Hosts sang their agreement in unison.

Only Lucifer did not sing. Instead the questions that had plagued his mind began to spin with such force and all at once, that he spontaneously implanted them in all of the Angels' minds. He then voiced a question to the Trinity.

"My Father, was I not the first created? Shouldn't it be thy desire that I shouldest be the King of this new inferior race?" As the question was asked, Lucifer sent an image of himself into the mind of each angel. In the vision he was sitting on a throne with this creature called man beneath him. On all sides of him were the other Angels and Man was under his feet.

Although he thought his ability was hidden, it was not hidden from the Trinity and in seeing the vision he sent, the Father sent His own vision...one of Truth. All the angels saw the Second Person of the Trinity on His Throne with a dominion that ruled all of Creation from the beginning until the end. It showed how ALL of creation was created through and held together by Christ. It was much grander than Lucifer's vision and each Angel was silenced by the unchallengeable truth of it. It sent a shock wave through all of the angels who had any reaction to Lucifer's vision and they repented in their minds to their Creator. Lucifer felt no such repentance. Instead he posed another question.

"If my Father, I cannot rule this humanity, may I then be His Mother?"

The angels, at this moment, had no concept of sexes or the difference between women and men. Angels were not privy to the reproductive nature of men, so the word " Mother" had no real meaning for Lucifer. He just wanted to replace the sign in the Heavens from the Woman to Himself, as he felt was only fair. He preceded Her in existence and he should never be inferior to Man and certainly not to the Woman, who was the inferior side of the race of Men.

Lucifer sent another image to the angels of Himself in the Heavens and the Woman at his feet. He also invoked many questions of why the Trinity would pick these Creatures to descend to...why not descend to the Angelic nature?

The voice of the Father was loving but firm.

"Thou knowest not the conditions of life and humanity. It is not possible for thee to comprehend ways which are far above thine own. This Woman will be placed above thee and all of creation under Her feet. All of the Heavenly Host will serve Her and all of Humanity for all ages."

At this point there was a brief period of time when Lucifer was able to converse with his brethren and plead the case which was forming in his mind. He made them all to know the unjustness of the Father's Will and that being placed beneath these humans was an insult to their very nature. He conceived an impossible plan; to make a throne for himself and place it above the Throne of the Most High. He spent this period convincing as many of the angels as he could to join him in this endeavor.

The 'good' angels all rebelled against any of the images being sent to their minds. They used their intellect to argue that this was the road to ruin. They reminded each of the doubting angels of the place of Hell, where the Father would not dwell, and the horrors within. Satan countered this by sending images of this Hell as being the new Kingdom that he would rule, and sent images of beauty and light. He sent visions of each angel sitting upon his own throne, and the Father grieving the angels' departure and prompting them to come back to the Kingdom of Heaven. He then showed these same angels that were refusing to leave this "paradise" that they now rightly ruled, that they would be jubilant in the absence of the Trinity. It was during this period that Lucifer realized he could not penetrate the mind of the angel, Bene't.

Up until that point, all of the angels, the 'good' and the 'bad' were susceptible to Lucifer's interference in their minds, but when the gift called FREE WILL was given, the 'good' angels closed their minds to Lucifer. He could no longer see if his images or suggestions were influencing them. Only to the 'bad' angels was he still able to communicate his will.

All of the 'bad' angels accepted his thoughts and visions and he looked into the mind of each one individually to see how committed they were to his cause. When he tried to enforce his will on Bene't and then read his mind, he heard only silence. This did not alarm him at first, because Bene't was the angel who seemed most in agreement with him. Bene't was the one who held as many conversations as Lucifer did with any angel that would listen to him. Every reason a 'good' angel gave him to leave this revolt, became ammunition for him to believe even stronger in Lucifer's Cause. He battled against so many of the brethren in his choir and his closest brother, Syree, could not convince him to see the danger of his ways. He did not believe the Trinity had any right to place an inferior creature above the Divine Nature of the Angels. He would not listen to any reason and instead stood behind Lucifer in all of his arguments.

When it became clear that the 'bad' angels were going to populate their own Kingdom, this place called Hell, Bene't was leading the charge. So Lucifer did not fear the fact that he could not read Bene't's thoughts or implant any visions into his mind. It was, though, the singular thing that bothered him as he approached the throne of the Trinity for his final stand.

After the battle in Heaven and the great victory of Michael, all of the 'bad' angels fell into Hell and earned their new name...demon. There was no more thought given to what Lucifer could or could not do in Bene't's mind, because they were preoccupied with the monstrosities they had become.

They were all terrorized to see their physical state and even more traumatized to see that Hell would never be a place of "light and joy" where they would all sit upon their glorious thrones. Instead, it was a place of darkness and fire and pain and suffering because the only thing Hell contained... was hatred.

Lucifer recalled all of these events in an instant, in the time it took Natash to take one single deep breath. Bracing himself for whatever nightmare would befall him now, Natash waited. Bene't waited too because he knew by the way Satan was staring at him that he was getting a new assignment.

CHAPTER TEN... BLINDING THE SHEEP

Tim Nethers left the Ditch in a hurry. Because of that freak Malaya, he was now late for a very important appointment at the Lodge. He would be shaking with rage if he wasn't giddy with satisfaction because in the morning he would never have to think about her ever again. She had been a thorn in his side since she was a child. And even though she had no part in Natash's death, he still blamed her for it. She had a power that he didn't understand. It far surpassed anything he'd seen in his circles and she could summon it up instantaneously. He knew she had dealt with Natash in some way when she was younger and he was sure she had "prayed" against everything the satanist did. Yes, the sooner Malaya was dead the better. He couldn't wait to see the aftermath of Carl's handiwork.

Visions of bones and torn flesh entered his mind. He was hoping that before Carl killed her that he would make her suffer first. The problem was that Carl probably wouldn't be able to think to make her suffer. His actions were always purely reactionary so he would most likely just kill her instantly. Tim grimaced in disappointment at the thought.

If there was anyone who should ever be made to suffer, it should be her. She had caused him and many other of the "Elites" of the world an enormous amount of trouble. When he found out that she had been captured and that they were sending her to him, he was ecstatic. It was a 'reward' for all the good work he'd been doing in the Ditch. At least that's what the higher ups in the Deep State had told him.

Malaya was a national security problem. No, more than that, she was a global security problem and if the world's Elite and their goal of a "One World Order" was destroyed...she would be the one to do it. Oh how he detested her. He despised her more than anyone in the world. He had hated her from the first moment he saw her. If truth be told, he'd never had a more visceral response of loathing for anyone. And because he hated almost everyone and everything, that was saying something. Oh tomorrow could not come soon enough.

He looked at his clock as he turned into the Lodge and was relieved to see he was going to make it in time for the ceremony. He got out of his car and looked up at the enormous building with no windows. He watched as other people began entering the building. He wouldn't be entering through the same door. No, he was a leader in this Lodge...'the' leader as a matter of fact. He was far too good to enter through their door. He was superior in every way to the men who came here. Even the ones who were close to his ranking did not come close to matching his intellect or ambitions.

He made his way into his office and changed into his Fowlin's garb. This was an important day and one he looked forward to each year. Today was the Induction Ceremony for the Initiates. Today, the Lodge would once again add to its number and grow stronger.

He was standing just off stage as the ceremony began. He watched as the men to be inducted stood up and made their way to the front. He was always astonished at the melting pot of the men who were a part of this and every other Fowlins Lodge. They were Lawyers, Doctors, Judges, Pastors, as well as every kind of blue collar worker in the book. They were rich, poor, brilliant and illiterate. The adjectives to describe them were as numerous as the stars. They came from every background and they all came for one reason...to enter this "fraternity of brothers." To them it was a social club of sorts, that allowed them to gather with men to bond. None of them had a clue of what it really was, or what they were about to do.

Just as Tim was thinking this, Bene't and Natash arrived at the Lodge. This assignment they were on was two-fold. The first stop was here and it would be a short visit. They were there to "confirm" the ceremony. This was something Bene't had done since these ceremonies began. He used to enjoy watching them and participating in them as well. This time though he felt nothing but repulsion, as well as sadness for what these men were about to commit to. On top of that, he had the Satanist Natash with him and he detested the man.

At present, Natash was beside himself with confusion. He knew what he was to do at the ceremony but what he didn't understand was why it still felt like he was in Hell.

When Satan said he was going "up top," Natash was so excited to be leaving Hell. He also saw the first light at the end of the tunnel since arriving in Hell. If he could somehow be used to help Satan damn more souls, then maybe Satan would reward him by lessening his pain. He was also relieved that while he was on his errands from Satan, he would be away from Hell. But just like when he thought his arrival into Hell would mean a sort of kingship for himself, and he'd been wrong, he was wrong again today when he realized he carried the pains of Hell with him.

It was the strangest sensation. He was fully there with the terrifying demon, Bene't. He could see the lodge, smell the smells in the air. He could reach out and touch the men who were present, even though they weren't able to see him. He could walk, talk and think in the space of the Lodge while at the same time he was completely present in Hell. He felt the pain and suffering and hatred and fear and he could see and feel the demons tormenting him. So even though he was at the Lodge, he was also in Hell. The little light he was clinging to slowly faded into his eternal reality.

The Ceremony was beginning. The "Ceremony Master" introduced Tim Nethers as the "Sovereign Grand Commander." Natash began to foam at the mouth and fell into a fit of jealousy as that title actually belonged to him. Tim Nethers was his second in command and the closest thing he ever had to a friend. But watching him assume Natash's title, only made Natash abhor him. He was filled with an all consuming rage and immediately rushed Tim to attack him. He was disappointed when his efforts proved fruitless and Tim didn't react at all to Natash's assault. Bene't would've stopped Natash if his actions had been directed towards any other human, but not this human. Bene't had groomed this particular vile example of humanity. He knew that no amount of Grace from Heaven would be able to save Tim's soul; he was too resistant to God and His Holiness. He was just as disappointed as Natash that Tim felt none of the attack, and after pondering it, Bene't thought he understood why nothing had happened.

When someone sells their soul to the devil, they actively refuse Grace and defame the Holy Spirit. As they continue down this path of worshiping the devil and insulting God, they have less and less access to Grace, which in turn increases their pace down the path of ruin. Bene't knew quite well the times in Tim Nether's life that God had reached His loving hand out to him, and how many times that love had been rejected. He had a lifetime of chances to change and he still chose the path to Hell. There was no turning back for him. He had embraced the darkness of Satan, and like Natash, truly believed he would be rewarded with a throne next to Satan's in Hell when he died.

As the ceremony began, each of the men stripped down to a garment that looked like a loin cloth. The first thing they were asked to do was to remove any ring, including their wedding rings. Then any religious jewelry, like a crucifix, necklace containing a cross or a Scapular were also removed. Tim loved this particular custom because unbeknownst to the men, they were removing any protection these items offered, especially the blessed items.

After they were divested of their jewelry and sacramentals, the men were blindfolded and a noose was placed around each man's neck. This was supposedly to mimic the death of the original Fowlin, but it had more significance than that. Tim explained to them that this meant the men were in "spiritual darkness," Bene't shook his head at this because even if they had accepted Christ as their Savior, they were now rebuking Jesus by admitting they were in spiritual darkness.

After this, they placed a sharp object on the left side of the men's chest to mimic cutting them. Bene't had been present when Satan inspired this part of the ritual to mock the lance being pushed through Jesus' heart while he was being crucified.

At this point each man was to swear an oath. If they were Christian, they would swear on a Bible; if Muslim, they used the Koran and if they were Jewish they swore on the Torah. Tim Nethers knew that as each one used a symbol of their own religion to swear upon, that this really meant they were replacing their religion with a vow to Satan. This oath made them Satanists. But none of the men realized this until it was too late and they had spoken the oath. The first man began...

"I swear on my Bible that my throat will be cut, my tongue will be torn out by its roots, my chest torn open and my heart plucked out. My body will be severed in twain and my bowels taken and burned to ashes if I violate this Fowlins Oath."

Natash began to shake violently. How many times had he heard this oath taken? How many men had he watched make this vow? And only now, after his experiences in Hell, did he realize what was happening. These men were making this "blood oath" to say that if they ever turned against the Fowlin's lodge, they would willingly accept these terrible things to happen to them. What they didn't know was that they didn't have to turn against the lodge or reveal any of the secrets. Whether they did or didn't, the result was the same...all of these things would happen to them in Hell. Natash knew this because he suffered all of them daily, as well as even more horrendous things. At the time he took the oath himself, he knew he was pledging his life to Satan. Unlike these men, he held no illusions that this was a benign

Lodge or Fraternity. He knew it was a denial of Christianity and especially the Catholic church. He knew it was denying that Jesus was Lord and King. He knew exactly what he was doing. What he didn't know was that even if you never broke ranks with the Fowlins, you still suffered exactly as the oath stated. How many Fowlins had he seen in Hell getting their throats cut, their tongues torn out by its roots, their chest torn open and their heart plucked out, their bodies torn in half and their bowels removed and burned to ashes? He saw this every second in Hell. These men had no idea that they had just secured their eternity.

Tim Nethers also knew that they were making a deal with the devil but he, like Natash, didn't understand that the punishment held regardless of if you betrayed the Fowlins or not. One might think Natash would want to stop the men from making the oath, but it had the exact opposite effect on him. He wanted them to make it. He wanted them dead so they could join him in his torment. He had no compassion, even for the ones who didn't understand their oath. He was so jealous of their life force. The fact that they still had time to change, to make a different choice, made him only wish death for them. If he could have caused them all to die then and there, he would have.

Bene't watched Natash and knew what he was thinking and feeling. And while he used to have the same reaction to men when they participated in this satanic ritual, now he only felt pity for them. If he could stop them from coming to Hell, he would. If he could tell them that by making this oath they would soon watch their lives come apart; their marriages fail, their relationships with their kids, grand kids and friends deteriorate, he would. He wanted to tell them they would lose their jobs and misfortune would follow them. Most of them would become physically ill. Before it was over, something traumatic would happen to each one of them. If they were wise, some of them would hit their knees and turn back to God. If they returned to their Christian faith they would find help and forgiveness there. But most would not come back to God. They would continue their journey to Hell.

And all under the guise of 'fraternal brotherhood.'

Once the sinful curses were spoken and the covenant was sealed, the noose was removed and each man was called a "brother" for the first time. Then, the blindfold was removed and each man was "brought into the light." As each man opened his eyes he would see only the Fowlins symbols in front of him. From this point on, the name "Jesus" would not be allowed to be spoken by them within Lodge walls. They have now agreed that all Gods, ie Mohammed and Buddha and Chrisna were equal to the Trinity. From now on, they would only be allowed to say that they believed in a "Supreme Being" not the One True God. What they didn't know was that the "Supreme being" they were now referring to, was Lucifer. He alone would be their God.

Bene't was always amazed at how easily they gave up their Christ, their Lord and Savior and chose Satan instead.

Tim Nethers was amazed they gave up Jesus as well. Some of them wouldn't understand that they were now a vital, active part of Satan's army until they died... but some would. Tim scanned the new members to ascertain which ones he could raise up to the higher ranks. Since Natash's death, they needed committed Satanists more than ever. They especially needed the wealthy ones to help further their cause with the Elites. As he looked around, only two men looked to be candidates.

One was a congressman, who Tim knew was involved in the pedophile ring that most of the Elites were part of. His responsibility was to gather up children from third world countries to insert into the ring. Yes, he would definitely be an asset. The second man, a rich business man that Tim knew had ties to the Mafia, caught his interest. Mafia men were always sought after, because where money and gain were the subject, there was loyalty in spades. And to be a part of the higher Orders, they must have loyalty first and foremost to the Lodge. So much of what the Elite Society did, required secrecy, and if there was one group of people who understood that, it was the Mafia.

The main philosophy of the Elites was the desire to create a One World Order. This One World Order would enslave humanity. They would control healthcare, food distribution, education, housing, employment and even families. Each "world citizen" would be tracked and controlled by whomever the Elite chose as their world leader. The top priority on their agenda was to destroy organized religion and especially the Roman Catholic Church. It was for the goal of the latter, that the Fowlins lodge was created. It's appearance as a benign fraternity of the common man, became the perfect cover for the malignant army the elite would need to further their cause.

Tim directed the Ceremony Master to pull the two men that had potential aside, and set up appointments with him for later in the week. Tim would begin their grooming immediately. He then excused himself and headed to his car. He was on a high. He always felt this way when he added to his Master's army. All thoughts of Malaya had left his mind.

Bene't and Natash also left. This time Satan commanded that they go to New York to torment Matthew. Bene't didn't understand the request because the man was no threat to anyone. He was so far gone in his addiction and his emotional descent that he was a shadow of his former self. However, Bene't knew better than to ask the whys of it. He assumed that Satan was just enacting his revenge. Any time anyone ruined one of Lucifer's plans, he never let it go. He continued to attack the human until the moment of death. Sometimes his attack had no power to affect the human. This was true only if the human had a strong relationship with Christ. He could try to hurt them in many ways; causing trouble in their relationships, giving them money problems, implanting people who would abuse them. The list was endless, but for the Christians who understood that the attacks were coming from Satan, no harm came to them. All they had to do was invoke the name of Jesus or appeal to the Saints, Angels or to the Blessed Mother, and Lucifer's efforts became like puffs of smoke. But for the unbelievers, like Matthew, his attacks were like bullets in the bulls-eye. The devil could send the demon of Addiction and the effect would be deadly.

Bene't watched the demons that were assigned to Matthew, celebrating his demise. Satan was determined to end his life as quickly as possible so Bene't and Natash were sent to expedite that process. But because God never leaves his children without his help and protection, HE was sending Matthew help...and some of them were already there.

CHAPTER ELEVEN...
"BEHOLD, I MAKE ALL THINGS NEW!"

Tezra sat next to the cat that had lived outside of Matthew's apartment building. The little orange tabby was named Samson and he had a very sweet disposition. He was born in an ally and would've stayed there if Tezra hadn't rescued him from certain death. An arctic cold front had made its way into New York City and the temperatures fell well below freezing. To make matters worse, the wind was powerful and the combination meant that nothing could live long outside without shelters. Even the huge buildings left no protection for anyone to survive long.

Tezra had been sent there to protect Matthew. He had been sent at the direction of Matthew's sister Tara. Tara, and all the Saints in Heaven could direct the Holy Angels in any way they desired to help their loved ones on Earth. The Angels were more than happy to comply and serve these special souls with joy and honor. After all, these Saints were of the same 'kind' as Jesus and because HE took their form, they were all elevated to brothers and sisters and had at their disposal the storehouses of the Lord, which included the help of the Angels.

Tezra had been sent by Tara, but it also was confirmed by Mitka and at the directions of the great Arch Angels, Michael, Gabriel and Raphael. Just like all things that work together for the greater good and are always timed perfectly in the Kingdom of God, Tara's request came in the same instant that Mitka sent Tezra to protect Matthew.

Because Tezra is the General of the entire Animal Kingdom, he uses animals in all his interactions with humans. He would often enter an animal's body and take control of their actions to benefit the children of God. One of the times he'd entered Sampson's body was on the day he rescued him from the deadly cold. This was also the day when Matthew had his worst health scare ever.

Matthew had been drinking so heavily the night before and woke up with an abominable hangover. He was stumbling around his house searching for something to stop the throbbing headache that wouldn't allow him to see. As he entered the kitchen he realized he was going to get sick. There wasn't time to run to the bathroom. He barely had time to make it to the sink before vomit projectiled across the room. Before he even made it to the sink he was alarmed because what was coming out was pure red and it wasn't vomit...it was blood. And then, to make matters worse, it wasn't stopping. He was throwing up buckets.

He moved away from the sink just long enough to grab the phone. Between each bout of gagging he would dial a number or two until he completed the call and someone answered the phone. It was Peter who was on the other end of the line and he knew by the lack of words and the sounds he was hearing, that Matthew was in trouble. He didn't even reply; he just called 911 on his cell phone and ran up to the Penthouse as quickly as he could.

When he got there the scene looked like something from a CSI television crime scene. Everywhere in Matthew's beautiful white kitchen, blood covered surfaces. It was on the counters, the floor, the appliances and even on the ceilings. Peter ran over to him and could only pat him on the back and reassure him that the ambulance was on its way.

Matthew was so happy to see Peter, but his prominent feeling was fear. This had never happened before and Mathew knew this was life threatening.

He heard the sirens, and that calmed him a bit, but he still had not stopped throwing up. When the paramedics finally arrived and Peter ran to the door to let them in, Matthew had his first moment of relief. He took a deep breath but decided not to move an inch. Not that he could walk if he tried. The loss of blood was making him nauseous and extremely unsteady.

He did get a glimpse of the mess though. Blood was everywhere. It was even on the cat. The paramedics made quick business of putting him on the gurney and they rushed him out the door.

The hospital admitted him because he had lost so much blood and he had to have a transfusion immediately. After all was said and done, the doctor came in and told Matthew that he had alcohol poisoning and that he would've died if he hadn't come to the hospital when he did. He also told him they would need to run tests on his liver and that he needed to plan on staying in the hospital for a few days. After the doctor left, Peter assured Matthew that he would have his apartment cleaned immediately and asked if there was anything else he needed. Matthew just shook his head slowly. Peter started to walk out of the room when Matthew stopped him.

"Hey, would you also call one of those animal groomers who come to the house and have them give the cat a bath...I got blood all over him?"

"Of course sir," Peter quietly closed the door and called his wife to make the cleaning arrangements. Before he hung up he said, "Honey please put Matthew on a prayer chain at church. He's really sick. I know his liver is involved and I know it's from the alcohol but I'm really worried about his mental state."

"But honey, why? You know when he's sober he's of sound mind," she said.

"I know that but something has changed...he thinks he has a cat!"

When Matthew returned home from the hospital, his apartment was restored to its former state. He breathed a sigh of relief because he needed that.

He needed order and familiar surroundings. The four days he had spent in the hospital were grueling. Not only was he sick, he was also detoxing from alcohol and there were many times he just preferred death to the cleansing process. He never once thought he would quit drinking though. As a matter of fact, the thought of the wine he was going to down the second he got home was what gave him the strength to get through the ordeal. Even when the doctor told him he had significant liver damage from drinking, he didn't see the need to stop.

When he walked over to the refrigerator to grab the wine he noticed feeding bowls on the floor. He looked around the corner that led to his laundry room and saw a litter box.

"Wait...I have a cat? Why do I have a cat?" He started to walk to the living room to grab his phone to complain to Peter when he remembered. He began walking around his apartment to find the cat. He looked in all the bedrooms, including his and then moved to the theater room, the billiard room, the music room and his office, but there was no sign of the cat. Matthew was getting annoyed trying to remember the first time he'd seen the stupid thing. He remembered it had been a very cold day. This little orange cat was sitting outside of the door to the bar Matthew owned. It just looked at him and Matthew ignored him. The cat, however, would not be ignored. He jumped up on the window sill after Matthew had gone inside and simply stared into the window. Matthew wouldn't have even noticed him if he hadn't been inspecting the window sills for their weekly cleaning.

As Matthew moved from window to window on the inside, the cat moved on the outside. And each time Matthew looked at the cat the cat stood up and placed his paws on the window and meowed. By the time they got to the last window Matthew was feeling sorry for the cat. It was obvious he was freezing and also obvious he was asking Matthew to let him in. The problem was that Matthew wasn't a cat lover, or an animal lover for that matter. He actually prided himself on the fact that he had never owned one.

When he and Tara were children they had pets, all kinds of pets. Tara was a huge animal lover and rescued every stray who crossed her path. But since he moved out of his childhood home he never even considered getting an animal. But he wasn't a cruel man and to leave that cat outside in these conditions would be cruel. He walked back to the door and the cat followed him on the window sills. Matthew opened the door and the cat was sitting there waiting on him.

"Well, come in you stupid cat." Matthew said as he held the door open.

"Follow me. You aren't staying here for very long, just until this weather breaks. And you're staying in the basement. There may be mice down there to keep you entertained."

Tezra followed Matthew inside. He followed him all the way to the basement. Matthew thought it was strange that the cat seemed to be following his directions. After he opened the door he turned around and gestured for the cat to go down the stairs. Tezra stopped just before going to the top step and sat down and stared at Matthew again.

"What? What now? You're out of the cold and I know there's food down there..so go!"

Tezra's eyes got huge and he let out the longest meow Matthew had ever heard. Except it didn't sound like a normal meow, it sounded like the cat was screaming NO. Matthew was startled and it made him laugh.

"What the heck was that?" he laughed as he squatted and patted the cat's head.

"Okay okay, you don't have to go. I have to go to the bar for awhile so you can hang out in the storage room and we will figure out something." With that Samson/Tezra followed him to the bar. This started a pattern that continued for a week. Even after the weather turned warm, Matthew let the cat stay in the store room of the bar.

On the night that Matthew poisoned himself with alcohol, he had inadvertently let the cat into his apartment. What he didn't know was that the angel inside of his cat was the one who took care of him that night.

As Matthew remembered the history with the cat he passed his bedroom and saw that his closet light was on. It shouldn't have been on at all and Matthew knew he hadn't turned it on. When he walked in the closet, there was the stupid cat, sound asleep. Matthew reached down to pet him and realized he was sitting on something. It was the journal his sister Tara had written him. The journal that had changed his life. The journal that sent him spiraling out of control. The cat opened its eyes and gave Matthew a soul searching look with it's giant eyes.

"Where did you get this? How..I know I burnt this thing." Matthew stated confusedly.

"Well this isn't the first time I've seen weird," he said as he picked up the cat. He was about to pick up the journal but instead kicked it.

"No way, I'm not going there...I need a drink." The cat jumped from Matthew's arms and ran to the kitchen and was sitting on the counter when Matthew got there. He opened a cabinet to grab a shot glass and turned to open the door to the liquor cabinet. The cat was sitting in front of the door on the counter.

"Move!" Matthew said. The cat didn't budge. Matthew tried to pick him up to move him and the cat growled. Matthew's hands flew off the cat.

"So that's it, huh? You aren't moving? I can move you...I can," with that Matthew bent down to get face to face with the cat and screamed at the top of his lungs

"MOOOOOOOVVVVVEEE!"

The cat didn't flinch but when the scream ended the cat turned his head sideways and with his ears laying flatly back he glared at Matthew. He took a paw and cleaned his face with two strokes...stood up and arched his back and gave a lazy yawn. He then turned in two complete circles and laid down, blocking the cabinet. He looked at Matthew one last time and quickly meowed "NO" and shut his eyes.

Matthew was so dumbfounded he started to laugh. He was angry that he couldn't get to the liquor but he was amazed at what the cat had just done. He had two choices. He could kill the cat, which considering it's uniqueness would be a waste... or he could laugh. He chose laughter. He started laughing and slid down the wall until he was sitting. He laughed until he couldn't laugh anymore then, he put his face in his hands and cried. He couldn't say how long it lasted, but when he woke up he was in his own bed and the cat was sleeping on the other side of his bed, with his head on the pillow and his body under the covers.

"Okay, I guess I have a cat." he whispered and then out of nowhere the tears started to fall again and he shut his eyes.

Tara wrapped her arms around her brother as she thanked the angel Tezra. She wished Matthew was able to feel her arms...to know she was there. But then Jesus came and wrapped his arms around them both and Tara was resting in His peace and the knowledge that He was in charge and that All was well!

Bene't and Natash had arrived at Matthew's apartment just in time to see Jesus, Tara and General Tezra comforting Matthew. Bene't and Natash witnessed the scene as they hovered outside of the bedroom window. Neither felt the desire to go inside when they saw the Christ. In reality, they couldn't have gone in even if they had wanted to.

In the past, Bene't was startled whenever he saw Jesus. Not only because he was in the presence of the Savior of the World, and being around HIM was a constant reminder of what he had lost, but it was the pain it caused him and all the Damned whenever they saw Him.

From the Fall of the angels on, all of the demons and especially Satan, felt physical pain whenever they saw God. It didn't matter if they interacted with the Father, Son or Holy Spirit, the pain always came and was intense. It was as if the part of them that felt the Grace and Love of the Trinity and the goodness of Heaven, was ripped out of them when they betrayed their Creator. And the hole that those gifts left behind was filled with all things opposite of God. Every negative emotion joined together to assault that emptiness. It rendered them all paralyzed with pain for the duration of the meeting. This just increased their hatred of the Father and of all the Heavenly beings; as if it was their fault that the Devil and his minions chose not to serve Humanity at the request of their Creator.

Natash, on the other hand, was not startled to see Jesus... he was terrified. The one meeting he'd had with the King of Kings had been at his own death. He was reminded of what his choice not to accept Jesus as his Savior had cost him. When he saw Jesus standing before him in the moments before his earthly body expired, begging Natash to believe and run into His open arms, it was easy to reject his Savior. After all, he had pledged his soul to Satan and was looking forward to the throne he would occupy in Hell. This gentle God had nothing to offer Natash in life and he certainly had nothing Natash wanted in death. Seeing Him caused him the same physical pain that Bene't and all the demons experienced. Ironically though, it did not cause a longing or a desire on Natash's part to wish he had chosen differently to love or accept Jesus. It just made him hate the Savior even more because even with all the nightmare pains he endured in Hell, the pain he felt seeing Jesus in Matthew's apartment was exponentially worse. The love that radiated from Jesus to Matthew was the worst pain Natash had ever felt. And he would rather take all the pains of Hell in that moment, than to have to be subjected to the Light of the World for one more second.

He started to move away from Bene't to see if it were even possible for him to leave but quickly got that question answered. Bene't knew all of Natash's thoughts. Just as in Heaven where Tara is in Jesus and she in Him, the law of Hell was the same. The Damned were in Satan and he in them and knowing the thoughts of the damned followed that law.

"You can't go!" Bene't growled as he grabbed the satanist's arm. Just as he said that, Jesus arose and returned to Heaven. Tara gave her brother one more embrace and thanked Tezra again. She then looked at the window and saw both Bene't and Natash.

Her posture changed from docile to fierce in an instant. She locked eyes with Natash and moved towards them. Natash had never seen a Saint since his death, and having Tara be the first one he encountered was shocking. She was encased in the same light of Christ and every part of her radiated goodness and love. Natash recoiled as she approached. Oh how their roles were now reversed. On earth it was Tara who recoiled from Natash and he was the one in control. He was the one with all the power and she would have never looked at him with the courage she did now. She was nothing but dirt under his feet and it infuriated him to see her clothed in glory, while he was reduced to...this.

Bene't didn't move. He was waiting for the moment they would be expelled from the property and hurled into Hell. The Saints in Heaven had the same power as Jesus. They were His heirs. They were Sons and Daughters of the King and a battle with them could never be won. The amazing part about this truth was that the living humans didn't understand or believe this truth and many of them never once asked for a Saint's intercession. Had they utilized this resource, all demons would have run from them in fear.

When Tara approached, she simply pointed at the crown on her head. The crown had several different jewels on it and there was a pattern of gold that was made by tiny little crosses. In the instant of her pointing Natash was flung to the ground and so was Bene't. Natash began to scream out in pain and Bene't knew that this was just the beginning of the torment they would both feel.

When a demon or the Damned are in the presence of a Saint of Heaven, the punishment is always the same, and it is the worst thing they can or will ever experience. It's not a physical pain as much as a spiritual one, but it delivers a torture that is unlike anything else in existence. The reason it affects them this way is because it is the story of the Redemption of Christ. An unimaginable, torturous reminder of the defeat of Satan. They were privy to a "silent conversation" between Jesus and Lucifer during HIS Passion, and the crushing proof of the Trinity's undeniable superiority over Satan and his followers, both Divine and Human.

Since God lives outside of time, the demons and the damned who witnessed this story were placed in the time of the Passion. This just made the experience all the more painful for them as they became part of the crowd who lived during that time.

The first thing they saw was Satan racing up to the earth's surface on the day of Jesus' circumcision. At the moment of that first bloodshed, that first wound, there was a change in the soul of every child and young person under the age of 12 on earth; and Satan felt it through every part of his being. It caused him great pain and he surfaced to see where the source of this came from. He noticed right away that every person under 12 had a new light around them, a new unnamed power. As he roamed the earth he couldn't find the reason for it or from where the source originated. No child had more power than any other so he was in a state of confusion. Since he couldn't find the answer from the children, he searched the mind and hearts of the adults and also his own remembrance and that's where he found his answer.

Ten days prior to this day, there were three Kings who were traveling to give homage to a 'New Born King'. He didn't get this information from the Kings themselves, for their hearts and minds were guarded by the Father and therefore he couldn't penetrate them. He instead got his information from Herod who had held an audience with the Kings. They told Herod they were following a star to find the child. Herod asked them to return once they found him so that Herod could also go to pay him homage. When Herod uttered those words, Satan was in the room. He was the one who placed the idea into Herod's mind, to have the Kings return. That way Lucifer could kill the child in case it was the promised Messiah.

When Lucifer looked to the sky he saw no star and that was because Divine Providence had blinded his eyes so he could not see it. He tried to follow the Kings but the Trinity had placed 10,000 angels around the Kings and they became invisible to him. All he knew was that they were heading in the direction of a small village near Bethlehem. Every time he tried to get close to the little village he was physically removed by Divine hands and he was forced to stay where he was. This enraged him.

By the time Jesus was born, the star was gone and so were the angels that blocked his advance, so he began to go from house to house, child to child to try and see the newborn King but he hit walls with each attempt. He decided to go back to Hell and consult with the demons to make a plan to find the child. It was while he was back in Hell that he felt the new power of the children and he surfaced to find the source that he now knew came from somewhere in Bethlehem.

For His part, at the moment of the first bloodshed during his circumcision, Jesus was redeeming the "Sins of Youth" and although the redemption would not be fully realized until HIS death and Resurrection, outside of time it was already completed and the children were receiving the Grace of HIS suffering.

Because of his frustration with not being able to get any closer on his second visit to Bethlehem, Satan then made another visit to Herod. This time he brought the demon of Pride and that demon worked on Herod and made him feel greatly insulted that the Kings had not returned to him with news of the newborn king. So in his anger and misdirected righteousness, he ordered the murder of every male child in Bethlehem, under the age of two. Immediately the Throne of God sent the ArchAngel Gabriel to speak to Joseph in a dream and tell him to arise and flee the village and take Jesus and Mary into Egypt. Although Satan was watching every family in Bethlehem he did not see the Holy family of Jesus, Mary and Joseph leave because they were again shrouded by the protection of the Angels.

After Bene't and Natash witnessed this part of the story, the scene changed and they now were present with Jesus in the Garden of Gethsemane. Here they watched as the contest between Jesus and Satan... and Good versus Evil, began.

As Jesus was kneeling on the ground alone, as all of his apostles had fallen asleep in another part of the garden, Satan was standing above him watching.

As Jesus began His prayer out loud, asking God to let the cup pass from Him if it be God's will, Lucifer was in a state of confusion. He was very suspicious that Jesus could be the promised Messiah. He had been completely torn between thinking Jesus was the Messiah, and in thinking John the Baptist was. These two men were pure of heart and he was not successful in his efforts to stop their preaching or their faith in God. This made him plot the death of both of the two prophets.

When John the Baptist died, Satan knew right away that he had not been the Christ because nothing was different in the world...Satan was still in charge of the Earth. So as he implanted the betrayal of Jesus into Judas' mind, he also felt that he was still in charge of the Earth. But he would not feel secure until the Nazarene was dead. He planned on not leaving Jesus' side until he took his last breath. But as Jesus prayed in the Garden, something happened that concerned him greatly.

As Jesus was praying, he began to sweat blood. It wasn't a little amount of blood, it was a lot. As this was occurring, Jesus was redeeming all the sins of the heart that had occurred since the beginning of time and all the sins of the heart which would occur until the end of time. For every sin against love throughout eternity, Jesus paid the price inside His own heart and because of the greatness of that sin, Christ's heart could not contain the blood, and it began to seep out all over His body in the form of sweat. As soon as Satan saw this, he simultaneously felt power leave him and he had his first taste of fear that Jesus could indeed be the Messiah. Although Lucifer wasn't sure about Jesus, he wanted to do the unthinkable and punish him physically if he were permitted.

After the pronouncement was made that Jesus should be scourged, Satan commanded his strongest demons to possess the bodies of the humans who had been given that task.

There were six men in all and they beat him in pairs of two. The beating that Jesus received was more severe and brutal than had been exacted on any human being in the history of the world. The demons had the force and strength of a thousand men and they beat The Savior of the World until he no longer resembled a man. They took out all the hatred they possessed in each blow. Many of the wounds were fatal but because Jesus was also God, he continued to live to redeem even more souls. In the suffering of the Scourge at the pillar, Jesus had taken upon his pure innocent body, the sins of the flesh. This encompassed every sexual sin, murder, sodomy and addiction as well as any other sin affecting or caused by our flesh.

At first, Lucifer was caught up in the blood lust until Jesus caught his eye and tried to stand after he had been beaten mercilessly. The look in the Savior's eye was not one of pain or anger, it was a look of complete and utter determination and Lucifer once again felt power leave him.

When the scourging ended, and the men were exhausted from it, Satan put another sick idea of torture in one of their minds. It was to fashion a crown to be placed upon our Savior's head out of a vine containing four and six inch thorns into a crown. This, to Lucifer, was a huge insult if this was the Christ, because he mocked His kingship. But the instant the crown was placed on HIS head instead of joy, Satan shuddered with fear as Jesus silently spoke the truth of what was occurring with...one...single...glance.

Lucifer was made to know the truth of what happened at Jesus' circumcision. He saw the star, the birth and the fleeing of the Holy family to Egypt. He understood that in the garden Jesus redeemed the sins of the Heart and that the Scourging redeemed the sins of the Flesh. He also was made aware that the barbaric Crown of Thorns upon Jesus' head really meant the redemption of all sins of the Mind and Spirit. The devil was made to understand that if people utilized the love of Jesus, the devil could never again make their minds "his playground," It was in this moment that Jesus revealed to Lucifer that when Lucifer was imposing his will on the angels before they had Free Will, that the Trinity was well aware of his actions and motives in the minds of the first children of God. Jesus made it clear that nothing was hidden to the creative mind of the Trinity. And the power that

Lucifer lost with that truth caused him to fall breathlessly to the ground.

Now Satan was panicked. He immediately went to Judas, making him feel a false remorse and compelled him to return the thirty pieces of silver he used to betray the Savior. When that didn't work, Satan went to the Scribes, Herod and Pilate and tried to implant into their minds that the Nazarene was innocent and should be set free. But because all of these humans were without Grace or Love, he could not build on emotions they no longer possessed. At this point there was no doubt in his mind that Jesus was the Messiah and that Lucifer's ruin was near.

The only thing Satan and his demons wanted to do then was to go back to Hell and be as far away from this death as possible, but this was not to be allowed. As they tried to descend, a giant chain bound them all together and stopped them from moving at all. And to Lucifer's horror he saw that someone was holding the chain...It was Jesus' mother...Mary...the WOMAN from the sign in the sky.

Lucifer was shocked beyond belief because when he looked into HER eyes, all power left him and he and the other demons could only move if SHE allowed it. It was clear that they were trapped and would be made to witness the events that would be their ruin.

As Jesus was carrying the Cross, HE continued HIS silent conversation with Satan. Satan was made to know that the Cross that Jesus carried was really HIM carrying the Sins of all the world. It showed the devil that HE would stop at nothing to help the "hated humanity" by carrying the punishment of their sins. Each time HE fell, Lucifer was made to understand that every time a human fell, if they came to Jesus for help, HE would pick them up and carry their sins again. And even though HE only fell three times, the devil knew that the number of times that humanity would be allowed to fall was infinite...unlike the one fall of the rebellious Angels. As he raged against this revelation he was shown the fairness of it. When the fallen angels fell, they had all knowledge of God and they still turned against HIM. These humans who would never see HIM or understand HIM, would still love

HIM through the eyes of faith and that deserved total forgiveness if they asked for it.

This knowledge enraged and angered the demons and they wished again to be released of the grip of the Great Lady Mary. Mary ignored their pleas to return to Hell and continued along the path of the Passion, adoring Her Son all the way.

At this point in the story Bene't and Natash were walking with the demons. To their utter dismay, they realized they were both connected to the chain that the Queen held.

They couldn't meditate on it too long because the horror of what was happening in the Passion captivated them.

Even though Satan now knew this was the Christ, he still was inciting the humans watching into a kind of fury. Lucifer realized that after the Passion, he would never again be able to touch the King of Kings. In his hatred, he wanted to do as much physical damage as he possibly could while it was permitted.

When they arrived on Golgotha and Jesus was being placed on the Cross, the demons were begging the Blessed Mother to release them. The horrors of Hell were more preferable than walking this road to their ruin. The only response they received was a tightening of the chain and a new wave of pain.

For Bene't, he was reliving the worst moments of his existence because he had been here before. Every single time a Saint in Heaven fought, they used the Passion as a weapon against the Damned and the Hounds of Hell. As for Natash, this experience was brand new and so much worse than even Hell. It was worse because by watching, it was crystal clear that he had chosen the wrong side. Watching the innocent Christ bravely dying for Humanity and specifically for him, was soul crushing. To think he chose an eternity of pain for whatever would have awaited him in Heaven, was unbearable.

Natash was well aware that his choice to become a Satanist was because he wanted power and acclaim. And he also chose it to rebel against his brother Zachary's weak God. But watching Jesus' Passion up close and personal showed him that Jesus was not only not weak...HE was the strongest Being in history. And the love that emanated from the Savior was overwhelming. But instead of feeling contrite at the sight of Christ's great love and the sacrifice He was making, Natash felt only hatred and anger.

He began to join the crowd of demons and humans that were present in their hurling of insults upon the Lamb of God. He blamed Jesus for not making more of an effort to prove who HE was. He shouted that if only He had given   Natash more power then he wouldn't have had to go to Satan. He complained that he didn't have the same chances that his brother and others had to learn that Christ was the better choice. He would have said more but he was silenced at the first strike of the hammer that drove the nail into Jesus' hand.

Then, none of the enemies of God spoke. They were rendered helpless and weak and were no longer allowed to use their senses the way they chose. They could only see and hear what the Father in Heaven allowed. They were to hear and understand the seven phrases that Jesus spoke from the Cross and their meaning and consequences would burn inside them for the rest of their eternity. The memory and truth of living with this experience was worse than all the tortures and agonies of Hell. Both Natash and Bene't would replay the silent conversation between Jesus and Satan forever.

The first thing that Jesus said from the Cross was "FATHER, FORGIVE THEM FOR THEY KNOW NOT WHAT THEY DO."

It was at this moment that the Devil knew that the very victory of the Second person of the Trinity that Lucifer was trying to avoid, was indeed occurring before his eyes. In this statement the devil knew that the "Father" Jesus spoke to was indeed the King of Heaven and the First Person of the Trinity. He was so baffled by Jesus asking the Father to forgive this disgusting creature called Man. Why would He ask that when they had beaten, tortured and reduced HIM to nothing resembling a man? Jesus answered this question by letting Satan feel the immensity of the love HE felt for

Humanity when HE turned HIS mercy towards the good thief.

After the good thief had defended Jesus by telling the bad thief that Jesus was not guilty of any crime, Our Savior slowly turned HIS wounded head so that HE could see the good thief, whose name was Dismas.

"AMEN, I SAY TO YOU, TODAY YOU SHALL BE WITH ME IN PARADISE!"

At this pronouncement, all of the demons were horrified and screaming in fury because it was as if Jesus had said to Satan, "Even up until the hour of their deaths, I will be waiting for them to repent. I will offer MY forgiveness for their sins and they will take the seats in Paradise which you have lost for all Eternity."

Satan was furious and pulled with all his strength against the chain which the Great Queen held in Her grasp. He could not fathom the reasons behind the Father's mercy to this inferior race. How could they be forgiven over and over when he and his fallen brethren had only ONE chance?

The next words were the worst yet for Lucifer to hear. These words were the cause of his greatest anxiety in regards to the Christ. Jesus turned his head and looked down at HIS Mother who stood bravely at the foot of HIS Cross with 'Saint John the beloved' and spoke in the most tender voice,

"WOMAN...BEHOLD THY SON. SON, BEHOLD THY MOTHER!"

Satan screamed in agony as he was made to know that Mary was indeed the Woman from the Sign they had all seen in the Heavens which had introduced Humanity to the Angels. When Jesus referred to Mary as "Woman", He did so for a two-fold reason.

One, was that to call Her "Mother" would bring Him comfort and joy and he purposely wanted to deprive Himself of even that condolence so that His suffering would reach the maximum possible level. Secondly, He wanted to name Her. In doing so, Satan would know for sure that this was the Woman the Father referred to in the Garden of Eden when HE told the serpent, "the Woman will crush your head."

Then Jesus sent each encounter Satan had ever had with Mary into his mind. This was to emphasize each time he had been bested by the Queen. He was shown that Mary was conceived without sin. He showed him that each time in Her childhood that Satan tempted Her he was defeated at every turn. He saw that Her marriage to Saint Joseph was a chaste one and that the Holy Spirit was Her true spouse. He saw that it was She that rebuked many demons and that even now She was sharing in the redemption of men by contributing with Her suffering more than any other mortal creature. He saw the great honor the Almighty had and would heap upon Her for the 'FIAT' She gave to God when She consented to be the Mother of the King of Kings. He was shown that She would be the Queen of Heaven and Earth and would be held above even the Saints and the Angels and that the powers of Hell would be no match for the power the Trinity would enact through Her. Then when Jesus said to John, "Behold your Mother," he was saying to Satan that Mary would be the Mother of ALL of God's children and She would fight on behalf of each soul that sought Her intersession. She could never be beaten by the Devil, and this, when She was just a mere creature and not Divine like the angels and demons. If a soul fled to Her intersession it would always be safe, as She crushed the devil and his army under Her feet.

Later the devil would devise a battle plan in Hell with the other demons to attack Her in many ways. The primary way would be to convince Christians that to call on their Mother would somehow be a slight to Jesus or replace the Savior by placing Mary above Him. Lucifer would succeed in convincing millions to believe the lie and it was only after their deaths that they would know the truth, Jesus WANTED His Mother to be honored and adored and glorified because it was the greatest insult to the Dragon; that a mere creature would be given this enormous power over him. And since power was what he craved most of all, Her being second only to the Trinity was the greatest injustice Satan could fathom.

The next words Jesus spoke came out in a heart wrenching plea,

"MY GOD, MY GOD, WHY HAVE YOU FORSAKEN ME?"

Lucifer understood this to mean that Jesus was looking into eternity at all of the souls who would not choose to profit from His Sacrifice. HE saw every human, angel and creature that existed and saw the believers and the reprobates. HE wanted every single one of them to be saved. HE wanted them to walk into the gates HE was now opening for them. HIS heart was wounded that not all would choose Heaven. The Father took this moment to show Jesus all of the souls who WOULD be written in the book of life. The Almighty Father did this in a clear vision. This made it so Jesus could see them all standing at the Crucifixion outside of time...much like in the way Bene't and Natash were now REALLY present at the holy event.

Feeling the only comfort HE allowed Himself during the Passion, Jesus looked with love upon the Elect...the children who would choose HIM.

He then turned HIS gaze upon Lucifer and said, "I THIRST!"

Satan understood from those two words that Jesus was not satisfied with only HIS Passion. HE made it clear that HE still "thirsted" to save all of Humanity and that if it were possible to heap more suffering upon HIS HOLY HUMANITY to save more souls, HE would. This spoke volumes in describing the love HE had for Man. The Devil and his minions were fighting each other like rabid dogs in order to flee from that love.

Jesus pulled HIS gaze away from the Traitor and the army of demons and left them all trembling in fear.

HE brought HIS gaze back to HIS Mother and with one final loving glance HE lifted HIS eyes to Heaven and said,

"IT IS FINISHED. INTO THY HANDS I COMMEND MY SPIRIT!"

Satan and the other fallen angels were then violently thrown into the deepest part of Hell where they would remain, unable to move, crushed to the fiery floor.

The last thing they were allowed to see was what happened when the soldier pierced the side of Jesus with a lance. As the blood and water poured forth from the Sacred Body, it not only rained down on the soldiers and the earth, it also penetrated the earth and came like a great deluge into the space of Purgatory. As it flooded that cavern with great mercy, it washed each of the souls residing there and made them Beings of light. They were shown that Jesus would soon descend into "Hell" and expiate all of them into Heaven.

Satan was in anguish at seeing the unfairness of the Father. How could HE allow those souls into Heaven when Lucifer had spent centuries trying to damn their souls and turning them away from God. The Almighty showed Satan that even after death, all of the souls that died loving God, would have a way to be purged from the sins left upon their souls through the cleansing fires of Purgatory.

HE showed him that the sacred water and blood from the Lamb's side would wash them clean and ready them for Heaven. This was the final nail in the coffin. There were no words to describe the howling and roaring in Hell from the defeated Betrayer of the Father.

After they watched Satan raging in Hell, both Natash and Bene't were back in front of Tara. She took that moment to rebuke them in Jesus' name and return them to Hell.

Natash's last thought was that he hoped he never had to live that experience again. He welcomed the pains of Hell, to the victory of Love he had just witnessed.

Bene't knew his thoughts and said, "This is the FIRST time, not the last, that you will experience the Passion of the Christ." Every time a Saint of the Father battles you, they will use the Passion as their weapon. It is impossible to win the battle and there is no escape from it. And each time you experience it will be worse then the time before."

The horrified look on Natash's face made it almost endurable for the demon. Bene't thrust his talon through the satanists arm and they made the descent to the abyss.

CHAPTER TWELVE....
THE EYES ARE THE WINDOW OF THE SOUL

Father Zachary looked at his watch. It had been 3 hours since he had arrived at Jacob's house and Madison was still asleep. She did not sleep peacefully. She tossed her head from side to side murmuring words he couldn't understand. Her brows were furrowed and she looked to be in pain. Jacob had assured him that the doctor said she would be okay. She was just so sleep deprived and dehydrated that her body needed rest and the I.V. fluid to restore her. The doctor had allowed her to come home with the I.V. since her sister, Priscella was a registered nurse and had rushed to her side the moment she heard Madison had been hospitalized. The hospital had only kept her for twenty four hours and then she returned home. They allowed baby Rachael to stay in the hospital with her since she was still nursing.

Priscella stayed on the companion couch in Madison's room so she could take care of the baby while Madison slept. Priscella had to help hold the baby in Madison's arms because she wasn't strong enough to hold Rachael by herself. Jacob wanted to stay with her as well but he needed to be at home with Maria, and since it was only for one night and the doctors assured him she wasn't in any medical danger, he felt good enough to leave her with her sister.

Zachary had been sitting beside Madison's bedside praying for Madison and her entire family. He was going to start a rosary but he was interrupted by a soft little sigh. Maria had walked into the room silently and sat next to the priest. He had no idea how long she had been there.

"Hello little one, how are you doing?" Father Zachary asked in a hushed tone.

"I'm ok. I just want mommy to wake back up." she whispered back.

The priest looked at the little girl and was struck by how peaceful she was. Every time he had seen her, she presented in the same way...peaceful and calm. She didn't share the rowdiness of children in her age bracket. She was far too mature in both demeanor and in the words she spoke. He always felt like he was speaking to someone far older and wiser. In fact, she eclipsed most of the adults in his circle when the subject of God was brought up; and that was saying something since that included many holy Priests, Monks and Nuns. There was something very special about her and he wondered, not for the first time, what God had in store for her life. Whatever it was, it would be spectacular.

He tousled her hair and replied, "She will honey, she just needs to rest for a little while longer."

Maria drew her knees up and rested her elbows on them while her hands cupped her face.

"I know. I think her bad dream made her sick." she said as a matter of fact.

"What bad dream, Maria? Did she tell you about it? I didn't know she had been awake enough to talk yet?" Father Zachary asked, extremely puzzled by the child's statement.

"She didn't wake up yet." Maria whispered again.

"Well then how do you know she had a bad dream, Maria?"

Maria sighed again and turned her head towards the Priest. "I think it's 'uppost' to be a secret that only I know how."

"Why do you think it's supposed to be a secret? Did someone tell you not to talk about it?" She had Father Zachary's full attention.

Maria stared into his eyes as if she were searching for an answer there.

She squinted her eyes as she looked at him. Her eyes then shifted to something beyond him and seemingly, she saw something she trusted.

"No one told me that, it just FEELS like a secret." She then looked over his right shoulder as if she were looking at something. She turned her head slightly to the side and then nodded her head yes.

"Okay I'm allowed to tell you." Father Zachary looked over his shoulder and tried to see whatever the child was seeing. He saw nothing there, but he did not doubt that she did.

"Maria, is there someone behind me? Someone only you can see?" he asked cautiously.

"Yes," she answered sweetly.

"Did it tell you that it was okay to tell me your secret?" he prompted.

"Yes," she said again with a little more enthusiasm.

"Can you tell me who it is?" he asked.

Without flinching her gaze at all she answered the priest. "It's my Guardian Angel. He had to talk to your Guardian Angel first to make sure we wouldn't get in trouble from God. It's okay, we won't get in trouble."

Father Zachary didn't move. He knew this child was special and in reality it didn't surprise him that she would have strong spiritual gifts considering who her mother was, but he was still taken a little off guard by the frankness of her discourse.

"Oh, I see. Well that explains it. How long have you been able to see Angels? Do you see other things too?" he asked her slowly.

Maria shut her eyes and thought for a moment. When whatever she was thinking about was confirmed to her, she opened her eyes again, stared at him and replied, "I think I see everything."

"Everything? Can you explain that to me?"

She looked up at the invisible Angel and after a second replied.

"I can see the Angels, all the different kinds. I can see the souls who are waiting in Purgatory until they have no more dirt on their souls and they get to go to Heaven. They come to Mommy for help and Rachael and I help them too." She paused for a moment and took a deep breath and then continued.

"And I can see the demons and the bad spirits too. They don't like me and they really don't like Rachael." Her eyes widened when she made the admission about her baby sister. Something darkened in her eyes as she continued.

"On the day Mommy had the bad dream, I had to fight the Devil. I don't like seeing the Devil."

"Wait, what, the Devil? You fought the Devil?" Father Zachary asked incredulously.

He was now on full alert and all of his attention was on Maria. As he was waiting for an answer his eyes were drawn to the bed. Madison had woken up and she was staring at him. Her eyes were huge, bloodshot and wet with tears.

"You have to help her, Father. She's in such great danger."

At first the Priest thought that Madison was referring to Maria. He thought she'd been listening to their conversation. He placed his hand over hers and tried to soothe her.

"Shh, it's okay Madison. I'm here. Everything is fine and Maria is okay too. You don't have to worry anymore." He barely finished speaking when Madison frantically replied.

"Not Maria Father...Malaya!!!!! You have to help Malaya!!! She's in grave danger. You and Jacob have to go find her." Madison was becoming visibly upset and her breathing became erratic.

"Ok Madison, I will help her, calm down now. Take some deep breaths."

As if sensing something was wrong, Priscella walked in the room and immediately took over.

"Okay you two...give me a minute with her. I want to take her vitals." Obediently Maria and Zachary left the room.

Zachary went to the kitchen to get a glass of water. He was standing at the sink when Jacob walked in through the back door. Noticing the color, or lack thereof, on the Priest's face Jacob went right to him.

"Are you okay Father...Is Mattie okay?" Jacob asked with concern.

"She just woke up Jacob." Jacob made a move to walk past the priest so he could see for himself the condition of his wife, but Zachary's next words stopped him.

"And the first thing she said was that you and I have to go find and save Malaya."

Father Zachary moved to the kitchen table and sat down heavily and continued speaking.

"When you called me last night and told me what had happened I knew I could waste no time in getting here. I still haven't figured out how she even knows about Malaya. I know for certain I have never spoken to Madison about her. Somehow she does know and now I need to decide what we should do." The priest sighed and looked at the floor, lost in concentration. Jacob squinted his eyes and looked at the priest.

"Father, what is going on? Who is Malaya and why is she in danger?"

Zachary sighed, took a deep breath and began. "It's been a long time since I even thought of her, which I am embarrassed to say, because it causes me shame. She isn't someone you can easily forget."

Father Zachary took a drink of water and then took another before he put his glass down. Jacob sat down at the table across from him and waited patiently for him to continue.

Neither of them heard or saw Maria as she also took a chair. And when she spoke both men were startled by her presence.

"She's an Indian Daddy."

Father Zachary whipped his head around to face the child, dumbfounded by what she had said. He looked at Jacob questioningly before he responded.

"That's right, Maria. She is an Indian."

Maria shook her head yes and gave the priest an encouraging look as if to spur him on in his story. Zachary replayed the conversation he had just had with her moments before Madison woke up and knew that there was more to this child than even he'd thought possible. He kept staring at her and then slowly pulled his gaze back to Jacob. He made a conscious effort not to ask Maria any questions about the how and why she knew that Malaya was an Indian. He would revisit that in another conversation. Because time was of the essence, he continued telling his story.

"Malaya is a Pueblo Indian from New Mexico. She was born on a reservation there. On the day of her birth I was there doing a mission. I had been there many times before and I became good friends with the chief of the tribe and of his wife Maleeya. They lived in a little village. It was made up of adobe houses, on top of a Mesa."

Father Zachary stopped when he realized Jacob wasn't sure what a Mesa was. He didn't even look at Maria because he thought she might already know, and he was trying not to get distracted by the child.

"A Mesa is a huge rock hill or mountain that has a flat top and the Native Americans would build their houses there. It was wise because they were well protected from their enemies and could see from all sides if they were under attack. They also liked to build there because it was closer to the stars and the "Grandfather."

Even though most Indians today live and dress much like people who are not Native Americans, this tribe was different. It was important to the Chief to keep as many of their tribal traditions as they could. So the tribe dressed, cooked and lived as closely as they could to their ancestors. They didn't hunt, but had livestock and gardens and only ate what they could grow.

The last day I was there, there was a huge celebration for the tribe because the child who was to be born, was the child of the Chief. When I arrived, Maleeya was already in hard labor and the baby would be born any minute.

As soon as the Chief heard I had arrived, he summoned me to their little adobe house. He asked me if I would go in and say a prayer of blessing over his wife. The tribe's Shaman was already in with her, as well as some of the women of the tribe who always assisted with the births. I was very surprised that the Chief had asked this of me because he was not one who had been convinced of the Christen religion. Only his wife had accepted that Jesus was the Son of God and her Savior. Aside from her there were just a few other tribe members who were willing to believe and give their life to Christ.

As soon as I went in, the Shaman stopped his chanting and gave me a death stare. He was not one of my biggest fans and he perceived my presence as an affront to him and the traditions of the event. He would've thrown me out if the Chief hadn't come in behind me and silenced any complaints the Shaman had.

Maleeya was in hard labor and had begun to push when she saw me. Even in her pain she motioned for me to come to her. I went to her side and grabbed her hand. When she could speak it was only for a few seconds and she just said, 'Bless my child Father.' I took out my holy water and made the sign of the cross on Maleeya's forehead and it was at that moment that Malaya was born.

She came into the world screaming her little head off. All of us gathered around the midwife as she held her up in the air and announced to the Tribe that the Chief had been blessed with a girl...an Indian Princess.

To say that the fact that the baby was a girl and that put the Tribe in an uproar, was an understatement. No one was pleased about it. They had been counting on the baby being a boy, who would someday become their future Chief. There was so much riding on this because the tribe had been praying for a strong leader that could lead them into the 21st Century with Prosperity. All of their prayers to their ancestors and the ceremonies they were performing, were for this end. So when it turned out to be a girl, you could almost feel the disappointment infecting the Tribe.

I went over to see the baby, and the midwife immediately handed her to me. Normally the Shaman would be the first to hold a newborn but when the midwife motioned for him to take her, he stood his ground and didn't move. He crossed his arms and turned his head in disgust.

When I first held her, I felt an operation in my spirit take place and I knew I was holding the soul of a Saint."

Father Zachary stopped talking just long enough to see if he had lost Jacob on anything and realized by the intensity of his eyes that Jacob was riveted. Maria had her arms on the table and was resting her head on them. Her head was turned towards the Priest and she was listening intently as well.

"I can't really explain how I knew it, but I did. She was the most beautiful little baby, with a head full of thick black hair. Her face was perfectly round and her cheeks were pink. She had completely stopped crying the second I held her but her eyes were still closed. I looked at Maleeya and was pleasantly surprised to see that at least she found joy in this child. She was smiling a radiant smile. If she had wanted a baby boy, there was no way to know it by her expression. She was thrilled to have a daughter.

I asked her what name she had chosen for the baby and she paused and looked at her husband. He was standing there with his head down and had yet to even glance at his daughter. Realizing that her husband was not going to respond, the new mother held her chin high and stated firmly,

"Her name is Malaya. It means, ``Small Beautiful Miracle." She smiled and leaned back on her bed, exhausted from the delivery.

I reached for my Holy Water and blessed the baby by placing the Sign of the Cross on her head. As soon as I completed the Cross she opened her eyes and something happened to me that I can never fully explain. Her eyes were two colors around the pupil. They were green but each one had a white design in it. At first I didn't see what the white design formed because I was entranced by her. I couldn't look away even if I'd wanted to, because looking into her eyes was a journey."

Father Zachary stopped talking and looked around, first at Maria and then Jacob.

Jacob was a little surprised to see the priest so out of sorts because he was always so serene. Maria reached out and placed her little hand on the arm of the priest, comforting him.

"I know it's hard...but you can say it, ask your angel to help."

The priest looked at her with first a look of alarm, which quickly turned to peace when she mentioned the angel. He took his other hand and placed it on top of hers and said,

"You're right little one, of course you're right. Let's pray together now." Maria nodded in approval and then reached her other hand towards Jacob to include him in the prayer.

"Dear sweet Guardian's, given to us as gifts from the Most High, please hear our prayer. I don't know how to explain what happened to me when I looked into baby Malaya's eyes because I don't know how to make sense of it...but you do. Thank you for your love and protection and continue to guide us each day...Amen."

Just saying the prayer relaxed Zachary and he watched as Jacob opened his eyes and Maria sighed and smiled.

"Okay, how do I start? Well when I was looking in her eyes I got chills all over my body. Not the kind of chills you get because you're cold...a different kind. I get these when I get an operation of the Holy Spirit. It's kind of like God touches my head and this ripple of tingles goes down my body. When this happens I know that God is confirming whatever is happening," he paused again to make sure he was being understood.

Jacob was still staring at him with those intense eyes. He didn't seem confused, just ready to hear the rest of the story. Maria rested her head back on her arms on the table and simply raised her eyebrows as if she were questioning why he stopped talking, but seemingly understanding the point.

"Well, after the chills, I saw her eyes move. Well... her eyes didn't move but the color in them did. She fixed her eyes to stare into mine, so they didn't move."

The priest closed his eyes, trying to clearly bring up the memory to the forefront of his mind.

"Yeah, so it was the color inside her eye that moved. It was like the color moved in little ripples and then it was like I was watching a movie inside her eye. The movie first showed me what looked like a scene from Heaven. I saw glorious white clouds with a brilliant ray cutting the sky in two. Then I saw angels flying in that sky and I felt an overwhelming feeling of love. The angels were flying up higher and higher and they ended up stopping in front of this huge white Cross that looked like it was made out of diamonds. At this point the clouds separated and I could see myself as a baby."

He turned towards Jacob and Maria and said, "You know how people say that their life flashes before their eyes when they have near death experience? Well this was like that except it showed me all the times God had intervened in my life to bring the truth of His existence to my soul." The priest sighed and had a look of awe as he remembered.

"The whole experience couldn't have lasted more than a few seconds but to me it felt like it was a long... long time. I would have just stood there holding the baby forever if she didn't break her eye contact with me and looked towards her mother. I carefully handed Malaya to Maleeya and stood back and watched mother and daughter meet face to face.

Maleeya looked at her child with the most tender love. She gently touched the baby's head and face as if she were tracing it into her memory. When Malaya opened her eyes and stared at her mother, I knew exactly what was happening to Maleeya. It was completely silent in the room as all this took place. When Malaya finally shut her eyes, Maleeya gasped and looked at me.

I had no words to say. I had no point of reference for what the baby could do. I just smiled and shrugged my shoulders and raised my eyes to Heaven. Maleeya understood that she had been blessed to be the mother of a special child. Finally, the Chief and the Shaman approached the baby and each took their turn holding her, but Malaya didn't open her eyes to look at either one of them. After the chief held her he handed her quite quickly to the Shaman. The Shaman shook a rattle like thing over her head and mumbled some chant but it was clear his heart was not in it and he quickly handed her back to Maleeya. At that point, it was made clear to us that it was time for us to leave, so mother and child could bond and rest.

I didn't see either of them again until that night. One of the midwives excitedly barged into the little room that I stayed in when I visited, and motioned for me to come. I got up and started walking to the door. She grabbed my arm and indicated to me that I should run.

I heard the noise as I got closer to the chief's adobe. There was yelling and screaming and pleading and wailing. I walked into chaos. Maleeya and the midwives were standing in front of the crib guarding the baby from the men in the room. It appeared the men wanted to get to the baby and it was clear that their intent was malicious.

The chief was trying to calm everyone down, but wasn't succeeding. The Shaman and two other Shamans I had never seen before, were yelling at the chief to move and let them have the child. I said a quick prayer and then held up my hands and using my loudest voice I yelled 'STOP!!!' I want you to know, I claim no responsibility for what happened next...this was all God. Everyone in the house stopped and became silent. As soon as I saw this, I stood between the two groups and motioned for all of the men to go outside. To my great surprise they listened and left the house.

Once we were outside, the problem began to spill out. Apparently the Shaman had returned after the birth to see the baby again and something he saw upset him. He called for other Shamans among the Pueblo Nation to come and help him decide what to do.

When they arrived and saw the problem, they were all calling for the death of the baby. The chief explained to me that they thought the baby was an abomination to the tribe. They felt she was a punishment from the Ancestors for some unknown sin they had collectively committed. I asked the men and the Shamans to leave me alone with the Chief and they all left without argument.

When we were alone, the Chief spoke. He looked exhausted and confused.

'Father Zachary, do you know the story of the White Buffalo?' I hadn't ever heard the reference and told him so. He explained to me that all Native American tribes have a legend about the White Buffalo.

'A White Buffalo is the most sacred living thing we could ever encounter. The significance of one being born must be interpreted by a holy man or Shaman. We see the birth of a White Buffalo calf as the most significant of prophetic signs. It would be similar to your weeping statues or crosses of light in your Christian religion. To us, the arrival of a White Buffalo is like Christ coming back to His people. The White Buffalo will bring all Native Americans together and we will be bathed in purity of mind, body and spirit. It brings us great hope for the future.'

I must have looked confused. I had no idea how this White Buffalo had anything to do with that beautiful baby in there. The Chief realized that and grabbed my arm and led me back into his house. We walked over to the crib and the Chief pointed at Malaya accusingly.

I looked at Maleeya for permission to approach the child and she nodded her answer. I walked over to the crib and looked at the baby. I wasn't sure what I was looking for so the Chief said, "Look at her eyes!"

I looked at Maleeya because both of us knew what this child could do with her eyes, but Maleeya shook her head NO, and spoke,

"Not that, Father" she gave me a knowing look that the Chief didn't notice. "Look at the color of her eyes."

I gasped when I saw it. I picked Malaya up and held her closer to my face and sure enough there it was. Inside each eye, there was a white portion inside of the pupil that made the shape of a perfect little white buffalo.

I sat down on the chair still holding Malaya. I understood the problem. I asked them what this meant to them as a tribe and it was the Chief who spoke again,

'Only the Holy Ones can interpret the sign of the White Buffalo and our Shaman saw the baby as a curse. He wanted to end her life but I forbade him to do it. He then sent word to the other Tribes in the Pueblo Nation to send their Shamans here to persuade me...I am NOT persuaded.'

He went and stood next to Maleeya and wrapped his arm around her as his wife began to cry. He then told me that the Chiefs of all the other Tribes would be arriving very soon to the Mesa. The Chief told me that once they arrived, if they all agreed, they could take Malaya and kill her and the decision would be out of his hands. He clearly did not know how to fix the situation and Maleeya was devastated.

I didn't even think, I just reacted. I told them I would sneak her out and take her somewhere safe. I knew it was the right thing when I saw the relief on both of their faces. So we made our escape plan and then the Chief and I left the house.

All the men and shamans were waiting outside the house and that was good, it was part of our plan. It was very important that they saw us leave, or rather saw ME leave. As I walked to the place I was staying to gather my things, I heard the Chief telling the men that I had suggested they leave the child and mother alone until the other Chiefs arrived. I heard them muttering but they must have agreed because when I came back out they were no longer yelling.

I made a showing of my leaving the mesa. I said I must go because I was late for another mission. I said my goodbyes and offered some blessings, but mostly they just ignored me because they had more important things to focus on. I let them see me leave the mesa and as soon as I was out of sight, I circled back through the trees until I was at the back of the Chief's adobe. Maleeya was there holding Malaya. She included a little bag of clothes she had made for the baby and also a necklace with a symbol of the tribe on it.

I felt so sorry for her. She was crying hard. I couldn't imagine her sadness in saying goodbye so fast after bringing her baby into the world. But Maleeya knew that the alternative was far worse. I took Malaya all bundled up in her papoose blanket and I told Maleeya that God would save her child. I told her that she would see her daughter again and I kissed her check and blessed her head before I left."

Father Zachary stopped talking and took a deep breath before he continued.

"Well I don't have time to tell you everything about the perilous journey I made with her, but it was not easy. We were almost discovered a few times and we actually had to hide in the trees when we were going down the mesa. The other Chiefs were coming up the mountain and there was just this tiny little group of trees that we could hide in. I was so afraid that the baby would cry but she was truly an angel and didn't make a peep. I heard them talking as they passed by us. They had already made up their minds to end the child's life. They saw her as a punishment from the Ancestors. They wanted her to die before other Indian Nations found out about her existence and blamed the Pueblos. After they passed us, I prayed for God to get us as far away as possible and quickly too."

The priest stopped, remembering something. "Huh, I had forgotten. After I said that prayer, out of nowhere came a donkey. He looked like one of the ones I had ridden down into the Grand Canyon. He even had a kind of crude saddle on. He came right to us and stopped in front of the trees and turned his head towards us. ' Zachary laughed, remembering. "I didn't even hesitate. I just grabbed his mane and carefully got on top of him. He turned around and took us down the mesa."

"I ended up riding that donkey all the way through the desert to the place I was going to hide Malaya. I took her to a monastery of Poor Claire nuns. The Mother Superior understood the reason I brought her to them and agreed to keep her safe and raise her in the convent."

"I was able to leave her there, quite confident that she would be safe. Needless to say I could never return to the Mesa, as I'm sure they suspected me." Zachary paused again to look at Maria and Jacob.

"I checked on Malaya through the years and she was thriving in the convent. Then one day I got a letter from the Mother Superior and she said that Malaya left and they had no idea where she was or what had happened to her. I have continued to pray for her protection through the years." His voice trailed off after that into silence.

Jacob was getting ready to speak when Priscella walked into the room. "She's asking for both of you."

The men got up and went to Madison.

Priscella looked over at Maria and saw that her eyes were closing. She looked at her watch and realized it was way past her bedtime. She scooped Maria up into her arms and took her to her room and put her in bed. She heard Rachael begin to cry and left to get the baby so Madison could talk to Jacob and Father Zachary. As soon as she took her, Rachael quieted. She gave a little yawn and then she too began to drift off to sleep.

Priscella decided to put her in the crib that was in Maria's room instead of the cradle in Madison's room. She turned off the light and left them.

As soon as the light went out Maria got out of bed and went over to the crib. She reached out and touched Rachael's cheek. She tried to be as soft as possible because she didn't want to wake her sister.

"No wonder your tummy hurts," Maria whispered. She withdrew her hand. "No wonder you can't sleep...she's just like you! You're such a good baby to do this for her...I love you." And with that, she climbed back into her bed and drifted off to sleep.

CHAPTER THIRTEEN...TICK TOCK...TICK TOCK

Syree stayed by the children all throughout the night. These two little souls were so precious and amazing. Syree told Mitka that he thought the girls communicated much like the angels do, but after Maria's comments he wasn't sure anymore.

He'd known Maria was able to hear things telepathically, but he wasn't sure how the infant was communicating herself to Maria. He had Mitka observe the two of them on several occasions. Rachael didn't make many sounds except through her tears of pain. She didn't coo or gurgle like other babies. She was either sleeping or crying, so it didn't seem she was communicating at all.

Could it be that she was like Malaya and somehow showed a "movie" like the Priest had described? The answer to his question was answered almost immediately as Maria sat up in the bed and spoke.

"It IS like baby Malaya. I can see things in Rachael's tears."

Maria took her hand and swiped at the hair that had fallen over her eyes. She was wearing a nightgown and her thick head of curly hair was a wild mess. Syree thought she was just adorable, and thanked the Father in a silent prayer for the grace in assigning him to guard the females in Jacob's house.

"I'm sorry little one, did I wake you?" the angel asked.

"Yeah I was kind of already awake and listening," Maria stated in hushed tones.

"What were you listening to?" Syree prompted.

"I was listening to everyone. Mommy and Daddy and Father Zachary and Aunt Priscella but also I was listening for Rachael. She isn't talking right now though and then I heard you." Maria replied.

"You were thinking about how Rachael and I talk. We do it through her pain. We did it the day she was born. She started to cry after she woke up from the first time she slept and as soon as she did, I ran over to her and that's when I saw and felt how she talked. She had a picture of Malaya in her tears and I saw lots of things Rachael knew about her...God told Rachael everything when he asked her if she would suffer to save souls who don't know who God is." Maria looked at the angel sadly. Syree wrapped his wings around her shoulder.

"Oh, I see," the angel said softly..."Rachael is a Suffering Soul."

"Yes, and Mommy doesn't understand, she keeps trying to fix her. She doesn't know that Rachael is doing this because she loves God so much. Rachael told me that God told her, she could stop any time but she said not yet. I want to tell Mommy but I don't think she would understand." Maria answered.

"Oh I think she will understand someday little one. Your mommy knows about Suffering Souls. She just doesn't realize that Rachael is one." The angel explained.

Maria thought about that and then moved onto other things. "Will you stay with us when Daddy and Father Zachary go see Uncle Matthew?"

Syree wasn't sure of that answer because although he heard the humans come up with the plan to go get Matthew to help them rescue Malaya, he had not been told by Mitka or any of the ArchAngels what part he would play in their journey.

"I don't know if I am to stay here or to go with them but don't worry if I leave, Mitka and all the Guardian Angels will be here."

As an exclamation point to Syree's announcement, Maria's Guardian Angel materialized in the intense white light he used to show himself. Like

Mitka, Syree also wanted to see the angel in his true form but the Trinity ordained that for now, they would all see him in this way. Syree acknowledged the angel and continued,

"No matter what happens, be not afraid...all will be well."

Maria smiled at the angel, "I'm not afraid. I just want Mommy, Aunt Priscella and Rachael to be protected if I have to go fight the devil again."

With that said all the angels emitted a protective light around the humans in the house and there was an overwhelming feeling of peace that came over all of them.

A few hours later Madison was awake and feeling much like herself again. The I.V. had been in for 24 hours so Priscella called the doctor to see if she could remove it. After hearing Madison's vitals, he consented with advice for them to call him if she wasn't feeling better by the next day. After they removed it, everyone went to bed. Priscella went to sleep on one of the couches and Father Zachary was asleep on the other.

By the grace of God, Maria and Rachael were both sleeping and for the first time in months the house was quiet. Madison quietly got out of bed, not wanting to wake Jacob.

She tiptoed around the bed and quietly made her way around it and out the door. She wanted to go sit in the living room, but knew she couldn't because she would disturb her guests. They really needed to try and find a bigger house.

Their current house was just a little box. The living room and the kitchen were in one space on one side of the house, and two bedrooms with a bathroom between them, was on the other. It completely lacked privacy. As she looked around she decided that when Jacob and Father Zachary left in the morning, she would get on the computer and start looking for houses for sale.

She walked through the tiny hallway and quietly went to check on the girls. This was the first time since Rachael's birth that she had slept through the night. She didn't want to linger long because she knew waking her and then comforting her with everyone in the house, wouldn't allow anyone to sleep.

Madison, in her exhaustion, was not aware that her prayer to Tara had been heard and the new Saint of God was actually holding baby Rachael in her arms so that she could sleep without much pain. Madison was so out of sorts that she wasn't even aware of Tara's spirit as being present. Little Rachael had her eyes closed but even in sleep her brows were furrowed.

"What is wrong with her, Lord?"

Madison didn't really expect an answer but she got one nonetheless. She couldn't explain how she knew, but she KNEW there was something wrong with Rachael's colon. As soon as morning came she was going to call the doctor.

Tara was happy Madison had heard her whisper to get the doctor to look at the child's colon. This thrilled the Saint. All the Saints of Heaven were filled with joy when some earthbound loved one called on them to help. Most of the time it was done in silence and under the cloak of invisibility, but each prayer was always answered. And if there was any sadness in Heaven, it was from the Saints who never were called on by their loved ones to help. For the Saints, helping was the greatest part of their growth in Heaven and they were always willing and able to help. So many humans though, knew not to pray to their dearly departed. They rather thought of them resting quietly instead of waiting to serve humanity, which they were well equipped to do. So, Tara came at the moment she was called. At the same time, she was able to be at Matthew's house protecting her brother and dealing with Natash. Humans always put such a limit on things and usually when it meant ignoring their family members who now sat with God, it was to their detriment. Tara blessed her dear friend as she watched her walk out of the room.

Madison tiptoed out of the girl's room and through the living room, through the kitchen and quietly out the back door. When she walked through the kitchen she looked at the clock, it was 2:30am. As soon as she opened the door she was met by a very startled dog. Their big Saint Bernard, Max, was not expecting anyone to come out of the house at that time of night and he started to bark in protest until he heard Madison's voice.

"Hi Maxy, don't bark, you'll wake everyone up."

Obediently he was quiet but he wagged his enormous tail and leaned into her so hard he almost knocked her down. Madison decided standing wouldn't work so she sat on the back step and started petting the excited animal. For his part, he was very happy to have some attention. Since the baby had been born, Max had been relegated to live outside on the chain until Jacob understood that he didn't need to keep the dog away from Rachael.

Madison tried to talk to him about letting Max stay inside again but Jacob was adamant that until they knew what was wrong with the baby, he didn't want to introduce dog hair into the house.

Madison agreed but she felt so sorry for the dog. She couldn't imagine what was going on in his doggie mind. Did he think he wasn't loved anymore? Did he think he was being punished? Madison gave him a big hug and tried to reassure him.

"I love you, puppy. I hope you know that you aren't in trouble and that we love you. Saint Francis, please explain it to him. I don't want him to be sad."

As if Max understood the prayer he made a quiet little "Ruff." And in reality he did understand, because the second the prayer was on her lips, Saint Francis appeared to the canine and communicated the message.

Madison had no knowledge of the Saint being there. Even with her gift of discernment, she rarely saw the souls of Heaven, that gift was given to her sister Priscella. Mostly she saw the Holy Souls in Purgatory who had no one to pray for them because their families on earth didn't believe Purgatory existed. It was these souls who came to Madison almost daily. She was glad she could help them because it broke her heart that they had no one.

Madison was much calmer now. For the first time in months, she felt she could think rationally again. Even though she was sending her husband and Father Zachary to find and help Malaya, and everything in her gut told her it would be dangerous, she was feeling relief that something would be done...and quickly.

She shook her head in amazement at the strangeness of God. Here she was, the most exhausted she'd ever been in her life, with a bunch of her own problems and God sent her this dream about a perfect stranger who needed help. She looked up in the starry sky and smiled at Him.

"Have your way then!" She sighed and started talking out loud.

"It WOULD be someone Father Zachary knew," she laughed a small laugh and looked up again.

"You're funny, Lord. But why give the dream to me? Why not Father Zachary? I'm not complaining Lord, I've been wanting to see him again, but not like this."

She gave Max another giant hug and looked back at the stars. Madison was always in awe of the stars. She and Jacob had gone to a Planetarium in Chicago on their honeymoon and Madison was greatly affected by the show they saw there.

When the show was over she had tears streaming down her cheeks. When the lights came up and Jacob saw that she was crying he was confused.

"Are you alright?" he asked.

"Oh I'm fine. I just don't get how anyone can see that and not be humbled. We are so tiny in the scheme of things and yet God loves us. I wonder how anyone can see that show and not believe in God." She wiped her cheeks as she continued.

"God is just so...big," not finding adequate words for her feelings, she waved her hand in the air.

"I'm fine honey. My soul is just touched beyond belief right now. Thank you for bringing me here."

Max looked up in the sky too but quickly became bored with it and lay down next to Madison. She continued to pet him, lost in thought. She was remembering the dream she had about the Indian woman.

When it began she saw this tall woman with long black hair walking in the desert. It was nighttime, but the moon lit up the dessert floor like it was day. The wind was cold and fierce and it was blowing her hair all over the place. The woman didn't seem to be affected by the wind, even though it seemed to Madison that she would've been. There was an enormous black cloud racing towards her fast and the Indian was walking right towards it. The cloud left the sky and touched the ground. It was huge and it roared as it sped towards her. As soon as it picked up speed, the woman started to run towards it.

Madison was afraid for her. No one in their right mind would see this thing and think of doing anything other than hiding. One look at this woman's face, and it didn't appear she was in her right mind.

She had a look of utter determination and it was a sight to behold. As she collided with the cloud, there was a huge explosion and all these black creatures started to form from the dust. Each creature was coming for her, but as they touched her, they exploded and vanished. After all the creatures were defeated, the scene changed. Now she was in a cage and it was clear she couldn't get out. She was trapped on all sides. Madison watched as a terrible monster approached the woman and began to attack her. Madison watched her getting torn apart limb from limb by the giant monster.

The woman began to scream the most agonizing scream and as she screamed, Madison heard a man laughing and calling out the Indian's name in a sing-song voice. "MALAYA.....MALAYA."

The man began to laugh and it sounded like a demon was laughing. Malaya was almost dead when she looked into Madison's eyes and said, "Help me."

That's when Madison began screaming her name over and over.

"Malaya...Malaya...help her...Malaya.!"

Right after that, Madison woke up in her house and in Jacob's arms. He was trying to soothe her but there wasn't a way to do that. Madison knew that something terrible was coming for that woman and that she had been chosen to help her. The only thing she knew to do was to tell Jacob to call Father Zachary, which he did.

Madison began to tell Jacob what had happened and that's when her eyes rolled back in her head and she passed out cold.

Jacob asked the Priest to call Madison's sister and ask her to come as quickly as she could and he called 911. Within 20 minutes, Priscella was there and Madison was on her way to the hospital in an ambulance. Father Zachary took the first flight he could take to get to them. Madison shook her head at the memory and closed her eyes

"Lord, in a few hours Jacob and Father Zachary will leave. I want to pray for protection over them while they are gone. You know it's been a long time since we spoke to Matthew, and he won't even answer his phone. Please help him be willing to help find and rescue Malaya. Also, Lord, thank you for letting everyone sleep tonight, it is much needed. Thank you for letting me know where to look to help Rachael. Please help the doctor listen to me. Send my guardian angel to his guardian angel and let only YOUR WILL be done. I love you Father and I thank you for my family and my life."

Madison gave the big dog one more hug and then she grabbed his head and got nose to nose with him.

"Don't worry boy. I'm going to find us a new home and you will be inside with us where you belong."

Madison planted a kiss on his snout and quietly snuck back into the house.

Madison was wrong about the dog, he wasn't upset about being outside. He liked being able to sniff the wind and listen to the sounds of the animals and humans around the neighborhood. The only thing he hated was the chain that kept him in the backyard. He wished he had been able to go around to the front of the house on the past two nights because the "black ones" were coming in and out of the house constantly.

He knew they meant harm to the humans and he wanted to go protect what was his. But he was reassured by the "white ones" that they were protecting the family. Tezra let Max know that his job was to give warning any time he saw a "black one." The dog knew that the "white ones" could win against them; Max could not and had the scars on his body to prove it. But that didn't mean he wouldn't try, especially when it came to his human children.

Even though he hadn't been close to the new human, he could still tell a lot about her from her scent and her cries. She was much like one of his litter mates who was the runt and was sick. Max's mother eventually laid on the puppy, killing it, because she knew it wouldn't survive. But Max knew it wasn't the same in the human world. Madison was always trying to get the baby well, it just wasn't working.

He still spent a lot of time with Maria because she visited him several times a day. She was also taking care of the baby...just like she took care of everyone in the house. They just didn't know how much... but Max knew.

He saw every being that she saw and could hear every time she battled them. The "black ones" hated her and wanted to hurt her and the baby. Maria knew this and wasn't going to let that happen. Max wished he could help her fight but he knew from the "white ones" that it wasn't his job.

He wasn't worried though, he knew how strong the little human was. He lifted his head and looked around and sniffed the air. For now everything was safe. He laid his giant head down and rested it on his paws and fell fast asleep. He didn't wake up until the morning when he heard the humans moving about. When he did, he sniffed the air and smelled a smell that told him that some of the humans were leaving. He sat up and sniffed the air. From Jacob's open bedroom window he could smell the suitcase that was kept in the attic. That thing Jacob carried always meant he was leaving.

Max was on alert because he didn't like Jacob being gone when the "black ones" were around. Max knew Jacob didn't see any of them but the "black ones" were afraid of Jacob. Not as afraid as they were of Maria, but they were afraid. If he was leaving then Max needed to stay on guard until he returned.

Both Jacob and Father Zachary were uneasy about leaving the house, even though they knew it had to be done. Jacob wasn't sure Madison could handle taking care of Rachael in her weakened state but Priscella had agreed to stay and help until the men returned. The problem was, they didn't know when that would be. This seemed like an impossible task. Firstly, because they still hadn't gotten a hold of Matthew and they weren't even sure he would agree to help them. He was the only one who had the resources to help find this Indian woman. And then the logistics of it all were a bit overwhelming. Although Jacob would never let his concerns show, he did ponder them silently.

For his part, Father Zachary had a different set of concerns that were all spiritual. He wasn't worried about Matthew, or the seemingly Herculean task of finding Malaya and rescuing her. He knew God had already planned each and every step of this journey and it would reveal itself as they went along. He wasn't overwhelmed by it at all and knew it would work out somehow. His concerns had to do with Maria, and really all the females in Jacob's house. He kept replaying the conversation he'd had with Maria about her fighting the devil. He had no idea what she'd meant. In reality, they were all fighting the devil on a daily basis but he had a feeling that Maria meant she was actually fighting him face to face. This bothered him because she had no business doing that, if indeed she was. The priest knew she had gifts, but no one had enough gifts to battle that Entity alone. Only a church sanctioned Exorcist would ever do that. The priest shook his head in thought. He realized he had no idea what Maria meant for sure, so he shouldn't jump to conclusions.

But how did she know about Malaya? Zachary had asked Madison if she'd told Maria about the dream she had about Malaya. Madison assured him she'd only told Jacob and then wondered why the priest was asking. Luckily he didn't have to answer because Jacob came in with a glass of water for Madison to drink, and Zachary took the opportunity to leave the room.

He knew that both Madison and her sister had gifts of discernment and would be able to sense danger while he was gone. He also knew they had bravery to rid the home of any demonic spirits should the need occur. But he still couldn't shake the feeling that something significant was going to happen while the men were away. He immediately took his concerns to prayer.

After the men were gone, Madison went to check on Rachael and was stunned that the baby was still sleeping. Not trusting that her slumber would continue, Madison took the opportunity to call the doctor. No one was in the office yet but she left an urgent message for them to have the doctor call her as soon as he walked in. As if on cue, the second she hung up the phone, the baby began to cry.

Maria and Priscella were at the crib quicker than Madison. Maria took Rachael's hand and shut her eyes. She was watching what Rachael was showing her through her tears and it had to do with the Indian. The vision the baby was showing her was interrupted when Madison walked into the room and picked up the baby.

"I've got her guys, but thanks. Maria you go get ready for school because Aunt Priscella is going to drive you there today."

Maria was unhappy to leave her sister but obediently went to her room and got ready. Madison made a quick job of giving Rachael a bath, putting her in a fresh diaper and clean pajamas. She went to the rocking chair in the living room and began to nurse her.

Rachael screamed through all of it, but settled down the second she started to nurse. Usually the baby would eat for twenty minutes and then the crying would begin again but this time she didn't even last for five minutes before a blood curdling cry began.

Madison did everything she could to try to help her continue to nurse, but Rachael kept rejecting it and continued to scream in agony. Madison put the baby on her shoulder and kept patting her back thinking maybe some air was caught in her throat and she needed to burp. When that didn't work, she tried the football hold but that had no effect either.

It was right at that moment that the phone rang. Madison saw from caller I.D. that it was the doctor's office. A very annoyed nurse wanted to know what was so "urgent" before she "bothered" the doctor with it. Madison lost all patience and said,

"Here, listen for yourself." She put the mouthpiece of the phone right to Rachael's mouth and the nurse's ears were blasted by the noise. After a few seconds Madison put the phone back to her mouth and said,

"Did you hear that? Is that urgent enough for you? I'm getting in my car and I'm bringing her to the hospital. Tell the doctor to meet me there because I want her colon x-rayed and tell him I won't leave there until it's done!!!"

Madison didn't care if she sounded rude or bossy or how she sounded at all. This doctor's office had done nothing to help her child and she was just over it. Luckily the nurse realized that Madison was serious and she told Madison that she was taking the message to the doctor right then. Madison just hung up the phone and went to get the diaper bag and other things she would need for Rachael.

Priscella helped them get in the car, and then with a promise to meet Madison at the hospital, she took Maria to school.

When Madison arrived at the hospital her regular doctor was waiting there for them. Rachael was still screaming and it was the most agonizing scream the doctor had ever heard a child make.

"Why do you think it's her colon, Madison?" he asked as they kept walking to the Emergency Room.

"It's a God thing. I just know it." Madison said as they made their way there.

"Ok, Madison, give her to me...let's see what's going on." the doctor said as he reached to take the baby.

He disappeared behind a door where a nurse was waiting to help with the x-ray. Madison leaned against the wall and slid down it until she was sitting on the floor. She put her head in her hands and started to cry. After ten minutes Priscella arrived and joined her on the floor and wrapped her arm around Madison. There were no words spoken between the two because both of them were listening to Rachael scream from the other room.

It seemed like an eternity before the screaming stopped and the x-ray door opened. The doctor stuck his head out and motioned for them to come into the room.

"I don't know how you knew Madison but you were right...it was her colon. It has been spasming and it is constant." He looked at both women as they waited for him to continue. He pointed at the monitor in front of them and explained.

"You see, Rachael's colon is about the size of your pinky, it isn't very large but it is spasming down to the size of the tip of a needle. It's extremely painful for her. It's a little like acid reflux except instead of the problem being in her esophagus, it's in the colon. I just gave her some medicine to stop the spasms and as you can see...it's working."

Both women went to the table to look at Rachael, and it was apparent that it was working indeed.

Madison gave Rachael a little kiss on her check. It was the first time she'd ever seen her daughter completely out of pain. It was a sight to behold.

"Do you feel better now angel?"

In answer Rachael opened her eyes widely and looked at her mother. It was as if this was the first time Rachael had ever seen her. Madison kissed her again and this time when she pulled away, Rachael smiled at her. This was her very first smile. Madison made a small laugh and said,

"What a beautiful little smile you have baby girl. Oh Praise God!"

Madison gathered her child in her arms and at the same time thanked the doctor for helping her.

"So all I have to do is give her this medicine and she will be okay?" Madison asked, a little skeptical.

"Yep, that's all you need to do. She should grow out of this. In the meantime I want to see her in a month to check everything again."

With that the women took the baby and went home. Madison noticed that Rachael was looking around at her environment. She seemed to be curious about everything she saw. In reality she was seeing everything for the first time. When she was still in pain, she could only focus on that, so she didn't notice much else.

Priscella and Madison spent the afternoon relaxing and regrouping. Madison called Jacob and told him the fantastic news and he was overjoyed and relieved. They lay Rachael down for a nap and Madison took that time to start her housing search. As she was searching for homes the door opened and Maria came through. Madison put the computer down and put her arms out to welcome her oldest child home.

"Hi baby...guess what?" Madison said excitedly.

"What?" Maria answered as she fell into her mother's embrace.

"Well let me give you a hint. What don't you hear right now?"

Maria listened and thought for only a second before she knew.

"Where is she?"

"Believe it or not...asleep!"

"Can I go see her mommy?" Maria asked.

"You can, honey but be quiet as a mouse."

Madison watched as Maria slowly walked and quietly entered their room. She walked over to the crib and sure enough she saw her baby sister sleeping peacefully. Maria was so happy for her sister, but she was more happy for her Mother. Madison needed to help Rachael, but she didn't understand that just because this pain was gone, it didn't mean there wouldn't be pain coming...because there would be...because Rachael wanted that.

As Maria was thinking this, the baby started to stir. Rachael turned her head and opened her eyes and was looking at Maria. The baby broke out in a huge smile, and Maria noticed she had a deep dimple in her right cheek.

"Well hello, baby!!! Mommy said she got you out of pain. Does your tummy feel all better?" Maria patted Rachael's belly and smiled back. Maria stuck her head in the hall and said.

"I'm sorry, Mommy but I woke her on accident." Maria said apologetically.

Madison looked at her watch and noticed it had been three hours since the baby went down for her nap.

"No, it's okay honey. She's been sleeping a long time. It's time for her to get up."

"Mommy, may I get her up? I'll be really careful." Maria pleaded sweetly.

"Hang on I'm coming." Madison watched to make sure Maria picked the baby up correctly and followed her to the living room just to be safe. Maria laid her on the couch, then ran back into their room and grabbed a diaper and the wipes so Madison could change her.

Rachael was smiling and cooing the whole time she was being changed. Priscella had left to go pick something up for dinner, so the three of them were alone. Madison was loving it. This was how she had pictured it during her pregnancy...the three of them hanging out together on the couch. It was turning out to be a great day and Madison said a silent prayer praising God for helping all of them. She felt very blessed.

Maria was very happy too. They all had a nice dinner and then the two girls had a bath and a story and it was time for bed. It was the first time that Rachael was put to bed at the same time as Maria. Madison wasn't even sure it would work, but Rachael was clean, fed and tired so she wanted to give it a try. She said prayers with both of the girls, kissed them and left the room to go call Jacob.

Maria looked at the crib and she had a perfect view of her sister through the crib spindles.

"Good night baby...I love you!"

Rachael turned her head and looked at Maria through the spindles and smiled a huge smile and then shut her eyes and went right to sleep. Maria smiled back and then looked up and began to pray silently. She was so thankful that this medicine would help her baby sleep. She was just getting ready to fall asleep herself when she felt the demon enter the room.

She opened her eyes again and looked at the demon. She knew this demon from when she had been in the cage with Natash. This one was named Rahoul. The only time she had ever seen him was when she was kidnapped. He was the demon that tried to kill her but Jacob and the angels stopped him.

As she watched him walk towards Rachael's crib, she silently sat up in the bed. The demon wasn't aware of Maria at all, because it was focused on the infant. Maria grabbed the Crucifix she kept on her nightstand and slowly picked it up. She got off of her bed unnoticed, and moved to the crib. By the time the demon noticed her, it was too late. She had held up the cross in its face and rebuked it in Christ's name to return to Hell...and instantaneously, it did.

Maria looked at Rachael and inspected her. It didn't look like she was hurt in any way and though she was relieved, she was also angry at the devil for sending that demon.

"I won't let you hurt her," she whispered sternly.

She then grabbed her pillow and a blanket and put it on the floor in front of the crib. She had every intention of sleeping there, just in case another demon came back. She immediately talked to the angels in the house and asked them to protect all of them. She was made to know from Mitka that they had been aware of Rahoul and were all prepared to battle him if he tried to hurt anyone in the house. Then he praised her for her courage in rebuking him. He told Maria that she could sleep in her bed because no demon would be back tonight, but Maria said she just wanted to be close to Rachael.

Maria laid down on the floor and the familiar bright light of her Guardian Angel encased her. She felt warm and safe and started to relax. In spite of that comfort, she wasn't asleep when the vision started...she was wide awake.

When it began she was transported inside of it. She was no longer occupying the space on her bedroom floor, instead she was in a funeral home, at a funeral. She didn't know any of the people at the funeral. The atmosphere was very still and the people all were trapped in their own thoughts. They weren't grieving normally. No one was crying or hugging or comforting each other. In fact, not a single tear was shed.

It was as if everyone there had lost themselves. They were standing and staring but at nothing in particular. Everyone's face was expressionless, without emotion. Something was wrong and it wasn't just that someone had died.

The room she was in was simple. It was a large rectangular room and the ceilings weren't very high. It reminded Maria of an oversized living room she saw once. It was crowded with people and she struggled to walk through the crowd as she made her way to the coffin. There was a fireplace and she stopped in front of it and watched the flames and the calming glow of the fire. It was the only calm thing about the place. She noticed a small log stuck between two other logs. The small log was sticking out and she grabbed the side of it and was untouched by the flame. Not understanding why, she grabbed the log and continued to walk towards the coffin holding the log like a torch. As she walked, people moved out of her way so she could get there.

The casket was black and simple, there was nothing fancy about it at all. When she looked inside she saw a woman, old and frail. Her cheeks were hollow and she held flowers against her chest. Her face was dark and ghostly.

She looked gaunt. Her hair was long enough to go past her ears, but not long enough to reach her shoulders. It was straight and gray. Her expression was emotionless and Maria had a troubling feeling about it.

She stood alone at the casket and wondered why no one was with the woman. They were all so distant and empty and no one would even look at her. She thought she knew the reason but she didn't want to accept it. Instead she turned her gaze towards the flame on the small torch she was holding.

The next thing that happened was strange. She had a memory, something she'd experienced before, but this time everyone in the room could see it. An oddly shaped portal-like screen appeared directly over the casket and it was showing exactly what she was remembering. Now all of the people in the room turned their eyes to the screen over the casket.

Maria had never left the room, but she wasn't in the room..she was only on the screen inside the recurring memory. In the memory, a demon was chasing her. It was large and black and was running on all fours. It's arms were much larger than its legs, and the way it was running reminded her of how a gorilla would move. Maria didn't know where she was or where she was running to, but she decided to stop, and she turned around and faced the demon. She rebuked it in Jesus' name, and a hole appeared underneath it and sucked it in. That same hole appeared beneath Maria and suddenly she was falling.

As she fell, she realized something was different. She was wearing armor. This armor was unlike any armor she'd ever seen. It was harder than a diamond but lighter than a feather. It was shining brighter than a star. She then realized that in her right hand, she was holding a sword.

The sword seemed to be one of a kind and specifically made for her. The blade was see-through but at the same time it wasn't. It was like looking at the sky at night. You're seeing everything and nothing at the same time. On the hilt of the blade, a rosary was wrapped around it and around Maria's wrist. She didn't have a shield. She didn't need one. On the front of the armor and the handle of the blade, was a crest. It was a cross.

She fell for what seemed like forever in a complete empty space. She couldn't see anything but the light of her armor. After some time, she finally saw something. Suspended in the air, was a massive floating ring. Inside this massive ring were Roman numerals 1 through 12. The only number that wasn't in a Roman numeral form was the number 6.

She didn't realize that it was a clock until she saw the moving hands. Every time a hand on the clock moved, it made a deep click sound. It was incredibly loud. She landed on the ring of the clock and it was so massive that she couldn't see the other side. The whole clock was rugged and the color of stone. She began to hear screaming and it was coming from everywhere. It didn't sound human. None of it did.

For unknown reasons, she thought she had to make her way down to this endless pit. She jumped off the clock and once again she began to fall. As she fell, stone walls came into view and she was able to grab the wall. She started to climb down. Each time she grabbed the wall, it would break into pieces under her hands and feet. It was so brittle that even the slightest touch would break pieces off. It should have been impossible for someone to climb either up or down the wall, but she did it with ease. Still, it took a very long time to make it down. She was finally able to make it to some ground.

She was now standing on a very narrow bridge. There was a line of these "things" on this bridge. Each "thing" was filled with every bad emotion possible. Some emotions for each being were stronger than others; some showed more anger, some showed more lust, greed and so on. Depending on what sin they were known for, they would inflict that on each other. They all hated each other. The worst part about them was that Maria was shown they had once been human. They still were, they just didn't look it. Many would shriek in fear and try to jump off the bridge. Every time they tried, it was like an invisible wall was stopping them. She couldn't look at them anymore, so she decided to keep walking. They couldn't look at Maria, and they couldn't lash out at her or hurt her, so she had no reason to be afraid. She was protected.

Everything was massive and it seemed to take forever to get to the end of the bridge. At the end of the bridge was a ring-like platform. In the ring stood a massive hand. The hand was bluish in color and the flesh on the hand was rotting. The fingers were deformed and there were strange markings branded all over the flesh of this hand. The hand would grab these "used to be" humans... one by one. It would squeeze them before disappearing down into the nothingness and returning to grab the next person.

Maria moved on and left that place and somehow she made it to a cliff. As she stood on the edge, she could see everything. Each cavern, each cave, each corner was visible, everything except for the bottom. Some areas reminded her of the honeycombs in a beehive. Except, each of these honeycombs was a different room with different methods of torture and punishment. The tortures were gruesome...too gruesome to describe.

The screaming was deafening. The demons here were ugly. They had no shape or definite form. The deeper anyone went in the pit, the uglier and stronger the demons became. The deeper she went, the more gruesome the torture. Death didn't exist here because everything was already dead. This was Hell and this was it's reality.

Suddenly Maria heard a bell-like sound ring. It was six o'clock. Everything froze and the shrieking stopped. It was dead silence other than the ringing of the bell. Then a flame erupted at the bottom and there was only one voice heard throughout the pits of Hell. It was a violent roar, and it was speaking in a language that Maria didn't know. Then, all at once, every demon and former human alike started running.

They all ran, without a sense of direction. One former human clung to a wall nearby Maria, and looked at her with intent to kill. Her eyes were completely white and it was like they were clouded in fog. Maria recognized this human...it was the frail old lady that lay in the casket.

Suddenly out of the bottom came this beast. It was massive and it devoured everything in sight, including all former humans and demons alike, as well as the old woman in the casket. Somehow though, it didn't get all the way to Maria before it sank back to the bottom of the pit. As it sank, the environment changed. Nothing looked the same as it did before. All the caves, caverns, corners morphed into something different than before. Maria realized this happened every time the clock struck six.

More wailing filled the pit and like hornets, demons swarmed out from the bottom. This time, they could see Maria. They all raced in her direction.

Maria traveled back the same way she had come. However, because the environment changed, so did the path she had to take back. She had to reach the top. This time she was traveling in a lake of lava. Waves were crashing onto her but she was unharmed. Her armor never let the lava burn her. She would pass by former humans groaning and drowning in the lava.

The demons that were after her laughed, then flew past her. They waited for her on the clock. The clock was the only thing that didn't change. Maria made it back to the rock wall, only this time it wasn't brittle. This wall had spikes protruding from it. These spikes were as sharp as the finest blade. There was no smooth surface on this wall. Along with the spikes were ledges sticking off the side of this wall. Each ledge was filled with a pool of blood.

Maria climbed her way back to the clock and by this time, it was almost six o'clock again. The army of demons waited on the hour hand. They all swarmed after her. This was the only time she used her sword. Each swing of her sword brought a roar of thunder and flashes of light. It struck throng after throng of demons as she fought her way to the center of the clock. Then the bell rang much louder than before.

The roar was heard once again, but this time, Maria could see eyes...all the way at the bottom. Such hatred consumed them. Then all the demons shrieked and started jumping off the clock until Maria was the only one that remained. The beast was coming for her now. It was too late though. A brilliant white light formed above her and from that light came a hand that grabbed hers.

Suddenly, she was back on earth and the beautiful light never left her. Every part of her body and soul were filled with love and peace. This infinite love greatly overcame the unimaginable hate that she had just witnessed. The Trinity protected her. He clothed her with His armor and she carried His sword.

Then she was back at the funeral. The fire on the naturally made torch was gone. The screen of her memories had disappeared. Everyone at the funeral couldn't believe what they had seen. The entire atmosphere of the room completely changed and Maria began to pray...

"I confess to Almighty God and to you my brothers and sisters that I have greatly sinned..." Everyone bowed their head, and in unison they all prayed with Maria...not with their voices, but their hearts. When the prayer ended, Maria was back in her room. She stood up to check on Rachael, who was still fast asleep and then she lay back down into the bright light of her angel.

Back in Hell there was an uproar. All the demons were furious that they hadn't caught the human child. All of them knew a great punishment would be waiting for them as Lucifer was beside himself with rage. He saw her on the way back to the clock and being stunned, he sounded the alarm for all the demons to give chase.

It was obvious that the Trinity, and probably their horrid Queen, was aiding her. No one entered Hell without Lucifer knowing it, and Maria had done just that. This putrid child had done it. If that wasn't bad enough, something even worse happened as she was almost at her escape. Bene't had just returned to Hell with the satanist, Natash and he arrived right as they had her surrounded.

All the demons worked together like a rabid pack of vicious wolves. They were joined and given direction by the Alpha, who of course was Satan. No order could be challenged or ignored…it just wasn't possible. But as Bene't entered the pit, he didn't even respond to the order. He stood there looking horrified and screamed,

"MAAAAARRRRRIIIIIAAAA RUN!!!!!!!!!!!!"

And in the instant he stopped screaming, all time stopped and everything went into slow motion.

Bene't turned his head towards Lucifer and Lucifer lifted his brows in utter surprise. Then his eyes narrowed, and he himself went after Bene't with an attack the likes of which Hell had never seen before.

CHAPTER FOURTEEN...
THE MORNING MIRACLE

While Maria was taking her journey into Hell...Jacob and Father Zachary had been thrown into a different kind of Hell, when they entered Matthew's world.

When they arrived in New York, they took a taxi to Manhattan to find Matthew's building. They had both tried to call him several times, but the calls went to voicemail every time. They hoped they would be able to find him once they made it to his house.

When they got there, they met with the door man, Peter. After asking lots of questions acquiring information on who the men were and what business they had with Matthew, the doorman consented to let them in. He asked them to wait in the lobby while he tried to reach Mr. Bradley. After several attempts at trying to call the Penthouse, Peter had the sinking feeling he knew right where Mr. Bradley was. Father Zachary noticed the deep sigh Peter showed and felt concerned.

"Is Mr. Bradley okay, Peter?"

Peter didn't have a clue why he felt comfortable enough with the Priest to answer honestly...but he did.

"Father, if I may be frank, I am very concerned for Mr. Bradley. He has been a mess since he came back from a long trip last year to find his sister. I think when he found that she was deceased, he just couldn't cope.

He actually spends most of his time in the hotel bar, which is right through those doors." Peter pointed towards the doors.

"Thank you Peter," Father Zachary replied gratefully.

"You're welcome, Father. I have to warn you though, he can get quite mean when he's drunk. And Father, I don't want you to think I'm crazy but my wife said that he was being haunted. I know that someone in your profession would be an expert on these things. I don't know anything about these things, but I would say that sometimes I think he's possessed. He is not at all the man he used to be."

Father Zachary thanked him and told him not to worry, that they were there to help Matthew. Then he and Jacob walked into the bar.

What they encountered was not what they had expected. First of all, Matthew didn't look anything like they remembered. He was no longer the clean cut professional man who dressed beautifully and had a sophisticated air about him. His hair had gotten long and it was obvious it had not been washed in awhile. He was dressed in jeans and a very dirty shirt that was wrinkled, and full of fresh stains. When he came into complete view, they realized he wasn't wearing any shoes and only one foot had a sock on it.

Matthew was standing at the pool table playing a big burly biker type who had skull tattoos all over his huge arms. The two were in a heated exchange. Matthew was accusing the man of cheating when Matthew went to the bar. Everyone around the table was trying to convince Matthew that the man did not cheat. But nothing could convince Matthew, not even the obvious anger of the man he was provoking could silence him.

Jacob, however, was very aware of the biker's anger. He knew from vast experiences that this man's anger had reached its boiling point, and it would just be minutes before Matthew would be in grave danger. It only took Jacob seconds to sum up the biker. He was bigger than Jacob but that didn't worry Jacob at all. He'd fought much bigger, angrier men with ease. He was coming up with the quickest way to take the man down when he stepped in between the two men and was now in a position to protect Matthew.

Matthew was yelling with his eyes closed and didn't even see Jacob come to his aid. He was still screaming when Jacob said to the biker,

"Don't even think about it."

The biker was surprised and really had no idea where Jacob had come from but he was so angry at this point, that he didn't care if he fought Jacob or the drunk guy he was playing pool with.

The biker quickly sized Jacob up... but he sized him up incorrectly.

"You need to move out of my way little man. This isn't your business."

Jacob had no intention of moving and quietly made that known with the dangerous "try me" look he gave to the biker. The look threw the biker off guard because he had seen it before, when he'd fought and lost fights with men his size. 'Surely this guy doesn't think he could beat me? ' One more look at Jacob's eyes told the biker that he didn't just think it...he knew it.

It had to be all the alcohol he'd consumed, because he didn't want to listen to that voice that said he should walk away...he should have.

The biker lunged at Jacob and missed. Jacob grabbed the biker's arm and twisted it behind his back so quickly and so roughly and with so much force that it seemed to anyone watching that the biker's arm would break. The biker immediately started to holler in pain and began begging to be released. If it had been a TAP OUT fight, the biker would've already been pounding the floor.

"Are you going to behave and leave this very drunk man alone?" Jacob asked, as he tightened his grip once more.

Through the man's groaning, he promised he would. Jacob decided for good measure he would escort the biker to the door.

"On second thought, I think it would be best if you just left." And with that Jacob threw the man out the door.

Peter, who had not followed them into the bar, was almost running to it now. When he walked in, Jacob was already back in the bar over by the pool table. Peter heard Mr. Bradley still yelling at the biker who was no longer there. Father Zachary was trying to get Matthew to open his eyes, so he would know that he was there, but Matthew just kept making a racket. Peter knew it was time to remove Mr. Bradly from the bar, but he was not looking forward to it. After last night, he had hoped that Matthew would be too hungover to come back down to the bar. He didn't realize that the hangover was the reason Matthew came. Peter made his way over to Matthew but then stopped when the duty of removing him was taken out of his hands.

When Matthew finally opened his eyes and saw the priest and then Jacob, he thought he was hallucinating. He knew they couldn't really be there. He thought they were demons in disguise and he began to back away from them, begging that they get away from him.

Father Zachary tried to speak softly to him and reassure him that they weren't there to hurt him and they just wanted to talk to him. In answer to this, Matthew picked up a bar chair and threw it at the priest.

Matthew didn't understand what he saw next, but right before the chair would've hit the priest, Matthew's cat jumped in front of Father Zachary and took the full brunt of the flying chair. As soon as the chair hit the cat, it fell to the floor with a thud. Even in his drunken state, Matthew knew that he had killed his cat. There was no way the animal could have survived the force of the chair. Matthew ran over to where the chair landed. Where he expected to see the broken body of his cat, he instead saw the cat grooming himself. As Matthew got to the cat, it looked at him and in a loud protesting meow he said,

"NOOOOOOOOOO." Then the cat put his ears back, hissed at Matthew and walked over to the priest and started weaving in and out of Zachary's legs.

When Matthew looked at the priest and saw he was still there, he still thought the priest was a hallucination. He looked around at something else he could throw at him and instead found Jacob standing face to face with him. He was startled and also thought Jacob wasn't really there so he started begging him again,

"Please go away...leave me alone. GO GO GO GO GO GO," Matthew kept getting louder and louder with each "GO!"

Matthew's eyes were crazed, and he ran over to the bar and grabbed a knife the bartender kept by the lemons. He didn't hesitate and ran back to Jacob and started slicing wildly in the air.

He tried to cut Jacob, but he missed each time. At one point, he used so much force that when he missed, he accidentally sunk the knife into his own thigh. He cried out when he saw what he did and pulled it out quickly. Blood began to quickly stain his jeans. That's when Jacob acted.

"Alright Buddy, you've done enough damage for one day...let's go." When Matthew protested, Jacob grabbed him by the neck and headed towards the door. Matthew was fighting so hard, Jacob finally picked him up and threw him over his shoulder, carried him out of the bar to the elevator. Father Zachary, Peter and the cat all followed them to the elevator. They all rode to the penthouse together. Matthew had completely stopped fighting because he had passed out cold.

Once they got inside Matthew's house, they took him right to his bedroom and Jacob carefully laid him on his bed. He asked Peter to bring him a tee shirt and after he delivered that, he sent him to get wash rags and hot water.

Jacob used the tee shirt as a makeshift tourniquet to stop the bleeding on his thigh. Then he cut off his jeans and began to clean the wound to determine if it would require medical treatment. After examining it, and pouring Peroxide on it, Jacob used some band aids to make a Butterfly bandage and decided that at least for now, the damage was contained.

He asked Peter if he could make some coffee. For his part, Peter was happy to be ordered to do something and not be solely responsible for Mr. Bradley. He was impressed with Jacob's medical skills and happy he took control of the situation. He also felt a kinship of sorts with the Priest. He felt they had known each other for a long time. Peter didn't understand it, but having Father Zachary there made him relax. He brought out a pot of coffee and three mugs, as well as a platter of cheeses, meats and fruit that he had just purchased for Mr. Bradley that very morning. He was happy he did too, because the two men eyed the food as soon as they saw it.

"If you want something more substantial, I can order room service for you." Peter offered.

With a wave of his hand the priest refused. "No thank you, this is plenty for now." He gave a quick glance at Jacob to confirm, and Jacob simply gave a nod of agreement as he filled his plate with the food.

"On second thought," Father Zachary said as he watched Jacob fill his plate, "Go ahead and order some..." The priest didn't even know what to request because he wasn't used to ordering room service. Because he was on a simple diet, he couldn't think of what would fill Jacob's obvious appetite. Luckily Peter came to the rescue.

"I think I'll just order an assortment, Father." He smiled as he left the room to order.

When all was said and done, they had their choice of chicken wings and salads, steak kabobs, rolls and desert. It was more food then Father Zachary had ever eaten at one sitting. Both men ate their fill while Peter prepared the guest rooms. He checked on Mr. Bradley once more before saying good-night to Jacob and Father Zachary. He left his number in case they needed anything during the night.

Jacob and Father Zachary were sitting in the living room watching as the lights of the city got brighter and the panoramic view stunned them. It was a while before either man spoke. Both of them were lost in thought, and mesmerized by the view. It was Jacob who broke the silence.

"So how exactly is he going to help us?" Jacob asked the question as he raised one eyebrow, pointed over his shoulder towards Matthew's room and a grin formed on his face.

Father Zachary laughed and said "Only God knows...and His ways are mysterious."

Both men smiled as they took another drink of their coffee. Jacob looked up at the priest and both his face and tone were serious.

"What do you suppose happened to him Father? He didn't strike me as a man who would lose his mind like that. He doesn't even look the same to me."

"Well that's because he's not." Father Zachary said.

"You and Matthew watched many of the same things when we last met and went to find Maria...things most people never see in their lifetimes. You came out of it more spiritually mature, and I believe that might be because you are surrounded by holiness." the priest said and then motioned towards Matthew's room.

"He doesn't have a Madison."

His comment touched Jacob and he smiled, shaking his head yes and then added,

"Or a Maria"

Father Zachary thought of that statement. He made a mental note to take the time to talk to that extraordinary little girl once they returned. He recalled their conversation and then remembered Maria had said that both she AND Rachael were suffering for souls. So the baby must also have strong gifts. And he wanted to ask Maria how she knew that Rachael suffered. He wanted to discuss all of this with Jacob but decided against it. He wanted to wait to talk to Maria first. He wanted to fully understand before he spoke to Madison and Jacob. He didn't know why he believed this, but he was sure that neither of them had any clue about their daughter's gifts. He simply countered back,

"Or a Rachael."

Jacob thought for a moment. The priest was completely correct. Everyone around Jacob could help him process what had happened. But Matthew had no one around him who understood God... who could answer questions. Jacob and Madison had many conversations about Maria's kidnapping, and all the supernatural things surrounding it.

Living with Madison was to constantly experience the supernatural, and talking about God all day long, had become a habit for Jacob as well.

"You know, if I didn't have my family, I guess I would've turned to alcohol to cope with what happened too." Jacob said, deep in thought.

After the men had spoken for a while they went in to refill their coffee cups; neither of them felt like going to bed.

Matthew woke up from his drunken stupor and met them in the kitchen. At first he was startled to see them. He shook his head and refocused his eyes. After looking from man to man he said,

"You guys are really here?"

It wasn't really a question. It was more of a statement to confirm to himself that what he was seeing was real.

"Hi Matthew," Father Zachary said. Jacob just stared at him and nodded his head. That made Matthew laugh.

"And Hello to you...man of few words," he chuckled to Jacob.

"So Padre, are you going to fill me in on what happened? Why are you guys here?"

"Well it's a long story," Father Zachary answered.

"Well I clearly have the time, so shoot...what's going on?"

"Well before we start, why don't you eat something and drink some coffee," the priest urged when he noticed Matthew was reaching for vodka and the bloody Mary mix.

Matthew immediately got angry and didn't even try to hide it.

"Look Padre, I feel like crap and I need to feel better quick...this is the best way and since you're in my house and I'm in charge, I think I'll be having a drink."

Jacob side stepped so he was suddenly in front of the cabinet holding all the alcohol.

"Yeah...I don't think you will." As if on cue, the cat jumped up on the counter next to Jacob and did his signature meow that sounded like he was saying "NOOO."

Matthew sighed and realized he wasn't getting that drink. He looked at Jacob wearily and said.

"I have nightmares about you."

"Good," Jacob said sternly.

Matthew laughed at that, but knew better than to push Jacob. This was not a man that you argued with and if Matthew were to be honest, he was glad they were on the same side of things, because Jacob scared him.

"Matthew, I just need you to be as clear headed as possible. We need your help and God led us here." The priest said softly.

"Oh well if 'GOD' led you here, then I guess I better behave." He said with utter disdain and disgust.

Jacob reacted to that and grabbed Matthew by his collar and slammed him into the counter.

"Alright ground rules. I don't want to hear you talk disrespectfully to Father again and if I were you, I'd be careful how you talk about God too." Jacob seethed.

Father Zachary intervened and put his hand on Jacob's shoulder.

"It's okay Jacob. He needs to get it all out. Please put him down." Father Zachary said a silent prayer for help and at the same time the cat said "Noooo" but this time he was directing it to Jacob.

Tezra had been inside the cat protecting Matthew for a while. He was very happy to see Jacob and Father Zachary again, but more than that, he was happy to see Syree who had journeyed with them.

"Welcome my brother, in the name of the Father, Son and Holy Spirit. I trust you traveled well." The angel of the animal kingdom said joyfully.

"Well enough, my brother. Mitka sends his greeting and thanks you for your service." Syree returned.

Tezra left the cat's body and stood next to Syree watching the humans.

163

He filled Tezra in on all the goings on at Jacob's house and Tezra did the same regarding Matthew. When Syree told him of Lucifer's attempted attack on the infant, and Maria's response, the animal Angel rejoiced in her.

"To see what the Father's Will is for that child, will be beautiful to behold. How very blessed we are, my brother."

Then he motioned towards Jacob. "And I see my little protege' hasn't quite learned to control his temper." Tezra said this about Jacob because he was gifted in his interactions with animals, and since Tezra was the angel in charge of the entire Animal Kingdom, he had a connection to any human who had special abilities with animals.

Syree smiled, "Not quite yet my brother...at least this time he was righteously angry."

Tezra told Syree that he would return to instruct Max, the big Saint Bernard, on what to do in the future if Satan came again. And then the angels prayed while the vicar of Christ, (the representative of Jesus on Earth), Father Zachary, tried to enlighten the two men in front of him.

When Jacob released Matthew, Matthew straightened his shirt and tried to compose himself. His pride was clearly wounded. Jacob grabbed a fresh cup of coffee and poured one for Matthew and motioned with his head that Matthew should move back into the living room. Father Zachary humbly followed Jacob's silent command and all three men went to sit on the large sectional couch. Even though Matthew complied, he was fuming at Jacob for the way he had treated him in his own home. He was very put out about it.

"Maybe if we just calm down, this can all be sorted out." Father Zachary said gently.

He looked at both of the men with the eyes of a father. One, a sad little alcoholic who didn't have a clue what was important in life and who was completely without direction. He had no idea how to cope with his life anymore and if he didn't accept God into his life soon, the priest doubted

Matthew would last much longer. The other was a stubborn, bull headed brute, who had learned to give his life to God but hadn't quite learned to tame his reactionary ways. The priest said another silent prayer and pressed on.

"Matthew, why don't you continue telling us why you're angry at God."

Matthew looked at Jacob as if to ask permission. Jacob didn't say a word, just stared at him. Father Zachary patted Matthew's leg and said,

"It's fine Matthew. Get it off your chest."

Matthew thought for a moment, and then seemed to get frustrated as he said, "Who said I'm mad at God? I don't even believe in Him. Because what kind of God lets kids be kidnapped and sisters get tortured and killed? What kind of God won't answer me when I try to talk to Him? And what kind of God allows people to be …."

Matthew put his face in his hands and stopped talking. Father Zachary was just getting ready to reply when Matthew stood up and started pacing in front of them.

"Everything that happened…it didn't really happen, did it? I mean, why me? Why you, Jacob…or you, Padre? Why would God choose us to show this stuff to? Why doesn't He show everyone in the world His miracles? What's the big secret? Can't He understand that we as humans need to see Him every day? How can He let angels and demons appear one day, and then just disappear from my life? What kind of Father does that?"

Matthew looked from the priest to Jacob waiting for a reply. He ran his fingers through his hair and was getting angrier. He looked at Jacob, "I NEED a drink!!!!"

"Nope," Jacob answered, then stretched his arms out, put them behind his head and relaxed back into the couch. This was maddening to Matthew because in that simple gesture Jacob said,

"No…don't even try it…I'm so sure you won't try it that I'm going to chill on your couch, looking cocky about it."

"I really hate you!" Matthew spat. Jacob yawned.

"That's your problem...not mine."

"Really, that's it? That's all you have to say? It's MY problem? You come into my house, keep me from drinking my booze, and boss me around and say it's MY problem? Are you even able to speak more than a few words at one time?" Matthew knew he was crossing a line but he just couldn't stop himself.

"Well can you? Or are you just stupid?" Matthew virtually spat the words.

Many things happened at once. Father Zachary saw where the conversation was headed and anticipated Matthew going too far, so he stood before the question posed was even finished to try to get in between the men. Syree, stood directly in front of Jacob as he was ready to rise and became like a cement wall that made it impossible for Jacob to move forward. Tezra jumped back into the cat Sampson and meowed "NOOOOOOOO" over and over.

Jacob was beyond furious. It wasn't being called stupid that angered him, it was Matthew himself. The guy had just disappeared out of their lives after the wedding and every time Madison tried to check in with him, he ignored her. Jacob was tired of hearing about how worried his wife was about this good for nothing drunk in front of him. When Madison was affected by anything...so was he. Standing there with his fists clenched and red faced in anger, he tried once more to move towards Matthew. The angel Syree, made that impossible.

So there they stood. Jacob frozen where he stood, ready to pounce as soon as whatever kept him frozen moved. Matthew was scared to death, and rightly so. Looking at the expression on Jacob's face told him he had made a deadly error. He couldn't understand though why Jacob had stopped. His expression said that he intended bodily harm.

But Father Zachary knew exactly what was happening. He could see Syree as clearly as he saw Jacob and Mathew. He would have stood there and stared if Tezra hadn't jumped out of the cat at that moment. Now Zachary couldn't look away from this angel.

Both angels were beautiful. Syree was perfect with his white hair and this intense white light that continually surrounded him. It was his purity that marked his appearance. It was how all of the ten thousand angels of the Queen's guard looked. Even though they were from many choirs, they all had this brilliant white hot light around them. So while Syree was stunning, it was the other angel the priest couldn't look away from.

Father Zachary had seen many angels and demons and supernatural things in his 54 years of life, but he had never seen an angel like this. He had seen this angel one other time. It was when he and Matthew were traveling in the desert and this angel sent them camels to ride for their journey. The priest was in awe of Tezra then, and here he was again, in Matthew's apartment.

Tezra was wild looking. He had long hair that looked windblown. He was covered in animal fur and he was huge. The furs just covered his torso. His arms and legs were bare so you could see how muscular they were. He wore moccasins of suede on his feet. His face was as masculine as a face could be. He had a square jaw and high cheekbones and bushy eyebrows that framed his beautiful intense eyes. But it was his overall appearance that the priest couldn't look away from. He looked untamed, like an animal. He had both a ferociousness and an innocence to him. The air around him was fresh and invigorating and was charged with electricity. He had a dazzling smile that made him look both childlike and like an old soul. The priest just couldn't tear his eyes away.

Matthew tore his fearful eyes away from Jacob to glance at the priest and knew something unusual was happening. Jacob stopped fuming long enough to follow Matthew's gaze.

"Father, are you okay?" Jacob asked, all anger left him and turned to concern.

"What are you seeing, Padre? What's there that we can't see? Tell us?"

Matthew was still scared but this time for another reason. He was on the verge of hysteria when he whispered.

"Are they back? Do you see the demons and Natash?"

Syree turned around and wrapped his wings around Matthew. The peace that immediately came over Matthew because of it, made him very emotional and he began to sob.

"No more...please God, no more."

With the wall gone, Jacob could move freely again and went and embraced his broken friend. He spoke softly this time.

"Mathew, look at his face. He isn't afraid. Whatever it is, he is happy."

Matthew looked at the priest again and saw that indeed, he was not upset at all.

"Okay, but why? Why can't everyone have this experience? Why doesn't God just show himself to everyone?" Matthew asked quietly through his tears.

Father Zachary replied without ever looking away from Tezra. It was the angel who inspired the priest to answer the question.

"HE does Matthew and I will show you." With that, Tezra and Syree both bowed deeply to the priest. The angels did this as a form of respect to the priesthood. These angels accepted a long time ago that they would serve humanity, not lord above them like the fallen angels. These angels knew that when the 'Word was made flesh," that humanity was elevated forever above the angels; and the men who were called to the priesthood, would be representatives of Jesus, so the angels always bowed to them. Even though not all priests were good or righteous, or in any way deserving of this respect, the angels continued to give it. After all, they alone were accountable for their actions and would answer to God if they didn't show the proper respect. And for all the bad unholy priests out in the world, they would be accountable for each of their actions that weren't Christ-like. And though there were far too many of those kinds of priests, there were more of the good ones and Father Zachary was even in a class above them. His whole goal every day and every moment was to represent Christ honorably. So when these angels bowed to him, it was because he was "running the good race and was a good and faithful servant." But that didn't make it at all easy for Father Zachary to accept. His humility far outweighed his pride. He thanked the angels and made a blessing of the Sign of the Cross over them and with that Syree disappeared and Tezra re-entered the cat.

When Syree released Matthew, he collapsed on the couch and stared into space. Without looking at anyone he said, "I think I'm ready to find out what brought you here."

"Finally," Jacob answered. Both men wanted to ask how the Father was going to show them God in the world, but they decided independently to leave the time to the priest.

Father Zachary sat down and told Matthew everything he had told Jacob and Maria about Malaya. Matthew listened in fascination.

"So Madison knows about this Indian and you don't know, how?" Mathew looked from one man to the other. He asked Jacob, "Doesn't that freak you out man? I mean I don't think I could handle being married to that."

"You couldn't...that's why you're not." Jacob answered.

"But how would she know these things? Who tells her?" Father Zachary was surprised that Matthew would be focusing on Madison's gifts and not the problem with finding and helping Malaya, but in a very patient voice the priest answered.

"Madison has been able to see, hear and feel spirits since she was a child. She also has had several prophetic dreams. Because she's so in touch with her spiritual side, she is able to pick up on things that none of us can. I believe the Holy Spirit sent Madison the dream, and HE also sent me to Jacob. Now HE has sent us to you, Matthew. God works through many people and Madison is just a gifted woman. God uses her to help souls, dead and alive. And right now Malaya needs help."

It wasn't that Matthew didn't believe him, he just didn't think he could live with someone who had those gifts. It seemed to him that the gifts would be more of an intrusion on her life than anything else. He tried to take it at face value and let it go. He ran his fingers through his hair again and asked, "Okay Padre, so what do you need from me? How can I help you find this weird Indian girl?"

This time when Father Zachary spoke, it was with a sternness that he rarely showed. He was clearly insulted and didn't try to hide his emotions.

"Matthew, Malaya isn't weird...she's what I call a super Saint. She was born to bring many souls to Christ. She has had to suffer I am certain, although I don't know the details of that...but I know she has. I don't know yet what you can do to help, but I'm sure God will let us know soon. One thing you need to know for certain, is that if God is bringing this extraordinary woman into your life, you had better pay attention. I believe any one who comes into contact with her will be blessed beyond measure. Please do not call her weird again. Good night."

With that, the priest got up and started to walk to his bedroom. He turned around once and said,

"Plan on going to sleep soon...I'm getting both of you up very early." And with that he disappeared into his room.

"Sorry, Padre," Matthew said with regret.

"Well I hated I pissed off the Padre," he said to Jacob.

"Yeah, it seems like you have quite the talent for that," Jacob said without sympathy.

Matthew looked at Jacob with disdain. He couldn't really defend himself because he knew it was a true statement. He just hated that it came from Jacob.

"What's your problem, Jacob? I mean it. You've been a jerk ever since you got here. What did I do to you?"

"It's what you did to Madison. My wife has been worried about you since the wedding and when you didn't respond to her calls, she got pretty upset. I don't like to see her upset." Jacob said with obvious contempt.

"Well I didn't know she was upset!!! How would I know that? I can't read minds. Anyway, why would she care?" Matthew asked pathetically.

"Yeah that's a mystery to me too. All I see when I look at you is a cocky, egotistical narcissist." Jacob snapped.

"Wow, don't hold back, Jacob. Tell me how you really feel." Matthew said with humor.

"It's obvious you don't know my wife at all. When God puts someone in her life, she has a connection with them for the rest of her life. It's some kind of spiritual thing that I don't understand, but she does. She can feel when something is wrong in people's life no matter how far away from her they are, or whether or not she's seen them for years. Then when that happens, she puts time and effort into praying and suffering for that person. I live with that. And you ignoring her isn't okay with me. Don't do it again."

Matthew knew by his demeanor that Jacob was serious and he'd been pushed as far as he could be pushed.

"Ok. I won't." Matthew said apologetically.

"Good, now you heard Father...go to bed," Without another word, Jacob got up and went to bed.

Matthew stood up and was stunned by the audacity of his guest. He picked up all three of the glasses on the table and headed to the kitchen. He was muttering to himself the whole way.

"Don't tell me to go to bed...this is my house...who do you think you are?"

He kept complaining all the way to his room but did so softly, because he didn't want Jacob to hear him. When he got in his bed the cat jumped up on the bed and walked straight to his head and sat down. Matthew looked at the feline and talked to him as if he could get advice from him.

"So you agree with me, right? Don't you think that guy's pushing it?"

Samson/Syree leaned into Jacob until his nose was almost touching the human and meowed.

"NO." Then the feline turned his back to Matthew, curled up in a ball and went to sleep.

"Fine, be against me...everyone else is," Matthew said and even as he heard himself saying it, he heard how ridiculous he sounded. He was sick of himself and sick of the victim he had become. He rolled over away from the cat and shut his eyes; hating himself as he drifted off to sleep.

It didn't feel like it had even been a minute between when Matthew shut his eyes and when Father Zachary was shaking him to get up.

Matthew noticed, as he opened his eyes, that it was still dark outside. He sat upright, thinking that something was wrong for the priest to be getting him up.

"What's wrong, Padre?" Matthew asked with concern.

"Nothing, come on. Hurry, or we will be late." the priest said.

Matthew couldn't imagine where they were going or how they could be late. He was going to ask, but when he joined them in the living room, Jacob already looked annoyed that they had to wait on him at all. Matthew decided to stay silent. When they left the building Father Zachary turned and asked Matthew.

"Which way do we go to Central Park?"

Central park? Why were they heading to Central park in the middle of the night? Was the priest crazy? Didn't he know this was New York City? Didn't he know that it wasn't safe to go there in the dark?

"It will be fine, Matthew." the priest answered as if Matthew had asked the question aloud.

He was about to protest until he looked at Jacob's raised eyebrow. It was mocking his fear. Jacob was silently asking if he was afraid. Well, heck yes he was afraid! This was stupid and reckless. But he'd be darned if he was going to show fear in front of his bully of a house guest. Instead he brushed past both men and took the lead.

"It's this way," Matthew said.

When they got to the park, Father Zachary saw a hill in the middle of a tiny grove and led the men to it. Jacob saw the fear in Matthew's eyes and whispered spitefully,

"Looks like the perfect place for a murderer to hide." He smiled at Matthew's shocked expression. And sat down next to the priest.

Matthew sat down too but not before looking all around him for someone who could be following them or hiding. He hated the fact that he was so transparent to Jacob. He wanted to take his chances and slug him, but couldn't because he would upset the priest...at least that was the lie he told himself.

All of them sat there quietly. Father Zachary put his finger up in the air and said,

"Listen...tell me what you hear?"

Matthew listened but didn't understand what the priest wanted him to say. Jacob shut his eyes and answered.

"I hear crickets."

"And Matthew...what do you hear?"

Even though he was annoyed by this stupid game, he decided that if Jacob could play it then so could he. He listened for a moment.

"I hear frogs and squirrels chirping." Their answers satisfied the priest and he smiled sweetly.

"Matthew, you asked me why God doesn't show miracles to everyone... why HE doesn't make HIMSELF known. I'm getting ready to show you that HE does show HIMSELF, and HE does it every single day, in every part of the world. You just haven't been paying attention." he paused for a moment as he looked down, grabbed a twig and broke it.

"The Bible tells us this in Psalm 113:3...FROM THE RISING OF THE SUN, TO THE PLACE WHERE IT SETS, THE NAME OF THE LORD SHALL BE PRAISED!

In the book of Revelation it states...THEN I HEARD EVERY CREATURE IN Heaven AND ON EARTH AND UNDER THE EARTH AND ON THE SEA AND ALL THAT IS IN THEM, SINGING: TO HIM WHO SITS ON THE THRONE AND TO THE LAMB BE PRAISE AND HONOR AND GLORY AND POWER, FOREVER AND EVER!! This means that all of creation will praise God every single day beginning with the rising of the sun. Gentlemen, I want to welcome you to the MORNING MIRACLE!"

"All you have to do is listen to all the animals making noise right now." the priest said excitedly.

They heard the crickets and the squirrels and the frogs and then they heard the roar of a lion. Father Zachary's eyes got huge as he asked,

"Is there a zoo nearby?"

Matthew looked confused but answered, "Yeah, the zoo is in the middle of Central Park...why?"

The priest broke out in a huge smile and started to laugh..."Oh my, this is going to be awesome. Good job, Lord!" he said as he looked up to the stars.

"So it's getting ready to happen. First you will hear all the animals stop making noise and then it will all go quiet...and then they will begin." the priest said, barely able to contain his joy.

"What will begin?" Matthew whispered.

"Just listen...here we go," the priest whispered back.

And just like Father Zachary said, all the animals stopped making noise. First the squirrels stop chirping, then the frogs stop croaking and finally the crickets stopped making noise and all was silent.

This wasn't a normal kind of silence. It was a heavy silence. It kept getting heavier and heavier and all the men felt like their ears were going to plug up. It was so quiet that it was uncomfortable. Each moment of it was almost painful and both Jacob and Matthew wanted it to be over. Just when they thought they couldn't stand the silence or the darkness a second longer, a tiny sliver of light peeked through the eastern sky. The instant that happened the animals began to make noise. First it was the birds who began to tweet in every direction and the legs of the crickets began to make sound. The frogs began to croak and the raccoons called out to each other. Then there was a roar, then two...then three. Everyone in the ape family joined the song and the elephants began to blow through their trunks. The cheetahs, the bears, the camels, the zebra's and every other kind of zoo animal joined the song. It kept getting louder and louder as the sun continued to rise. It kept going until it reached a fever pitch, and as uncomfortable as the silence was, the noise became so loud that none of them could hear anything but the animals. Matthew was starting to cover his ears, but Father Zachary grabbed his hands and shook his head no. And when the sun had completely risen the animals one by one, became silent. This happened until once again there was nothing but silence. By now all three men were standing up. Jacob was smiling the biggest smile either the priest or Matthew had ever seen on his face. He was beside himself and so was Matthew, because from the moment of the total silence until the song rose to it's crescendo, the Holy Spirit could be felt by all of them.

"THE MORNING MIRACLE... brought to you by God...every....single...morning!"

Father Zachary fell to a sitting position and was laughing. In all the times he had gone out to worship God with Nature, he had never been by a zoo. The experience needed to be felt to understand the intensity.

"Wow...just wow", Matthew said as he sat next to the priest. It was obvious how Jacob felt as he turned his face towards the sun, closed his eyes and just continued to smile.

Father Zachary watched as the sun lit up Matthew's face and he saw something there that had never been there before...belief. He put his arm around Matthew and said, "See, Matthew, God is here...HE'S everywhere. And every morning, no matter the season, no matter where you are, you can come out and see HIM in the Morning Miracle."

Matthew couldn't speak. That was the most beautiful thing he had ever experienced. He actually knew he had felt God for the first time ever. It was a calmness that enveloped him and he just knew that everything from this point on in his life was going to be okay. For the first time since learning that Tara had died, he didn't want a drink. He didn't need it anymore. He knew that whatever nightmare he'd been through in the last year, was over. He was wide awake and he was...happy. He couldn't see the stunning animal angel, Tezra, standing behind the priest and he couldn't see his sister Tara as she wrapped her arms around her brother and praised God for his conversion. He didn't know it was her that whispered the idea into his ear, but he felt like she was close. He shut his eyes and let the unfamiliar feeling wash over him like a cleansing balm. "I miss you sis...and I'm ready now. Just show me what to do." The idea came to him instantaneously as he stood up.

"Come on guys...we have work to do," he said with complete resolve. All three men left the park with Matthew leading the way. Any thought of fear or the man he was before, was gone. He had an Indian Princess to rescue.

CHAPTER FIFTEEN...
HIS MERCY IS BOUNDLESS

Tim Nethers was furious. All he wanted to do was return to the Ditch and recover Malaya's remains, but he had been called away to a mandatory meeting of the Elite Fowlins in Scotland. He had been summoned by the Royal Arch Fowlin who would promote him to the title of King. This was a title that Tim had wanted for years and was happy to be getting it, but the timing could not be worse. He wanted to get back and see the evidence of torture that Carl had put Malaya through. He knew that there wouldn't be much evidence there, because Carl was a cannibal. He called and inquired about Malaya's "well being." He laughed when he phrased the question that way. To say he was disappointed with the answer was an understatement.

The report back to him was that there was no sign of her at all. This told Tim that the insane Carl had eaten all of her, including her bones and clothing. When he asked for the guards to search the cell, they claimed they had, but Tim knew they were lying. There wasn't one of them that would go near Carl's cell. They were all terrified of him. They had to use long poles to push his meal trays to him. Sometimes, Carl would grab at those, and try to pull the guards with it. He got a hold of one once and almost succeeded in keeping it. The guards kept calling for backup to pull it away from him. It ended up taking 19 men to get it out of his cell. So Tim knew good and well, that no one searched Carl's cell.

He sighed heavily. Just like everything else, he would deal with it when he returned. But there was one perk about this trip, and that was that he could tell the other Satanists, of the world, that he had killed Malaya. She was no longer a threat to them. This news would be most welcomed. Not that any of them knew her well, only Tim did. They knew her by reputation only, but knew that to have someone like her in the world, was a danger to their agendas and plans for humanity. She had to be eliminated.

On the long plane ride, Tim could think of nothing but Malaya. Although he knew she was finally dead, her involvement in his life had been detrimental and he was permanently scarred because of her. The knowledge of her death did nothing to quiet his mind when he thought of her.

He thought back to the first day he had met her. They had both been taken as children by a group of the world's elite who were part of the MK-ULTRA mind control experiment. He was seventeen years old and she was fifteen. He had been bred by his mother to be a part of a satanic cult and he was actually scheduled to be sacrificed to Satan as an infant. For some reason, one of the women saw something in him that marked him for greatness in the Satanic world, so he was spared. No one ever told him what marked him and he really didn't care. He was compliant with his life, because he felt the power of Satan as a young child, and it thrilled him. He was attracted to evil and only felt comfortable when he was immersed in it. So anything that happened to him as a child was readily accepted, as long as he felt the power of darkness. It was the power of light and goodness that he couldn't tolerate. He was introduced to that light, the first time he met Malaya.

She had been kidnapped somewhere in the desert, and was brought to the facility, which was hidden in the Catskill mountains of New York. The place was completely covered by foliage and couldn't be seen from the air or from the ground. If you didn't know it was there, you would never go near it. The bushes that surrounded it on the ground were heavily thorned and so dense. To try and get through them, would rip the human body to pieces.

The only way in, was through a trap door and a long underground tunnel. Children had been kidnapped and trafficked through this place since the late 1960's.

Someone told Tim once, that a Congressman was murdered because he had found out about the facility and what they were doing and was getting ready to expose them. He planned to close it, and imprison all of the players. Tim knew it was true too because one night he saw the murdered man with his own eyes. It was this night that he met Malaya and she had seen the dead man too.

The Elite could not allow the Congressman's plans to close the facility to transpire, so he had to be murdered. Until his death, the Congressman thought it was just a problem within his country.

He had no idea the scope of it, until he was shown it after his death. He was heartbroken to know that it was a worldwide problem and that closing the facility in New York was just touching the tip of the iceberg. After quite a while of purging his sins of infidelity in Purgatory, he had enough people on earth who prayed for the repose of his soul, and he was able to pass on to Heaven.

Once he was in Heaven, he was able to battle many of the demons and evil men and women who dwelt in the New York facility. Each time, he would use the Passion of Jesus as his weapon and many lives were saved because of his battles. He would spend all of his time, until the Final Judgment to this end, and was thankful God grew his soul in this way.

The night Malaya came, they had her eyes covered with a blindfold. Tim had seen them bring in many other children and they would be screaming or crying or begging for their mothers. This made Tim hate them on sight because he thought, even as a child, that this made them weak and stupid. So when they brought Malaya in and she was completely silent, he was intrigued by her.

They put her in the same cell as him. Most of the time they would keep other children away from him because he loved to torture them. So unless it was for a punishment they knew he would inflict, they rarely put children near him.

Malaya sat Indian style in the middle of the cell. She didn't move or speak, or try to free her hands, which were tied behind her back. She just sat there quietly. Tim jumped up and started circling her, but he didn't speak to her. He wanted to first see if he could scare her. When his movement around her didn't do the trick, he started to kick at the dirt floor and have it rain down on her head. Even with this happening, she didn't move. Finally tired of his game he went over and untied her blindfold. He moved back then and watched as it fell down her cheeks and finally into her lap. She opened her eyes very slowly and simply looked at the floor. She looked left and then right to get a general assessment of her living situation, but she never raised her eyes to look at him.

"Hey... what's your name?" he demanded her to answer.

"Malaya," She said simply.

"That's a stupid name." he sneered, hoping to upset her. His hopes faded as she quickly shrugged her shoulders. He was going to ask her something else but she beat him to it.

"How long have you been here?" she asked, turning her head away from him and looking at the entire room.

"I don't know. My whole life."

"What is this place?" She asked, still not looking at him.

"It's called home, idiot." He sneered.

She sighed and then asked sweetly, "What's your name?"

"It's Tim Nethers, not that it's any of your business. You won't be here long enough to care anyway."

"Where will I go? Where will they take me?"

"You sure ask a lot of questions for someone who's probably gonna die!" Tim said, waiting for her to break down in tears. But much to his dismay, she didn't.

"I doubt it," she said with surety.

Tim was taken aback. She was only fifteen, but displayed the confidence of an adult. Maybe she hadn't been kidnapped. Maybe she had been born into this, just like he had.

When you were born into this life, you were never allowed to act or speak like a child. You were treated like an adult in every way. If you didn't act like an adult, you were punished and sometimes killed. Tim had seen it many times. Sometimes they let him be the one to do the killing... he loved that. He didn't like that she was so brave. It made him hate her instantly.

"Maybe I'll be the one to kill you," he said in his most hateful tone.

She actually laughed. She then began trying to untie her hands. He walked up to her and kicked dirt in her face. It got inside her eyes and her mouth and covered her cheeks with dirt. She spit it out of her mouth and continued to try to untie herself.

"You better not laugh at me no more. I kill people all the time. They put kids in here for me to hurt. I will hurt you," he said vehemently.

"You would need an army!" she said in a tone far too confident for the situation in which she found herself.

"I have an army. I have bad people here that will help me and I have other bad things that can hurt you too," he said defiantly. He had never met anyone like her. He wanted them to come back and take her out of his cell. He wanted to hurt her. She was just a stupid girl who was defenseless but something told him that hurting her wouldn't be possible.

"Do you mean demons?" she asked, still never once looking at him.

He backed away from her then, almost as if she had slapped him. Angry and very confused, he wondered how she knew about the demons? Could she see them too?

"Yes, I can see them Timothy," she said slowly, with exaggerated patience. "I have always been able to see them." She paused for effect and then asked,

"Can you see him?" She nodded her head in the direction of the cell that was the farthest from them.

And that's when Tim saw the slain Congressman. He was standing there staring at him. Just as Tim was ready to speak, he was silenced as he was drawn into the Passion of the Christ. Malaya wasn't aware that the spirit was showing Tim the Passion, but she had seen Heavenly spirits do this before. She knew that she wasn't meant to know what was happening and that was okay. It just meant that her Calvary had arrived and God was protecting her. It only lasted a few minutes and then Tim was on the ground crying and sobbing.

Tim hadn't been privy to the exact vision that Tara had shown Natash and Bene't, he was just shown a little glimpse of Jesus' sacrifice and that was enough to send him over the edge. A good person would have been changed by the vision and had a beautiful conversion, but not Tim. He had made a decision when he was very young that the devil would be his master. So seeing Jesus crucified, only made him feel hatred for the Savior...not love, gratefulness or compassion. He was only crying because it shocked him to see such a thing, not because he felt love for the Lord.

"I guess you did see him," Malaya said when he quieted down.

Tim answered by picking up a pile of dirt and throwing it at her. It hit her in her face again, but this time she wiped it away. Tim noticed her hands were free and was going to ask how, when she held them up in front of her face and said,

"Oh, how did I get free? Can you see him?" she asked motioning to the right of her. He flinched before he looked in case it was the slain Congressman again, but it wasn't. He looked but couldn't see anything.

"Hmm, that's interesting. He's really beautiful." Malaya looked up at the huge stunning angel that was her constant companion and smiled.

Tim was angry that he couldn't see anything and rudely asked, "What is it?"

"It's my Guardian angel. You have one too but yours is in pretty bad shape. It looks pretty sad," she said quietly.

"I don't have an angel...I don't want an angel. I like the demons," he seethed.

"Yeah I can see that. That's a shame though because I think you were born with the mark."

This immediately got his attention. How did she know about the mark? Could she describe it to him? What did it look like? He didn't want to appear weak. He wished he could pretend he hadn't heard her, but he couldn't...he had to know.

"What does it look like?" he asked begrudgingly.

Malaya raised her eyebrows but didn't look at him. He at least had heard of it and so she asked her guardian angel to take over the conversation, because she wasn't sure how to explain it and she wasn't sure what he knew.

"I don't know."

"What do you mean you don't know? You just said I had it. Can't you see it? Everyone tells me about this mark but no one tells me what it looks like," he said furiously.

"That's because only the devil and God know what it looks like. I do know this. Every kid in this place has it. I have it too. It's something we have the instant we arrive in the womb." She glanced at him to see if he was still listening and he clearly was.

"Do you want to know more?" she asked.

"Yeah, tell me now," he blurted out.

"Well, those of us who have it, have been created by God to do something big in our lives. The devil goes in and looks at us inside the womb and sees that mark. He tries to kill us all. He hates us."

Now Tim knew she was wrong. "Not true. I was supposed to be sacrificed and I was saved because of that mark, so the devil obviously doesn't want to kill me. You don't know what you're talking about."

Malaya sighed and continued. "He does want you dead...he wants your soul. He wants to use you and have you waste your life on him...which is exactly what you're doing by the way."

"How do you know what I'm doing? You don't know crap!"

She took another breath and began again, "If you believed in God and loved Him, what just happened to you, that freaked you out so much, would instead have made you sorry for your sins and want to ask God for forgiveness. But instead, you were repulsed by the vision. So I know that you are being controlled by Satan. And it makes me sad that God is still trying to extend HIS MERCY and LOVE to you and you keep rejecting it."

Tim didn't even know what to say. She was right about all of it and he didn't understand how she knew what she knew.

"I want you to shut up right now or I'm going to shut you up," he said angrily.

"You would need an army, Timothy, and no matter how hard you try, you will never have an army as big as my Father's Army."

This enraged Tim and he started to lunge at her. He didn't even get two steps before he was thrown back against the wall. He got up and came at her again and the same thing happened. The third time he asked Satan for help and he got just a little further before he was thrown against the wall once more.

Malaya just looked at him sadly and said, "Give up Timothy. You can't win and God will keep reaching out in love for you. I'm going to pray every day that you realize you're on the wrong side of things." She still hadn't looked at him. She said goodnight and then laid on the ground and went to sleep.

Tim sat there most of the night just watching her. He had never hated anyone as much as he hated her, and they'd just met. Every hour he would get the courage to get close to her to try and hurt her but each time he was only allowed to go so far. He finally gave up and decided to go to sleep himself.

In the morning he woke to the sounds of breakfast being brought to the cells. He sat up and rubbed his eyes and immediately he looked towards

Malaya. She was sitting Indian style with the blindfold on and her hands tied behind her back not saying a single word. Tim rubbed his eyes and jumped up and ran over to her. She was in the exact same place she had been when they first brought her in. How did her hands get retied behind her back? How was her blindfold back on her eyes? Tim rubbed his eyes again and it occurred to him that he must have dreamed the whole thing. He had pretty much convinced himself of that, until he saw all the scrapes on his arms and legs from being thrown against the wall. He didn't know how to process what had happened. He had no explanation for any of it. He was just getting up the nerve to ask her a question when they brought them breakfast. He thought for sure they would remove her from his cell because they had never left anyone with him for more then a few hours and she had been there all night. But instead of taking her, they took him.

There were three handlers that came to get him. At first, he was too busy watching her to notice them and when he did, he was even more afraid. The two men and one woman were looking at him like he was sick or something...or crazy. They took him in a room and put him in a chair. They then began to play for him a video tape from his cell the night before. It began with them bringing in Malaya and her sitting on the floor exactly as he remembered. It then went to him walking around her and then kicking dirt in her eyes. And then nothing was the same.

The film just showed him going crazy. He was shouting at her...and then he was looking at someone else and then he was screaming and finally sobbing. And it showed him talking to her and getting angry and running at her and then being thrown at the wall. And finally it showed him going to sleep. And the whole time the film showed Malaya just sitting there without moving at all.

The handlers wanted him to explain. He had no reason to lie to them, so he told them everything that had really happened and that she had some kind of special powers. They questioned him for hours and then returned him to his cell. Malaya was still there but she had her blindfold off and her hands untied. She was sitting in a corner quietly. She didn't raise her head when they put Tim back in the cell. He walked right over to her and asked,

"What happened last night? How did you do that? And don't act like you don't know what I'm talking about because I know you do." He was almost screaming at her. He didn't notice that the handlers were still standing outside of the cell watching the exchange.

"Don't be angry, Timothy. I can't really explain it because you aren't willing to open your soul to God. If you had even a little amount of Grace, I could explain, but you've already sold your soul. Unless you change your mind and give your life to Christ, you will never understand." She stated kindly.

"I'm never going to change my mind, and stop calling me Timothy!" he raged at her.

"Well okay then, I guess all you really need to understand is if you continue to go against My Father's army, you will always lose. I'm still going to pray you have a change of heart."

He started jumping up and down in protest. "I don't want your prayers and there is no army stronger than Satan's!"

As he said this many demons materialized and came to his side. He couldn't see them, but he felt them. Malaya could see them, and they were getting ready to attack her. She showed no fear and stood up to her full height. She still had her eyes downcast but when she lifted her head and leveled her gaze at the enemies of God, they all scattered to the wind as she called on the name of Jesus to throw them into Hell. She waved her hand in the air and all of them were gone in a matter of seconds. She sat back down.

Tim screeched at her as she stood and called on the name of Jesus, but as soon as she waved her hand, all of his power was gone. That's when he noticed the handlers still standing there.

"Well did you see that? Was the video tape running for that?" He could tell by their faces that they had not seen what he saw. He started to get hysterical and started insisting they take him away from her.

He was in such a rage, that they decided it was best to remove him. He was out of control and the girl had done nothing. She had sat in the cell the whole time, silently looking at the ground. It was clear to all of them that the experiment with Tim's mind control had failed. He needed another session right away. As they were dragging him away, Malaya called out his name and kept telling him to turn back to God and he would be forgiven. She heard him scream until he was far away from the cell.

The next time Tim saw her, it was in the lab. This was the place where the kids were given drugs and hooked up to electric shock machines for their "modified behavior classes." Although Tim knew it was necessary for him to gain strength, it still was very painful because no matter how you did on the tests, you were going to be shocked repeatedly until they broke you. Each time it took them longer and longer to break Tim. He actually had gotten so used to the treatments that, although they were painful to him, he was learning to enjoy the pain. More often than not, the handlers had to stop the session so they didn't accidentally kill him. If it were left up to Tim, he would never ask them to stop. It was in this setting that he next saw Malaya.

When he realized she was going to go under the shock treatments for the first time, he reveled in the opportunity to watch her writhe in pain.

They brought her in blindfolded again. Tim wanted to know why they kept her blindfolded. It didn't make sense to him. It wasn't like she could find her way out of this place if she wanted to. It was too much of a maze with it's labyrinths of hallways and corridors. He watched as they removed the blindfold and hooked her up to the machines. She wouldn't open her mouth to take the drug they tried to give her, so they waited until she was tied securely to the chair before they gave the drugs to her through a shot in her arm.

The drugs were meant to keep her sedated so that she could withstand the shock treatment. Tim had been given them so many times, that he had built up a tolerance to them and they no longer affected him at all.

The handlers working with her, were waiting for her to respond to the

drugs before they began. Fifteen minutes went by and she wasn't affected...
then twenty minutes and finally at thirty minutes, they decided to give her
another dose. She spoke then, but not to anyone particular as she was looking at the floor.

"It won't work on me, no matter how much you give me."

Tim didn't realize it but his mouth opened and his jaw dropped. He
gasped in amazement. He had never heard anyone speak to the handlers like
that, and never with the challenge she just gave them.

"Is that right?" one of the men asked as he approached her again with
the needle.

He started to inject the needle, but stopped in his tracks as he made the
mistake of looking into her eyes. He took two steps back and without looking away from her for even an instant, he dropped the needle.

Tim watched as the man began experiencing something, but he had no
idea what that was. The handler put his hand up to his mouth, covering it in
shock. He then began to shake his head back and forth, saying "NO" over
and over again until he was crying so hard, he was inconsolable. That's when
two more handlers rushed over to try and reattach the blindfold on Malaya's
head. The first woman grabbed it, but in the brief glance she gave Malaya's
face to get her bearings, she also locked eyes with her and the identical thing
that happened to the man started happening with her. The third handler
realized what was going on, and made sure she kept her eyes down as she
approached Malaya. She took the blindfold and shut her eyes while trying to
feel Malaya's head and put the blindfold back on. She had almost succeeded,
but she accidentally attached the blindfold under Malaya's eyes. When she
opened her eyes to check her success, she found Malaya staring at her and
she too, was rendered useless.

Tim watched the scene in fascination. He didn't understand what Malaya was doing with her eyes. He wondered why he hadn't been affected
when she had looked at him. But then he wondered...had she looked at

him? Remembering his time with her in his cell, he knew she had not.

As if on cue, Malaya took just that moment to glance his way. All of his questions about what she was doing, were answered. He felt a warmth heating him from the inside out. It was probably very pleasant for most people, but Tim began to panic at its onset. The next thing that happened was like watching a movie. It started as God created him and placed him in his mother's womb. He saw that the Father had touched his forehead and when He did, something began to appear there. It looked like a tiny Cross, but it was lit by a white light and Tim knew immediately that the source of the warmth he was feeling originated from that Cross. The next thing he saw was the devil looking inside of the womb and seeing the Cross. Satan did something akin to a cat hiss when he saw it, and backed his face out of the womb.

Then he witnessed his birth and he saw the Guardian Angel that had been assigned to guard him. The angel was strong and beautiful, but to Tim, he was a hateful thing to behold. Then he saw vision after vision of his life. He was shown each time the devil had intervened to take his soul, and how God answered repeatedly to battle him. God's efforts were always stronger, but Tim noticed he stopped looking at them in each vision. He only wanted to watch the black efforts of the demons. As he rejected God, he had less Grace to help him fight. When he finally chose the devil as his master, all Grace left him. His Guardian Angel still stayed, but only to stop him from doing all the damage he wanted to do to others. The last vision he watched was his meeting with Malaya in the cell. This time he did see her Guardian Angel. He was made to understand that Malaya's sole purpose in being in the facility, was for God to reach out to Timothy once more and bring him back. It was so much to process, and Tim's cries joined the chorus of tears already in the room.

"Tell your Father, I will NEVER come back to Him...I've made my choice." he spat at her through his sobs.

Malaya looked at him with pity and sadness. She then released her hands from the ties that bound her and stood up. As she walked away from the chair and Tim, all the handlers were still wailing on the ground.

"Goodbye, Timothy. I've no doubt we will meet again." And with that she walked right out of the lab and the facility.

There had been many rumors surrounding her escape, but none of them were true. Only Tim and the three handlers knew what happened, and they weren't talking. Two of them had a change of heart and tried to escape the facility and leave. They were both caught and finally killed. Tim heard that even through the torture and pain, they were witnesses to Christ to the very end. The third one, a woman, refused to talk about what happened, but made it known that she wasn't going anywhere. And because of her strength and loyalty, they made her Tim's sole Handler.

Because it was a failure, no one ever spoke of it again but it put Malaya on the top of the Elite's Kill list, but they could never find her.

The flight attendant interrupted Tim's thoughts and asked if he was ready for his dinner. He accepted the offer and asked what time they would be landing. After hearing they were just two hours away, he tried to relax and concentrate on the award that lay ahead of him. But no matter what else he tried to think about, he kept seeing her eyes and remembering his time with her. He wasn't quite sure why he had an unnamed fear in his gut, but he did. At least he reassured himself, it was over...she was dead.

Father Zachary, Jacob and Matthew were hard at work in the Penthouse. None of them really knew where to start, so the priest made them hold hands and pray together for God's guidance. After some time, they got their first clue.

"Where in this country would someone be held to be tortured?" Jacob asked as he rubbed his forehead.

The question came out of nowhere. It came right after their prayers ended and it surprised all of them.

"Why do you think it would be a place of torture Jacob?" Father Zachary inquired.

"Well, Madison kept screaming that she was going to be killed by monsters. She made me believe Malaya was in a lot of pain and being hurt. So where would something like that be done?"

All three men thought. "Maybe a hospital?" Matthew offered.

"Probably not. That would have too many people as witnesses. Even if it were a hospital for the insane, there would still be nurses, doctors and aides that wouldn't allow a torturous murder to occur." Jacob replied

"What about a prison?" Matthew suggested.

"Maybe," answered the priest. "At least there they would have the ability to hide such a thing. All I know is, it would probably be a secret place. If anyone else discovered who Malaya was to the Native Americans, and what she could do with her eyes, it would be a place not many people would know about."

"Who would know about such a place? The Government maybe?" Jacob asked.

"Matthew, do you have any connections in the Government? Any friends that could help?" the priest asked.

Matthew thought for a moment and then grabbed his phone to make a call. At the same time Jacob's phone rang...it was Madison. They had a few moments of small talk and then Madison asked if they had found her. Jacob reported where they were in the search. In the background he suddenly heard Rachael scream. It was a familiar sound and meant she was really hurting.

"Is she okay? I thought the medicine was working?" Jacob asked.

"It is working. I don't know what's going on. Hang on, it might be time to give her more." Madison put the phone on the table and went to get the medicine. Jacob could hear Rachael screaming and he also heard Maria's sweet voice trying to calm her down.

"It's okay...it's okay. You're okay, baby. What?"

Jacob didn't understand who Maria had posed the question to. He tried to listen harder but all he heard were little murmurs. Finally he heard the phone being picked back up and was very surprised that it was Maria who spoke and not Madison. He also noticed that he no longer heard Rachael crying.

"Daddy? Are you there?" Maria asked.

"Hi baby, how are my girls? Is Rachael better now?" Jacob asked.

"She's fine now. But Daddy, she's in the Ditch." Maria said.

"Who's in the ditch, honey? Did Mommy fall in a ditch with Rachael? Did something bad happen?" He couldn't fathom why she would use the word ditch, because there was no such thing near their house. Jacob was immediately seized by panic.

"No Daddy, not Rachael. Rachael told me she's in the Ditch." Maria answered impatiently.

"Maria, I don't understand what you're trying to tell me...can I speak to Mommy please?" Jacob couldn't begin to make sense of what Maria had said.

"No Daddy...listen to me. Malaya is in the Ditch!! That's where they put her. You have to hurry, Daddy. You have to go get her." Maria sounded more upset than Jacob had ever heard her.

"Okay, honey I heard you." Jacob said, still utterly confused.

"Repeat what I told you out loud Daddy, it's important...please!" Maria insisted.

"You said, Rachael told you that Malaya was in the ditch. Is that what you said?"

Jacob looked over at the priest and shrugged his shoulders like he had no idea why he was asked to repeat it. He wasn't prepared for Father Zachary's look of shock, and they both were surprised when Matthew dropped the phone and said,

"What did you just say?"

Jacob repeated it aloud again and Matthew reached to pick up the phone. Father Zachary walked over to stand, while Matthew spoke into the phone,

"Hang on Burt..." He then turned towards both men with wide eyes and explained.

"I'm talking to my friend Burt. He's very high up in the CIA. He was searching all the places in the country that would house people who were wanted by the Government. I told him it would probably be a secret location. He just told me that there was only one place like that and it was right here in New York...it's called the Ditch."

All three men gasped. Father Zachary said "Praise you Father...You are so Good!"

Jacob spoke back in the phone and told Maria thank you, and to tell her Mommy he would call her back later. Matthew got back on the phone with Burt and asked how they could find the place. He also asked what it would take to rescue someone from there.

Mitka praised Maria and Rachael for helping Malaya and assured them both that Tezra and Syree would protect Jacob, Matthew and Father Zachary.

Madison walked back into the room and gave Rachael her medicine. She totally forgot she had been on the phone with Jacob. She looked at both of her beautiful daughters and was overcome with a feeling of bliss.

"How about we order a pizza tonight, Maria? I feel like we should celebrate."

Maria agreed and didn't question the fact that her mom had forgotten the call. She knew that her mother's Guardian angel had made her forget. Madison had been too sick recently to have all this knowledge right now. Her angel knew she would never rest or go to sleep, if she knew what had just transpired.

Maria bowed to her mother's Angel and mouthed "Thank you" with a tiny giggle. The Angel smiled back.

Maria's Guardian Angel, however, wasn't smiling and was on full alert. He had been with her all during her journey into Hell and knew that the Betrayer would not rest until he had his vengeance. He communicated his knowledge to Mitka and to all the other angels there. Mitka sent a message to Tezra that he needed to come quickly, his assistance was needed. Without a moment's hesitation Tezra jumped out of the cat's body and informed Syree that he alone would protect the men. Syree praised the Trinity for this new turn of events and asked protection over all the humans involved.

CHAPTER SIXTEEN... THE CHOICES WE MAKE

Matthew's friend had no idea how to help the men get into the Ditch. It was a maximum security facility that required the highest security clearance to enter.

The only hope they had was the man had a cousin that worked there that he could call. He wasn't giving them much hope though. He said it was virtually impossible.

Father Zachary laughed at that, when Matthew's face fell at the news.

"Come on, Matthew, don't despair. Nothing is impossible with God. After all, look how quickly He let us know where she was...and who HE gave the information to, to tell us."

Both Mathew and Jacob spoke at the same time.

"Maria!"

Father Zachary looked at them both stunned. Didn't they know the truth? Didn't they understand that it wasn't Maria... that it was the infant Rachael? Didn't they know that they had been handed a miracle?"

"Uh, no...it wasn't Maria," the priest spoke cautiously. Both men looked thoroughly confused. Father Zachary was going to elaborate but Matthew's phone rang. It was the cousin.

"Yes Hello, my name is John Waters. My cousin Burt told me to call you guys. He said you knew something about a girl prisoner in the Ditch?" the man said.

"Yes, that's correct," Matthew said. "Burt said you might be able to help us find a way in and help us find a way to rescue her...is that right?"

There was a pause on the line before John spoke. "Listen sir, no one wants that girl out of there as much as I do, but I can't see a way to do it. They only let employees, and some members of government in there. Other than that, they don't let anyone else in."

Matthew had the phone on speaker so that all the men could hear and they gave a collective sigh. Then Jacob snapped his fingers.

"John, do they ever let Clergy in for any reason?" Jacob smiled as a light went off in the minds of the men.

"Yes, they do, if they are requested by a prisoner before their death. The problem is, they only use one guy who is a family member of the director. It would be suspicious if anyone else came, although I'm willing to try it if you are." John said.

"Well, can we get one to request that three Priests come for a visit?" Jacob asked.

"I will try to arrange that sir. That just might work. Give me an hour and I'll call you back with the arrangements."

With that, John hung up the phone. He had a spark of hope in his heart that he might save the girl. It just dawned on him that they had better do it the next day though. He'd been told that Tim Nethers had to go on a short trip and John had no desire to try to rescue her with that maniac around. He also knew that if they pulled it off, it would be the last day he would be working in the Ditch. With all of the surveillance, they would know right away who did it. But John didn't care anymore. He owed that girl his whole life. He had felt God for the first time in his life because of her. If doing this for her meant that it ended up costing him his life, he was going to do it.

The Captain had just turned on the "fasten seat belt" sign. The plane was making preparations for its final landing at Glasgow Airport in Scotland. It could not come quickly enough for Tim.

During his dinner he had a moment of clarity. He was gripped with a fear that Carl had not killed Malaya. As he thought back on all her time with him, the detail that stood out the most, was that she could not be made to do anything she didn't want to do. If she wanted to escape from Carl or the Ditch, she could do it as easily as she had done it when they were children at the M.K. Ultra facility. He should have thought this out. He should have had her bound and chained and had 20 guards on her at all times. He knew Carl was a monster, but he had also seen Malaya do things that were beyond explanation. He was kicking himself for not putting her under protective detail. He should have burned her eyes out of their sockets and stood there to watch Carl tear her apart. Why didn't it occur to him before he was half a world away? He asked the flight attendants to phone ahead and get him on the next flight back to New York. He also needed to call the Ditch and send guards in to watch her and report back to him before he boarded the plane back home. When the plane finally landed, he jumped up and demanded to be the first one off the plane so he could make his call. He told the flight attendant to have his luggage transferred, and he ran to the gate of Departure while he was making his call.

Everyone at the gate was watching him. It was impossible to do anything else because he was yelling at the top of his lungs. He asked to be connected to Patrick O'Dey's office. The secretary was too scared to tell Mr. Nethers that Mr. O'Dey had quit, so she just patched him through to the manager on call.

Tim barked his orders at the man and told him to place all available guards in front of Carl's cell. He didn't want there to be the slightest chance that she could escape. The last thing he heard should have given him comfort, but it did nothing to calm him.

"Yes sir, Mr. Nethers. I will get right on this. Have a safe flight." John hung up the phone with a smile and total resolve in his heart. He said a prayer, thanking God that Tim Nethers didn't recognize his voice. He should have and if he had, he would have spoken to anyone else there, besides John. But by some stroke of luck he wasn't recognized. It wasn't "luck" at all. It was angelic assistance; because John's Guardian angel spoke through his voice box. The angel arranged it so the last person Tim thought it would be would've been John.

"Not on my watch," John said as he picked up the phone and called Matthew.

Bene't was not conscious of anything but torment. In all of his existence, he had been through many horrors in Hell. He'd been through the Machine Cavern, he'd been attacked by a throng of demons, he'd been left in the Lake of Fire, but nothing could have prepared him for the perpetual torture inflicted on him by Lucifer.

From the moment he had been caught trying to save Maria, his life had been one blur of pain, with just momentary glimpses of his tormentor, Satan. In all of their existence, Bene't had never known Lucifer to be in this kind of rage. The only time he had seen something close, was after the Christ's victory on the Cross.

When Jesus descended to Limbo and Purgatory to release the souls in those prisons, and it was made clear that none of Satan's ambitions would ever come to fruition, he raged. Every being in Hell paid for that rage too... no one was spared. Lucifer was beside himself that he'd missed all the signs. He had misinterpreted everything...Sacred Scripture, the words and lives of the Prophets, who Jesus was...who the hated Woman was. And because he had been wrong, everyone in Hell would pay the price of his wrath with pain. That time, Satan inflicted some of the pain himself, but he left it mostly up to the seven Legions of Demons. Then, everyone understood his rage... they all knew why.

But none of them knew why he was in his current disposition. That knowledge was solely between Bene't and Satan.

This time, Lucifer was taken completely off guard. He had no inkling that Bene't had some relationship with that putrid child. He hadn't processed yet that Bene't must have feelings of Grace to even care at all, that fact still escaped him. He wouldn't have understood it anyway because when the demons made their choice to fight the throne of the Trinity...all emotions and feelings, other than hatred, left them. They became beings of darkness and that meant a darkness of their hearts and all that implied.

The fact that the little girl had entered Hell without his knowledge, and that he knew not why she had come, or what it all meant, infuriated him. To add insult to injury, she was able to somehow escape, and he didn't understand that either. But to have her surrounded and then to be betrayed by his second in command...Satan had never felt any hate like that before.

All his thoughts collided in an instant...the fact that he had never been able to read Bene't's mind... Natash's account that Bene't could not best Maria when he kidnapped her while she was in the cage...Bene't's quick response to volunteer to guard her and her disgusting family...him witnessing the child's birth. It all made sense now and Lucifer couldn't stop attacking him! He was so vicious and cruel and out of control, that every punishment ever rendered in Hell before that moment, was nothing compared to the punishment Bene't experienced now.

As his nightmare continued, Lucifer kept demanding that Bene't explain his thoughts. But to his credit, Bene't did not satisfy one demand of Satans. He remained silent. The only thing he could do was try to focus on something other than what was happening to him, but the pain was so severe that to think was beyond his ability. He had a brief moment where his heart cried out for help from Heaven, and almost immediately, something happened. He saw Jesus during His Passion. Bene't watched as the King of Kings never once spoke in anger or hatred towards any of his abusers. Like the light of a firefly, the vision was over as quickly as it had begun, but it was enough. Bene't held onto that example with every fiber of his being. It would be the thing he credited with the keeping of his sanity.

When the Prince of all Evil finally exhausted his anger, he allowed Bene't to heal and come back into his whole being. Lucifer sat across from Bene't and glared daggers at him. When he spoke, Bene't thought they were the worst words he could ever hear.

"When Divine Providence allows...you will kill that child and together we will bring her back here where you will be assigned to torture her for all eternity."

"NO!" Bene't said in desperation.

"Oh yes, my son. And if for some reason you are allowed to disobey me in this, you will be witness to your brother demons obeying me. I promise you, it will be the most inhumane death of a child any of us have ever witnessed."

There were no words to describe the despair Bene't felt. It was beyond comprehension that he would witness Maria's death, let alone play some part of it! What had she ever done to deserve what was coming? She was a precious little light of God in a very dark world. Bene't had learned so much from her and the one thing that stood out was her beautiful faith. She understood God in a way few did. Why Satan thought he was above this child was beyond him. She was not born in the Kingdom like himself and Lucifer. She hadn't been witness to all they knew. She would never have the intellect of an angel or a demon. She would never have their strength. But when Bene't compared her to any of the demons, she was far superior because she believed without having these things. She loved and followed Jesus and she had never met HIM or the HOLY SPIRIT or the FATHER face to face. It was as if she had one grain of sand that represented all she knew of God and Heaven, and the demons had all the rest of the sand in the world. She took that one grain and used it to love and honor her God and to believe everything she believed; and that made her far superior to all of them...especially Satan. She chose correctly...to love God and they... did not. And it was the love of the Trinity that made all that possible when Jesus descended to save humanity from its sin.

Humans were the true children of God. They had all been tested and tried and the demons failed the test. They failed even after knowing ALL possible outcomes. The humans knew no outcomes, yet they passed the test of faith. And now Satan was going to destroy her and it was Bene't's fault. He had failed her by first failing his Heavenly Father...the sweet Holy Spirit...and the Savior who tried to save them all by showing them every choice and its consequence.

This knowledge of failing the Trinity was a more excruciating pain than if he had gone through the torture which Lucifer had just inflicted on him all through eternity.   He wanted to disappear or never be created for the heart wound he had inflicted on all of Heaven and its inhabitants. This was his Hell...knowing he couldn't go back...he couldn't change it. As he sat there, something happened which had never happened to him before. He was having a vision that he knew was being sent to his mind from Satan.

The enemy of God was showing him every possible way that they could kill Maria. It was one horrendous murder idea after another and there was no way Bene't could make it stop.

Lucifer knew that he was finally able to affect Bene't's mind and this knowledge thrilled him. He didn't know the reason for the timing of it, and he didn't even try to question it.   Instead, he just reveled in it and continued to send those revolting images to his second in command. Each time Satan showed him a way to murder her, it was Bene't who was killing her. Bene't could barely stand the pain of it. He felt his heart was going to explode from shock. In the last version of Maria's murder, Bene't was getting ready to end her life and Satan put the vision in slow motion and did a close up on Maria's face; the emphasis being on the total betrayal she felt. All the expressions on her face. He saw so many questions in her eyes, all which begged him,

"WHY?...Don't you love me anymore?...Won't you defend me anymore?..

Did I not love you enough? Was I not a good enough friend to you?...Don't you know how much I love you?...don't you know how much I love you???" and then Bene't struck the final blow...she was gone. He had killed her.

Satan began to laugh hysterically as he ended the visions. He knew that this was far worse for Bene't then the physical torture he had punished him with earlier. He decided then and there that he would do nothing else but this to Bene't, until the end of time.   He laughed again at the defeat of his General. He screamed, "JUSTICE...FINALLY!!!"

Bene't could not move, he could not think or feel...he was truly broken. He knew beyond a shadow of doubt that Maria would die, and it would be at his hands. There was nothing he could do.

CHAPTER SEVENTEEN...
DIVINE MERCY/DIVINE WILL

Carl was hungry. He didn't remember the last time he had felt hunger. He didn't remember the last time he had felt anything. For him, it was as if he had been trapped in a nightmare from which he couldn't escape. This dream world was made up of murder and pain, darkness and despair. It was filled with frightening entities that directed his every move. He was like a marionette, a puppet on strings. Each move...each thought was out of his control. He was manipulated by these dark beings and the control over him was so complete and thorough, that Carl lost the ability to think or act independent of them. He didn't know when it had occurred, but there had been a moment when he had just given himself over to it and let the entities use him for whatever means they desired.

It was then that he completely lost himself, and he didn't even care. His life prior to that moment had been so horrific, that this seemed like the perfect end to his evil life.

He had been born into a Satanic cult and he was born to be used and abused in many satanic rituals. If he had parents, he didn't know them. He only knew the people who had tortured him. He didn't even know how he had survived his childhood. He should have died many times over. When he was a child, he was full of anger and hatred. He fought with everyone around him and that included the adults. One in particular was a doctor that had been using him as a human guinea pig since birth. This doctor had pumped him full of experimental drugs that would never make it to a public platform. They were too dangerous and had many adverse side effects... most of them psychotic. That didn't stop the sadistic doctor from using them on Carl in the name of "worshiping Satan."

The problem was there was a side effect that the doctor never expected. The combination of the drugs had caused Carl to grow to an incredible height and weight. The drugs also caused his muscles to develop rapidly, so rapidly in fact that they seemed disproportional to the rest of his huge body. He looked like a picture of the "strong man" in a traveling circus who was billed as one of the 'Wonders of the World."

He got so big, so fast, that all of the doctors were afraid he would hurt someone, and with good reason. The doctor who had tortured him became his first murder victim. The doctor came to give Carl a shot to calm him down one day but the second he was within Carl's reach he was grabbed. Carl broke his neck and killed him. He then plucked both of the doctor's eyes out and ate them. This is how the staff found him a little while later. From that moment on, they made a decision to administer drugs to subdue him on a daily basis.

These drugs caused Carl to become like a zombie who could do nothing but stare blankly and drool. He was becoming a problem and they considered him a failed experiment. Since they didn't know what else to do with him, they put him in the same mind control facility that Tim Nethers had lived in. Tim had never seen him there, but he had heard rumors of the 'Monster" his handlers had created.

They would program his mind to kill and to kill on command. This was the time when Carl gave his soul to Satan and completely surrendered his will to the demons. He had been chanting his allegiance to the devil from the moment he could speak because he was forced to do so. So to allow them to take him over felt like the only thing he could do.

The handlers released him on the public and he killed many of the people the Elite had on their "Kill List." They only decided to imprison him in the Ditch because he was starting to be a problem for the NYPD. He needed to be hidden and taken off of the public's radar. Many unsolved murders were attributed to some serial killer that could never be found. Only the Elite knew that Carl was to blame.

He spent the rest of his life in a cell that had straw on the floor, as if he was an animal. He used the hay to defecate in, like an animal because in truth, he was more animal than human. They had made sure of that. He spent his days in a daze, never knowing what day, month or time it was and he didn't care. He had no awareness of the other inmates at all. They were just shadows and noises to him. The only time he was conscious enough to notice other people was when the guards came to give him a bath.

A bath wasn't exactly the correct term, because it was all done with a hose. They had a fire hose on the wall and, because he couldn't be trusted around other people, this was the only way they could get him clean. They turned it on Carl once a week. Because it was in close proximity to him, the power of the water pressure should have knocked him down unconscious but because he was so large at 6 feet 9 inches and over 400 pounds, he was able to withstand it somehow. It was only during this time that Carl noticed anyone. Something about the pressure and cold temperature of the water kind of woke him up. He had had the hose turned on him just a few hours before they put someone in his cell with him.

This had never happened to him before. He saw them throw something in his cell and then he heard someone laughing. He heard something about saving some bones, but he didn't understand what that meant. He didn't understand most things. More than anything he operated on basic instincts, and right now those instincts were telling him he was hungry.

He got up from the floor and moved toward the person they had put in his cell. At first he had a thought that it hadn't been a person at all, but just a heap of blankets. To say he was disappointed was too simple...he quickly became enraged. And like an animal he started to kick at the blankets, lifted up his head and growled in the air. It was a fearsome sound and all the other inmates wondered if the girl had just been killed. None of them could have seen him kill her though, because Carl's cell was the last one on the block. His cell had nothing across from it but a concrete wall. It was too far away from the other cells to ever see anything that occurred in it.

Carl lowered his head again and when he did he had a surprise waiting for him. The blanket wasn't a blanket at all, it was a sort of cloak and a woman was wearing it. She stood squarely in front of him and was less than a foot away from him. She was looking at him and had the sweetest smile on her face. She showed no fear as she said,

"Hello Carl."

As she spoke she reached her hand forward as if she wanted him to shake it. He had never had anyone do this to him, but somewhere inside of his foggy mind he had a memory of seeing it done. He looked down at her tiny hand and then at his large one and watched as he reached his hand and joined it with hers.

The first thing he thought was how hungry he was and he was finally touching his food. He had every intention of pulling her towards him, breaking her body and consuming her. Just as he made the motion to pull her towards him though, he could not do it. It should have been so easy for him because even at her substantial height, she was like a child compared to him. So he tried again, and this time she spoke during his failed attempt.

"Carl, can you look at me please?"

In all of his life, no one had ever spoken to him with a kind voice and he was drawn to look at her. When he did finally lock eyes with her, he could see the color in them begin to change and then move. Pretty soon he was watching his life story play out in her eyes.

Malaya, for her part, had never felt such strong demonic power. She could see all of the entities that were not only around Carl, but living inside of him. The demons raged when they realized Malaya could clearly see them. It was at their direction that Carl was going to kill her. They were unable to enact this or any of their other desires though, because Malaya traveled with not just her Guardian Angel, but a throng of angels. These angels came from the Choir of Powers and were the brothers to Mitka. These angels are called Warring Angels. These are the ones who fight not only demonic spirits, but Damned souls that prowl the earth with deadly intent against humanity. These angels had been with Malaya from the moment of her conception. They were there because Malaya was the "White Buffalo" to which all Native American prophecies eluded. Her presence in the world, let the Native Americans know that their delivery from slavery and servitude and isolation was at hand. The problem was that none of them expected the long awaited Savior of their people to take the form of not only a human, instead of an actual buffalo, but in the form of a woman. Like many prophecies, the waiting people had been expecting something other than what actually came. The Jewish people were expecting a rich King with many armies to come and battle against all of Israel's enemies, to not only free them, but raise the Jewish Nation to the forefront of every nation in the world forever more. They were looking for a 'Worldly" King, so when the son of a poor carpenter, who remained poor His entire life, became the Savior of the World, they did not recognize Him.

Much the same happened with Malaya. Each tribe believed that when an actual white buffalo was born, the Great Chief would be born and unite all the tribes and return to them what they had lost. There had been several white buffalo calves born in their history, but in retrospect, they never produced the leader they sought. So when a girl child of a chief was born with little white buffalo shapes in each eye, they felt that the Great GrandFather in the sky was punishing them with her. She was an abomination. Like Jesus, God the Father decided to bring her into the world in a very unusual way. This kept her hidden from the arrogant and learned and especially from Satan and his minions.

Malaya was created for one purpose and one purpose only...to bring all of the Indian Nation to the truth that Jesus Christ is Lord and Savior of the World. No amount of demons could ever stop her from fulfilling her destiny, not in this cell, or anywhere else. She was too well protected and gifted. The demons were powerless against her, unless the Father allowed it for the growth of her soul. So even though Carl was surrounded by more demons than she had ever encountered in one place, she courageously ran into the black demonic cloud that Madison had seen in her dream. She had one thing on her mind...she needed to rescue Carl.

The movie that Carl was watching was the story of his soul. It began in the beautiful halls of Heaven. He was shown how and why the Trinity had created him. He saw the unfathomable love the Father felt while creating Carl's soul. He was made to know that God had given him a plethora of extra Graces, more than was given to the other Children of God. He was shown that he would need all of them because the life that he would live, would be primarily lived in darkness. He watched as God showed him what his life would be like and why God would allow the great suffering that would come his way. After God showed Carl these things, the Father then showed him an alternate life he could live. This life would be lived in light and would be with a family and friends and he would be happy. God showed Carl both outcomes of each life and God told him he could choose which one he wanted to live. When Carl watched both choices he didn't even hesitate.

He chose the one that landed him in this cell. This filthy place, unfit for human habitation, with this Indian woman standing in front of him was his choice. After he had seen everything God wanted to show him through the eyes of Heaven's White Buffalo, Carl collapsed on the floor and fainted.

When he woke up, his huge head was resting in Malaya's lap and she was rubbing her fingers through his hair while she was singing to him. Her eyes were closed and she sang with a beautiful voice. She sang a song about the love that God had for the world. Carl stayed still, just basking in a peace that he had never experienced. Another thing that became immediately apparent was that Carl's body was different. He was still just as huge, but his body was clean. He reached his hand up in front of his face. Long gone were the filthy nails and the dirt and blood, urine and feces that normally caked them. He then reached up and touched his face and there was no trace of any facial hair. He reached up to touch his hair and noticed that it was very short. At that point he sat up and inspected the rest of his body. He had no way of knowing that while he was unconscious Malaya's angels had cleaned him and groomed him, and put him in fresh clean clothes.

There wasn't a mirror in the cell but there were two windows, and if you stood in just the right place the reflection of one played into the other and acted as one. When Carl saw his reflection he gasped. He did not recognize himself even remotely. He looked so different and he was very surprised to see that he was really very handsome. He looked at Malaya with a question in his expression. She replied with a simple nod in the direction of the corner of the cell. When he looked he was shocked to see many demons hunched against the wall. They were trying their best to get as far away from Malaya and Carl as they could. They weren't making any noise because the angels from the Choir of the Powers, wouldn't allow anything but silent submission. Carl thought they wanted to leave but couldn't for some reason. He didn't have any sort of fear of them because they had been his constant companions since he came into the world, but when he saw them, they were huge, menacing and terrifying. Nothing compared to what they appeared now.

Carl looked at Malaya and in a voice he didn't recognize as his own, said, "You saved me. How can I ever repay that?"

Malaya gently touched his arm and said, "I didn't save you, Jesus did. He paid all of our debts with His love."

Tears stained Carl's face and he understood completely. "Do you know what happens next? What you showed me about my creation...is that my new road?" he asked in awe.

"Yes Carl, that's your new road."

Carl fell on his knees, and for the first time since he came from his Heavenly home, he began to Praise his Creator. Malaya knelt beside him and joined her Praises to his. As they began to pray, every other inmate heard them and each in turn fell to the floor and joined with them in prayer. By the time the guards would return the next morning, the Ditch would be an entirely different place.

Tezra acknowledged the big Saint Bernard named Max. He asked permission to enter him, to hide from the enemies of Hell who in that very moment were approaching the house of Jacob. Without hesitation Max agreed, and jumped towards the angel to merge with him. Tezra removed the chains that held them in the back yard and as one body they silently crept towards the front of the house. When they reached the porch they stepped up and placed themselves in front of Jacob's front door.

Anyone passing by would have just seen an enormous dog sitting on his porch and that is what the hounds of Hell saw as they approached. Max began to growl as the demons got closer. Suddenly the front door opened and Madison stepped out. She had just finished the dishes after she put the girls to bed. It had been a very long day for her. She had worried about Rachael all over again. The medicine had worked for a little while but then it just stopped. Madison had called the doctor and he told her to increase the dosage slightly and he would see them in the office after the weekend. She tried it, but Rachael was still screaming in pain and nothing, not even nursing her could comfort her.

Maria had finally intervened when Madison could no longer stand up with her and she said, "Mommy, let me hold her for awhile. It's okay if she cries."

Normally Madison would have argued but she literally couldn't stand up any longer and for safety's sake, if nothing else, she consented. As soon as she placed the baby in Maria's arms, Rachael stopped crying. Madison stood back and was trying to analyze why. Was Maria holding the baby differently then she had? It didn't seem so. The strange thing was that Rachael was never calm when she was on her back, she always needed the pressure on her stomach. Maybe it was the fact that Maria was smaller and Rachael felt safer because of that. It really didn't make any sense. Madison was going to ask Maria what she thought and that's when she really saw her daughters.

Maria and Rachael were looking at each other and neither of them were moving. Madison was fascinated.

"Maria? Are you okay?"

Without moving an inch, and without breaking her gaze with Rachael, Maria whispered,

"Shh Mommy...I'm Watching."

Madison knelt down next to them and whispered back,

"What are you watching? What is happening?"

It took Maria a second to answer because she was concentrating so hard on what she was seeing.

"Look in her tears, Mommy."

Madison wasn't exactly sure what she meant by that but she looked at the tears that were falling down the baby's cheeks. She didn't see anything there. Then she raised her eyes and looked at Rachael's eye and sure enough, right there in her tears, something was happening. Madison moved closer to her so she could see better and as she saw it she gasped.

Inside of her baby's tear she was looking at something akin to a movie being played on a tiny little screen. Inside that screen she saw Malaya inside the cell with the monster. It was a brief vision because then Rachael screamed out in intense pain. Madison immediately reached for the baby but Maria stopped her.

"It's okay, Mommy...she's helping. She will be okay. Just wait."

Helping? Helping who? Helping Malaya?

"How is she helping her, Maria?" Madison asked in awe.

Maria turned her head and looked at her mother.

"With her pain, Mommy. This is her gift."

Madison slowly tore her eyes away from Maria and looked at Rachael. A bunch of little snippets of conversations she had had with Maria came flowing back and the puzzle began to make sense.

"So this is how she tells you things?" Madison asked cautiously.

Maria shook her head yes. And then both Mother and daughter watched as Rachael continued 'helping.'

After a short time, Rachael stopped crying and the movie ended and just like that she fell asleep. Maria began rubbing her eyes and Madison decided that it was time to lay them down to sleep. She wanted desperately to talk to Maria about all the things they had just witnessed, but she could tell that a conversation would need to wait.

Madison reached down and touched Max's giant head. It always made her feel better when Jacob was away to have the dog close by. He made her feel safe. As she petted him so many questions flew through her mind. How had she missed that Rachael had this gift? Why did Maria notice it first? How long had Maria known about it? Why didn't she tell her earlier? As each question formed, the answer to each was the same...Madison had been too exhausted to notice anything. When you put your purse in the freezer because you are sleep deprived, it's not a stretch that you wouldn't notice much in the physical world, let alone the spiritual one.

Madison sat down next to the dog and gave him a huge hug. She buried her face in his fur and said, "I love you Maxy, Come on let's go to bed." With that Madison opened the door and ushered in her pet. Not once did it occur to her that Max was still relegated to the back yard. Nor did she question the why or the how of him being off his chain and on the front porch. As soon as she locked the doors she checked on the girls and went to bed. Max and Tezra stood guard in between the two bedrooms waiting for Mitka's instructions.

Father Zachary helped Jacob and Matthew get dressed in their priestly garb. He made a call to a local affiliate of his order and asked to borrow two outfits. They wore long dark hooded robes that were the assigned attire of the Friars or Monks in his parish. He chose these robes because they covered all of their heads, and with the security cameras that were in the Ditch, they didn't want to be recognized by anyone. These robes allowed for them to lower their heads and walk without any part of their faces except their chins, showing. There would be no way anyone looking at security film would be able to recognize any of them.

"Well, how do I look?" Matthew asked Jacob as he spun around slowly. "Am I rocking it?"

"No." Jacob said, as he gave him an annoyed stare.

"Wow, fine. I should have expected that from you. What do you think Padre?" Matthew said as he repeated his spin.

"Well I think you look like the real deal. How about when all this is over, we talk about making that your permanent uniform?"

Jacob laughed out loud, "Right!"

"What is your problem?" Matthew interjected "Didn't I apologize for not calling Madison already?"

"No, as a matter of fact, you didn't."

Matthew was going to protest whatever he said but stopped himself when he realized the truth.

"Oh..ok..I guess I haven't have I?"

He walked closer to Jacob and looked him in the eye,

"I'm sorry man...really and truly sorry. I hope you can forgive me." He then stuck out his hand to seal the apology.

"I will forgive you when my wife does," Jacob said as he walked past him and towards the door. "We better go, Father."

Father Zachary walked through the door with Matthew on his heels.

"Why do you gotta be so hard all the time?" he muttered under his breath as he passed Jacob. He wasn't at all surprised when all he heard in return was silence.

When the men arrived at the Ditch, John Waters met them at the gate. He was a little taken aback by their appearance, but he didn't really have time to process it.

"We gotta move guys. I just got word that our Warden has landed at the airport. This isn't a dude you want to meet and I don't want to see him either. He's already gunning for me. I can't be here when he gets here so we've gotta hurry this up," John said a bit more panicky then he wanted to sound.

"We've got less than 30 minutes until he gets here."

And with that the men started to walk quickly towards the entrance. Once inside, they were ushered through locked gate after locked gate. Each time the guard on duty gave John a questioning look, but that was the extent of it. No one stopped them or impeded their progress. In no time at all, they reached the cell block that held Malaya.

As they arrived at the final gate, the guard on duty greeted the men. He looked pale as a ghost and quite shaken. He looked at the priests and then at Waters.

"Did Nethers authorize this?" he asked as he pointed to the priests.

All of the men froze and John Waters hoped his voice sounded convincing.

"Would I be standing here if he didn't you idiot? Now let us in already."

The guard opened the gate and let the men pass, but he grabbed John's arm as he whispered,

"Do you think these priests can tell us what happened in there?"

The guard was clearly spooked. John had no idea what he meant by "what happened in there" but grisly images of Carl killing Malaya rushed to his mind.

"Well, that's the plan," John said as he motioned for the man to step back.

"Stay here. There's already too many cooks in the kitchen if you know what I mean."

The guard backed away waving his arms up in the air, "You couldn't pay me enough man...you couldn't pay me enough."

With the guard's admission, the men entered the cell block with heavy hearts and great sadness. They must be too late...Malaya must be dead. But what they saw instead astounded them all, and John most of all.

The normal vulgarities one would hear upon entering the block were replaced by singing. It was the song version of the Lord's Prayer and every single inmate was singing it. As they passed each cell the prisoner in that cell was on his knees, his hands were folded, his eyes were closed and his voice was raised in song. John didn't know what to think, but this was the last thing he'd expected to find. Matthew and Jacob didn't question it too much because they actually expected some kind of weirdness...it seemed to always occur around the little priest.

Father Zachary however HAD expected something miraculous because that was how GOD always worked in Malaya's life. He laughed and said "Praise God!" He said it in a low voice prudently remembering that they were under surveillance. But he wanted to shout from the rooftops what the glory of God was accomplishing. As they moved through the cell block the priest gave a blessing to each cell and each man within it.

When they arrived at Carl's cell, John was walking backwards. He was holding one of the bars of Carl's cell before he knew what he was doing. He realized too late that he had made a fatal mistake, as he noticed the huge shadow that was suddenly upon him. He didn't even have a fraction of a second before the huge hand closed upon his. He shut his eyes and waited for death.

Death, however, did not come. When he realized he wasn't dead, he slowly opened his eyes and looked up at Carl. The wonderment on his face was clearly evident as he beheld a strikingly beautiful man, instead of the hideous monster he used to be. He couldn't look away even for a moment. He wanted to speak but he couldn't. Carl spoke instead,

"John, I can not allow you to hurt this woman. I will not allow anything or anyone to hurt her ever again. Is that why you're here..to hurt her?"

Carl's voice was soft and very gentle. John answered him as he shook his head,

"No Carl, I, I mean we are here to rescue her."

"Oh that's good...that's very good. Please come in."

Carl spoke as if he was an elegant butler welcoming them to his estate. All four of the men entered the cell block. Out of a dark corner Malaya came and made her way immediately to Father Zachary. She knelt in front of him and kissed his hand. She rubbed his hand on her cheek and then kissed it again.

"How many times will you rescue me, Father? Please bless me and bless my new friend Carl."

Father Zachary fulfilled the request and then said, "It's time to go my daughter, we must hurry."

"You're right of course," Malaya said, as she cocked her head to one side, seeming to listen to something no one else could hear. "He's already here."

With those words everyone reacted. All of the men, including Carl and Malaya started to run down the cell block. John was afraid that they would never get out in time and all of them would be killed. He knew that there was only one way in and out of the Ditch and if Tim looked at the surveillance cameras he would know exactly where they were and would be coming for them. Malaya got in front of all the men and led the way. When they got to the first guard he was in a very deep sleep. The men all thought he was just resting, only Malaya and the little priest could see that his Guardian Angel was responsible for his slumber. It was the same story with all of the other guards as well.

As they came out of the last gate, they were now in a very big open space. John knew that Tim would be waiting for them. Right as they stepped into the common area, Malaya turned around and put her index finger to her lips, asking all of them to be silent.

They all complied and entered the space. What they saw was Tim Nethers and all of the guards looking right at them. But their reaction to the group's entry into the common space was not what any of them expected. They were standing right in front of Tim's group, but it was as if Tim and the guards couldn't see them...and they couldn't. Malaya had called on all of the guardian angels in that place to form a circle around them. They were invisible to everyone except each other. So the group stood still and watched as Tim and the guards moved past them, went through the first gate to intercept them.

No one said a word. They just slowly walked to the entrance of the Ditch and walked outside. Their cloak of invisibility continued to cover them when they met the guards on the outside of the building. They walked to the van they had brought and all of them silently got inside and then drove away. No one spoke until there were miles between them and the Ditch.

Tim Nethers let out what could only be considered as a primal scream when he got to Carl's cell block. As soon as he opened the door, the songs of the prisoners became louder. He covered his ears with his hands and ran to the end of the block until he reached Carl's cell. When he saw that no one was there, he went inside and kicked around the hay looking for bones. When he realized he had found none he looked wildly at the guards.

"Did he kill her? Did he eat her?"

He asked this of all of the guards. He ran from man to man, grabbing them by the shirts and lifting them off the ground as he spat at them. No one dared to answer him. He continued to rage and finally belowed her name in hatred.

"Where did they go? What happened?"

Tim picked up his phone and called the guard in the control room. He screeched at the guard to get him every video from the last 24 hours. He and the guards ran to view them. Tim watched them all. He could see the one where he had thrown Malaya in the cell with Carl and that was the last time there was any footage of her. When he analyzed the film from Carl's cell, he could only see Carl. There was no trace of Malaya on the footage. He could see Carl talking to no one and then he watched all of the other inmates fall to their knees simultaneously. His rage was bubbling over as their singing began. The fact that some of the most evil men on the planet were worshiping God, was a direct result of Malaya's presence there. Somehow she had manipulated every single one of them.

Tim put out an all points bulletin on Malaya and Carl. The problem was that no one would ever recognize the new Carl, and he had no picture of Malaya he could fax on the bulletin. Tim had no idea that Carl looked different or that he wouldn't recognize him if he were standing right in front of him. In his frustration he re-watched all of the film as he waited for someone to call him and tell him they had been captured. He would never receive that call.

Maria lay there pretending to be asleep when her mom came back into the house with Max. She did so because the quicker her mother thought she and Rachael were sleeping, the quicker Madison would go to bed for the night. And Maria needed her to sleep. She watched as Malaya had been rescued in the last tear Rachael shed before she fell asleep. So just knowing all of her loved ones were safe, calmed her. But she was not ready or able to go to sleep, not when there was a demonic force making its way towards her house.

As soon as she knew Madison was asleep, she got up and tiptoed over to the crib to check on Rachael. Her little baby was sound asleep and perfectly safe. Maria looked up at Rachael's guardian angel and sweetly asked him to let nothing happen to her and she also asked if he would keep all the demons out of their room. After bowing to the angel she looked up at Mitka who was always with her and said,

"They're here," Mitka nodded.

The two of them walked into the living room where Max and Tezra were waiting. Maria petted Max and then bowed out of respect to the angel.

"Thank you for protecting my puppy," she said.

Tezra made the Saint Bernard's head rise up and down in reply. Maria's Guardian angel was close but neither Maria nor any of the Angels could see him..it was more of just sensing him and that wasn't normal. Mitka and Tezra united the question of the angel to Michael. Michael answered them both telepathically with two simple words...

"Divine Providence." That was enough to say to the angels that God's planned "Will" was sufficient. Both angels silently praised their Creator. Everyone in the house waited for the traitor to make his stand.

Bene't was bound with a tight long fiery metal chain. It was excruciatingly painful and each time he moved in any way, the pain answered back with a new torture. He was in deep deep despair. He knew that this would end his being able to feel his heart and his emotions. He knew that when he enacted this vicious crime of taking Maria's life, that anything good in him would forever be gone. He looked at her through the window of Jacob's house. He could see clearly that she was poised for battle, because she knew who and what was outside waiting for her. Bene't tried to pull against the chain but Satan himself was holding the other end, and each time he tried to get free, he was bound tighter and his pain intensified a hundred fold. The pain was tolerable to the anguish he felt knowing he would face Maria momentarily and she would know his betrayal.

Satan just laughed and laughed because now he could read the mind of his second in command, and hearing his pathetic thoughts disgusted

Lucifer. Never would he have imagined that Bene't would care about these filthy humans. He had no idea when it had begun, so he didn't know how long Bene't had been betraying him, but it answered a lot of questions he had always had since they lived in the Kingdom. At this point Satan was more interested in Bene't's punishment, than how long it had been going on...It couldn't come soon enough.

Mitka and Tezra and the Guardians were all told to stand down until directed by the Throne of God. They were going to be granted total invisibility, and they were told they were to allow anything that the demons did to Maria. Although they were alarmed, they knew that the Almighty was NEVER wrong and they trusted HIM completely.

When the Traitor and the hounds of Hell entered the house, it was clear to all of the holy angels that Bene't was there under duress and he was being forced. The big demon lowered his head and tried once again to pull at the chain. He didn't want to see that sweet, innocent face look at him. Satan read his mind and roared...

"Look at her!!"

There was no way to disobey the order, as he was bound by the hierarchy of Hell.

Bene't raised his eyes and stared at Maria. He was once again taken back by the beauty and innocence of her courageous little face. He had expected to see shock in her eyes as they entered, and if Lucifer gave him a chance, he would try to tell her that he didn't want to hurt her but he had no choice. But Maria wasn't looking at him...she was almost looking through him and her sight was intently fixed on Lucifer.

"Get out of my house!" she said as she squinted her eyes in anger.

Every entity in the house was shocked at her bravado...especially the demons who had never seen her before. All of them shifted their heads towards Satan to see how he would handle such insolence from anyone, let alone a 'female' child of Humanity.

Lucifer looked around the house and tried to see or hear the enemies he knew were present, but he had no inkling where they were hiding. He just saw the putrid child and her dog. He wanted to end her life right then and there. It took enormous restraint not to act on his desire. The only reason he was able to refrain was because he wanted Bene't to do it. He wanted to see the betrayal on the child's face...and the torment on Bene't's. He sent a ghastly image into the big demon's mind about how to murder her slowly and make it the most torturous way he could imagine.

By Divine Providence, all of the angelic beings were able to see what Lucifer had in mind. They also noted the complete anguish Bene't was feeling because he was being forced to be the murderer. Mitka and Tezra again silently posed the question to the Throne as to how they should proceed. It was made clear to them that they were to let the demon kill the child. A wave of sorrow touched all of the angels, but they also knew from centuries of obeying their God, that they would see the wisdom of HIS WILL.

Bene't was forced to move closer to her and when he did, Max immediately attacked him. The attack was short lived though because Satan threw the animal hard against the wall. The dog had the wind knocked out of him and he lay there panting. Maria was telepathically informed by Tezra, that Max was fine and she shouldn't worry.

Maria, however, wasn't worried...she was furious.

"I said, get out of my house...you don't belong here!"

Even though talking to a demon was the last thing any Human Being should ever do, Mitka was instructed that he was not to intervene in any way. So if there was a conversation between the Betrayer of the Father and this tiny little Saint, they were to allow it.

Satan moved closer to the child and made himself smaller and less threatening. Then he spoke.

"How about we play a little game. If you win, I will leave this house and never return. But if I win, you must tell me how you got into Hell and what you were doing there. Oh and if I win, he will kill you." Satan motioned towards Bene't.

Bene't might as well have been invisible to her, because Maria didn't seem to see him or even know he was there. As for the angels, every one of them wanted to tell Maria not to fall into this trap that the devil was presenting to her. But Maria had her own thoughts on the matter and decided to answer him.

"What game?" she asked as she stood her ground.

Lucifer's glee was evident. He knew he had her and at the end of this game, she would have sold her soul. He changed the tone of his voice to sound very kind and fatherly. He really shouldn't have bothered because he wasn't fooling anyone with his false sweetness, least of all Maria.

"Here's how it works. I am going to ask you a question and then you will ask me a question, or challenge me to do a task which you believe is impossible for me. If I can't answer your question or complete your task, then you win...if I can answer it, I win and you die." Satan said in a soft demeaning voice.

Maria didn't even hesitate, "Ask me."

All the supernatural beings in the room were stunned by her swift response. The demons were shocked because she showed no fear of Lucifer. They had only seen a few humans throughout history, who were that courageous. The angels were petrified because they knew that Satan didn't lose THIS particular game, and the child was no match for him. And Bene't knew that at the end of the questions, regardless of who the victor was, Maria would die at his hands.

Lucifer started to wring his talons in anticipation of the child's soul being under his control for eternity. He started to speak.

"Do you know who I am?" he asked Maria softly.

Maria answered in a strong forceful voice, beyond her years and completely void of any softness.

"The Betrayer of My Father."

Satan was taken aback that she had called HIS Father, HER Father. This child had no claim on the first person of the Trinity!! Nothing about her deserved to even KNOW about HIM, let alone call Him FATHER! If it were possible, her comment made him loathe her even more, and already he was concocting the punishments he would heap upon her in Hell.

"No," Satan condescended, "I am the first born of MY Father. I am the first creation and I am the most beautiful of all of HIS creatures. I am the wisest of all HIS creatures. I am the strongest of all HIS creation. I am all knowing. I am the crown Prince of Heaven and the only rightful heir to HIS throne. There is nothing I can not do!"

When Lucifer finished he looked at Maria for some kind of response but she only answered with her eyes, as she rolled them in boredom. She waited for him to speak again because she didn't see any need to respond to his lies. He had not expected for her to dismiss him, or humiliate him in front of the other demons. His hate raged on, but he kept his composure long enough to trap her.

"I told you that there is nothing I can't do...and it's true. I have become stronger than MY FATHER. If it were not true, why isn't HE here rescuing you?" Maria just continued to glare at him.

"Is THAT your question?" she asked angrily.

"Oh how I will suffer you when you become mine," Lucifer thought as he stared at the rancid child.

"No, my question is just this...since I am invincible and can do anything, can you challenge me with a task that you think I can't do? Once I accomplish what you ask of me you will lose, and I will take you immediately with me to Hell." Lucifer had lost patience with the human child and it was evident by how he spat the question at her that he could no longer mask his hatred.

Maria looked down when she was thinking of what to ask him... when it hit her. There was only one thing that she knew of that he WOULD never do or COULD ever do. All the supernatural Beings in the room were waiting with bated breath for Maria to answer. Not one of them believed Maria could find something the enemy of the Trinity wouldn't be able to accomplish. None believed she would find a task that would allow her to win this contest. All of them were surprised when a very slow smile crossed her face, as she figured out what question to ask.

Maria positioned herself so she was standing right in front of Satan. Everything about her posture showed that she was calm and fearless. She spoke each word clearly and distinctly for emphasis. She did not break eye contact with Lucifer as she spoke.

"I want you to go back to Heaven, to the time God showed you the sign in the sky of the WOMAN, and tell MY Father that you WILL SERVE HUMANITY! I want you to take back every horrible thing you and the other fallen angels have done and NEVER fall from Grace. I want you to go back and be OBEDIENT to MY Father and NEVER...EVER fall from Heaven."

Maria stood smiling triumphantly at Lucifer! She knew she had just won the game. All of the angels and demons were astounded by her challenge, because it was truly the ONE thing that the Deceiver could never do, nor would it ever occur to him to do.

Bene't was in tears and silently thanked the Father for her response. He was so relieved that he didn't need to kill her. Lucifer was in shock because he knew the child had indeed been the victor. She did what he thought impossible and found the one thing he couldn't accomplish. He was stunned and for the first time, he felt vulnerable but before he could respond to that, his thoughts were interrupted by Bene't's thoughts. After hearing Bene't "Praise the Father" he raged at him...KILL HER!!!

Instantaneously, all of the angels prayed to GOD to let them intervene, but GOD did not consent. So they changed their prayer to let the child feel no pain in her death, because they knew what was coming.

Bene't was upon her before she could blink, and he began to enact Lucifer's plan. He covered her eyes with one talon so he couldn't see her feelings of hurt, betrayal and pain. With the other hand he began to remove her skin, and within moments every muscle in her body showed. He then grabbed her intestines and began violently ripping them out of her body. He ripped out her lungs, her uterus, her kidneys and finally her heart. He did it as quickly as he could to mitigate her suffering and in less than 3 seconds it was done. He held her lifeless body in his arms and presented her to Lucifer. As he did that, Maria's Spirit left her body and that's when she finally looked at Bene't. It wasn't a look of betrayal, or anger or hatred, or even pain. It was a look of pure unconditional love. This was the nail in the coffin as Bene't begged,

"Please Father, shield mine eyes! Close thy vision to me. Have Mercy I plead!"

God looked at the Angel with a burning fire in His terrible, beautiful face.

"It is My Mercy which demands it continue...Behold!"

"Noooooo! Noooo! Father this is not my will. I will not live this existence away from THEE! I desire THY WILL...THY KINGDOM...THY DIVINE PROVIDENCE ONLY AND FOREVER" The Angel was beside himself with emotion as the Trinity showed him every... possible.... outcome... of his future, IF he had made the eternal choice to fall with Lucifer.

"My Son, My Will is to share with each of MY first born children, every possible future you can choose. I desire that each angel, from every Choir of Angels, may see and weigh every possible detail in that future. I do this out of love and to give all of thee the knowledge thou require to make thy choice. I do this because thou canst claim that thou didst not know or understand the consequences of thy actions. Every one of thee will retain, not only the knowledge of THY futures, but knowledge of each future of thine angelic brothers.

This GRACE will only be granted to MY ANGELS. I will not extend this knowledge to the children of Humanity. They will rely on Faith alone, and that will make the Love they give to Me, more valuable and pure than that of all of the angels combined. They must live blind of the complete knowledge of the Trinity, the Angels, and the creatures of the Heavenly Kingdom. Then, when their mortal life ends, the reward for that faith will be beyond measure. I now require thy choice to be made...Bene't, do ye choose Love?"

Bene't grabbed and clung to the robes of the Father and was sobbing.

"I choose THEE my Father...I choose LOVE! Never permit me to be separated from THEE, even for an instant. Hide me in THY everlasting arms. I give permission to infuse my Will with Your Divine and Eternal Will and to act only within the desires of THINE Eternal WILL."

As soon as the words were spoken, the Father pointed and said,

"So be it...Behold!"

In THIS future, the one that Bene't ultimately chose, he was back in Jacob's house...in the living room. Everything was the same minus, Bene't being there in his demonic form.

Satan was there with a hoard of demons and he watched as all of the supernatural Beings were waiting for Maria to answer the question the Traitor had asked. As she repeated her challenge, it was once again clear that Lucifer had lost the game. Bene't watched as Satan demanded Rahoul, (not Bene't) to "KILL HER!!!"

This time though, it was Maria's voice they all heard next as she beseeched, "BENE'T help me!!!!"

And then Bene't was transported into the room. He was no longer the repulsive demon that he would have been, if he had chosen to fall with Lucifer. He was once again an Angel from the Choir of the Virtues. His golden hair was shoulder length and had highlights of light dancing through it. His beautiful face was purely masculine with a strong square jaw, a straight Roman nose and a skin tone that glowed. His most remarkable features however, were his ice blue eyes; they seemed to be made of light. They didn't reflect the light, the light emanated from them and the blue color was otherworldly. Bene't was once again one of the "Shining Ones." He rose out of the floor and was the most brilliant white of all of the angels there, including the Generals. He came with such force, it felt like the little house was in the middle of an earthquake. Bene't immediately went after Satan, pushing him and all the other demons back to Hell.

During their descent, Bene't compared the life he would've led as a demon and the one he was living now as Maria's Guardian Angel. Watching the moments he would've had with Maria, if he had chosen Satan instead of the Trinity; and comparing them to the life he chose, moved his soul with such gratitude. He began watching every scene of Maria's life.

He saw himself standing in her kitchen the very first day he met her. She was staring at him and asked her mother if demons missed Heaven; and at the same time, he saw the reality of his life now. Instead of Bene't being the one in her kitchen, it was another demon, Rahoul who was the subject of the question.

The next moment he saw, was when Maria had been kidnapped by Natash and was thrown in a cage. In his demonic state, he was summoned by Natash to kill her but in his Angelic state, it was again Rahoul who was the demon summoned to kill her, and who failed his mission. It was Bene't, as her Guardian angel, who stood guard so no one could hurt her. He saw the time that the devil had been in her house, and Maria's Guardian angel chased Satan to Hell. It was then that Bene't realized that HE was Maria's Guardian angel. HE was the light no one could penetrate...HE was the one whom the other angels couldn't see. And HE was the most blessed of all creatures to have been saved by God's Mercy.

On his way back to Jacob's house he realized that all of the angels and demons would have known what he had just been shown. They had seen the alternate life choice he could have made. Lucifer knew it as well, and that brought true joy to Bene't's heart. He began to Praise God for saving him from the Hell he DIDN'T choose.

As he arrived back at the house, Mitka and Tezra had their wings wrapped around the child. Mitka and Tezra both told her how well she had battled their enemy and how proud they were of her. As soon as she saw Bene't, she reached her arms for him and asked him to pick her up. He immediately complied.

"Thank you for rescuing me Bene't. You are my very best friend," and with that Maria yawned and promptly fell asleep. Bene't looked at Mitka and Tezra with relief. Mitka was the first to speak.

"It could have been so different." All three angels smiled. Bene't was next,

"Praise be the Father, Son and Holy Spirit for Thine great Mercy shown unto me, unto all of THY children. How unbelievable that even one of our brothers would willingly choose an eternity absent of HIS great MERCY and WILL!"

All of the angels put Maria to bed and then they blessed her, baby Rachael and Madison. Bene't would never leave Maria's side. He spent all of his existence in utter gratitude for the privilege of being her Guardian. It could have been a very different night if he had not made the decision to choose LOVE. He prostrated himself to honor all the gifts showered on him by the Trinity; because of this, there was no other Angel in Heaven or Earth who was more grateful than Bene't. It would be peaceful in the house of Jacob this night.

CHAPTER EIGHTEEN...INFUSING THE WILL

When Father Zachary, Jacob, Matthew, Carl and Malaya arrived at the house of Jacob, they found the house dark, quiet and peaceful. Jacob made quick business of putting the men in the living room on the sectional couch. He made two twin beds on the couch and the men crawled in them. He didn't have a big enough bed to put Carl on so he made a palette on the ground with an air mattress for his comfort. Jacob apologized for the roughness of it, but Carl assured him that it was Heaven compared to what he was used to. He motioned to Malaya towards the restroom and told her he would get her room ready. He had every intention of moving Maria into bed with them and giving Malaya her bed, but he needn't have bothered. Maria had already made a bed on the floor next to Rachael's crib. Her bed was all turned down waiting for a guest. There was even a little piece of chocolate on the pillow. This was something Madison did every time they had guests. It made Jacob smile that she would've done this when she didn't even know that he was bringing company. Madison must have told her, he thought. "But wait, did I even tell Madison?" He was pondering the question when Malaya walked out of the bathroom wearing one of Madison's robes and nightgowns. They were a little too short on her but fit her perfectly otherwise. She held up a piece of paper and showed Jacob. It was from Maria and it said,

"Dear Malaya, Rachael said you would be coming so we put our

Mommie's clean pajamas and a robe for you to wear after you clean up. We put water on your night stand in case you want a drink. And a candy on your pillow."

Don't worry about any demons finding you here...they aren't allowed here anymore. Good night."

Jacob read the note and smiled. He was far too tired to process the meaning of it as his exhaustion had reached its limit.

"Goodnight Malaya. If you need anything please come let me know," Jacob left to see if Madison was awake and was a little sad she wasn't. He crawled into bed and fell asleep holding her.

Before Malaya got into the bed she looked down at Maria and to her surprise saw the little girl smile at her. She knelt down on the floor and smiled back,

"Well Hello there. I'm sorry if I woke you." Maria sat up and said,

"You didn't...we were waiting for you." When Malaya looked perplexed Maria nodded her head in the direction of the crib. She then quickly stood up and offered her hand to Malaya. The White Buffalo grabbed her hand and they stood above the crib. Malaya, this is my baby sister Rachael...Rachael, this is Malaya."

The baby smiled and cooed and tried hard to make words. Her eyes never left Malaya's.

"Hello you gorgeous little thing." Malaya whispered. She reached out and touched the baby's chubby cheek. Rachael smiled and kicked her little legs and arms in reply. Malaya turned her head towards Maria and inquired,

"Did you say in your note that Rachael told you I would be coming to your house tonight?"

Maria smiled and looked at her little sister,

"Yes, she knows all about you."

Malaya let the baby grab her finger as she continued speaking with

Maria.

"How does she know all about me?"

Maria grabbed Rachael's other hand as she explained.

"When Rachael was born, God asked her if she would suffer for you... if she would help you by suffering. God showed her your face and showed her many things about what you were born to do. He told her that many demons would be attacking you to keep you from doing what God wanted you to do. He showed her that her suffering, linked with Jesus' suffering, saves people's souls. Rachael told God that she would suffer to help you. My mommy doesn't understand the promise Rachael made with God about you. She keeps trying to fix Rachael...but that isn't what Rachael wants. She wants to be your helper for her whole life." Maria finished by moving her long curly hair away from her face using her entire arm.

Malaya looked at Maria and then at Rachael in complete humility. She had been taught an enormous amount of information about God in her lifetime, but this took her completely by surprise. She never would have dreamed that a little baby she didn't even know, would be willingly suffering for her. She grabbed her heart and tears fell from her eyes as she felt unworthy of the effort from the newborn. She was touched beyond belief. But something occurred to her and she asked Maria.

"How does baby Rachael tell you these things Maria?"

Maria yawned and then replied, "You can see everything Rachael is thinking inside of her teardrops. It's like a little movie in there. Father Zachary told me and Daddy that you talk through your eyes too..so Rachael is like you."

Malaya looked at Rachael and locked eyes with her. Rachael watched as Malaya showed the infant all about her life from the moments before she was conceived and placed into her mother's womb. Then Rachael shared the moment that the Father asked Rachael if she would suffer for Malaya. Then Malaya saw all the moments when Rachael's pain made a path for Malaya to win battles with the devil and his minions.

"Oh thank you, sweet baby. I praise God for your existence. I praise God for your willingness to suffer on my behalf. How blessed I am to be helped by you. Thank you for the sacrifice you are giving to me with your life of pain. You are filled with so much love. I will cherish you always."

Malaya reached down and kissed Rachael on her cheek. Rachael cooed and kicked and smiled in response. Malaya thanked Maria for allowing her to sleep in her bed and then all three of them went to sleep.

In the morning, when Madison woke up, she had no idea how full her little house had become. She tiptoed through the living room and went in the tiny kitchen and made some coffee and started making breakfast. From the looks of the man sleeping on the floor, she would need to make a lot of food. As soon as the smell of brewed coffee was in the air her guests began waking up. Father Zachary was the first one to join her in the kitchen. She hugged him and told him to sit down and then brought him a cup of coffee.

"It looks like you brought me a house full!" Madison stated.

Father Zachary chuckled and answered, "God has been very good to us, Madison. I'm anxious for you to meet Malaya...and Carl."

Madison joined him at the table and asked, "Is she okay Father? And how is Matthew?"

The little priest shook his head, "They are both fine Madison. We have a story for you as I can only assume you have one for us."

Madison was getting ready to tell him all about Rachael being able to communicate through her tears when Jacob and Matthew entered the kitchen. She ran to Jacob and kissed him and told him she loved him and was so happy he was home. Then she turned to Matthew and went to hug him. After the brief hug Matthew held her at arm's length and looked at her.

"Maddie, I'm sorry about ditching you guys. I've kind of been in my own private Hell. I hope you can forgive me."

"Of course I do! Just don't ever do that to me again or I'll hunt you down!" Madison laughed. And then they were interrupted by Carl walking into the kitchen. Jacob immediately introduced them and invited Carl to sit down for breakfast. A few minutes later Malaya walked into the kitchen holding Rachael with Maria in tow. Madison was stunned by the beauty of the Indian woman. Even with no makeup she put any super model to shame. Madison reached out and hugged her and said,

"Welcome Malaya! We are so happy you're here."

Malaya was overwhelmed with the way this family, who had never met her, was treating her like she was family. She noticed Carl must have felt the same way and she was humbled to God the Father, for bringing all of them into her life.

They all ate their fill of breakfast and made plans. Malaya knew that the enemies of God would now be looking for her and Carl. After a long discussion they decided that the last place they would look for her, would be her home on the Mesa in New Mexico. Malaya had not returned since her birth but she knew that is where she must go. Whatever future God had for her, it would be in the heart of the Pueblo Indian people. Since all of the airports, train stations and buses would be watched, they decided that Father Zachary and Matthew would drive them there.

Before they left, Father Zachary took Rachael and Maria out on the porch. He had so many questions for the little girl. Maria told him everything about her, about Rachael and about her battle with demons and the devil. To say that the priest was stunned would be a gross understatement. He prayed over both of the girls and asked for special protection for the entire family. He gave his phone number to Maria and asked her to call him any time anything happened. She promised she would. He told her that she also needed to tell everything to her mother and father. And with that, Father Zachary, Matthew, Carl and the White Buffalo left the house of Jacob.

EPILOGUE 1

Bene't was overwhelmed with all his possible futures. When the Father was finished showing him, as well as all the other Angels all their possible futures, there was a brief pause in Heaven. Each Angel weighed the things they had been shown and they all had a decision to make.

Bene't looked around at all the first Children of God and watched as a very clear line was being drawn. The "Good" Angels all chose The Trinity and gave their fiats "Serve Humanity." Each one was as powerfully affected by the experience as Bene't had been.

On the other side, the "Bad Angels" made the incredible choice to still believe that despite what they had been shown, they could somehow best the Trinity.

Bene't looked at Lucifer. Even after being shown the impossibility of his desire to raise a throne for himself that would be above the Trinity, his "PRIDE" would win the contest against his intellect. He made it clear he was choosing to battle Heaven.

Lucifer caught Bene't looking at him and his eyes narrowed. Bene't held his gaze and there was a message being silently spoken between the two.

"Traitor!!!!" Lucifer accused. "I will destroy you first!"

Bene't was not impressed by the threat and silently spoke his own message.

"I will meet you in battle... for every second of eternity! I will stop at nothing to defend The Trinity, The Christ and His Holy Mary and His Holy Church!"

The two Angels were unconsciously moving towards each other when the booming voice of Michael broke the silence.

"WHO IS LIKE UNTO GOD? MAY THE LORD REBUKE YOU I HUMBLY PRAY!"

The Great Archangel, by the power of God, thrust Lucifer and the other Fallen Angels into Hell. All the good Angels watched as the Fallen Angels morphed into the beasts they had chosen to become.

Bene't watched as Lucifer changed from the most beautiful Angel ever created into the terrible dragon that represented his true character.

Bene't fell upon his knees and began to Praise the Trinity for showing him each choice and thanked the Trinity for their Divine Love in extending such Mercy.

A great light came from the Trinity's Throne and filled all the Angels who remained with a new wave of Grace and Peace.

EPILOGUE 2

Tara watched as the crosses came closer to her. She could not take her eyes off of them. Jesus continued his explanation,

"These are the ones who took My command to their hearts. When I said 'Take up your cross and follow Me', these are the souls who wanted to emulate Me as closely as possible. My Father saw their love and granted that they would share My cup of sorrow and suffering. Each of these souls chose this life BEFORE they began their earthly journey. It is the greatest honor any human Soul can obtain... to be chosen to suffer to save Souls. These Soul's spend and consume themselves for Souls willingly.

In life, these are the Souls to whom other humans attribute My 'unloving' heart. They will say of Me, 'How can a loving God allow this person or that person to suffer? Why does He allow extreme poverty or famine or abuse? I don't want any part of a God like that!" Jesus' countenance changed to one of sadness and Tara put her hand in His to comfort her Savior. She could feel the pain He felt of being misunderstood by Humanity. Then the King of Kings continued,

"It is the greatest irony that these men do not understand that each of these Souls chose this life, out of their love for ME. And because of that the Father has placed them above all the Saints and Angels in Heaven. These Souls were selfless in every way and had just one desire and that was to share in the Redemption of Man. They accomplished this through linking the pain they felt... with the corresponding pain I felt during MY PASSION. They made their pain a prayer and offered it up for souls who do not believe in God; or to suffer alongside another soul, to assist them in carrying their burden. They are not afraid to suffer! They have chosen to give their entire lives as gifts back to the Father. They put every dream, desire and ambition down and exchanged them for whatever the Will of the Father has planned for their lives. These beings are the greatest examples of Love."

Tara took Jesus' hand and kissed it and then she rose and began walking towards the Crosses, along with Him. She scanned the faces of these perfect Saints until she found the one she sought and when she found her, Tara had the great privilege of being the first to welcome Rachael into her Heavenly home.

COMING SOON: THE HOLY SPIRIT GENERATION

ACKNOWLEDGEMENTS

The first person I want to thank is my husband, Stacy. Oh how we have learned to suffer to save Souls. To all of my children for their support in this work. I would like to thank my youngest daughter Shae for the book's cover and for somehow picking out of my brain the exact way I see Angels and Demons. I also want to thank my middle daughter, Myia, for providing some very important content to the story that is so personal to her. I want to thank my oldest daughter, Aubrii who was my first inspiration for Maria. I want to thank my sons Levi and Seth for being the inspirations for two of my new characters in "The Holy Spirit Generation"; I thank my son-in-law Max and my grand-daughter Makayla for the same reasons.

I thank my parents for the love and instruction that has made up so much of who I am today. My brothers Sean and Joe for their help in my edits, and enormous patience for the things I still don't know. My brother, Jimmy for giving me character references which will be noted in the final book of the series. I want to thank my sister Caroline for all she does for our family, our extended family and for answering the call to the amazing life in God she is leading. (Go get 'em Lazarus)

I want to thank my best friend Priscilla who is my soul mate in our walk with Jesus. You have never left me alone and are a constant source of support and understanding.

I want to thank Joy for your wisdom...Audrey for the laughter...Ellen for the soft place to be myself...and Amy for renewing the friendship of my youth...Kelly B and Cathy C for being there for me and my family. To my other girlfriends, Glenda, Mary Grace, Teresa W, Mary W, Susie B and Mary Elizabeth. We may not see eachother often but you are always in my thoughts and prayers.

To my new friends, Kelly T, Candy, Linda, Alma, Chris, Maria, Maureen and Marcy. I am looking forward to seeing what God has in store for all of us.

I also want to thank my oldest sister Beth, who passed away in 2015. You are so missed and so very loved. I know you are up there bossing everyone around and directing the lives of your whole family on earth. This book is dedicated to you. I miss you Betsy!

I want to thank Father Tony again as my inspiration for Father Zachary. I don't have to see you or talk to you very much because God linked our souls years ago, and serving you through prayer has been one of the biggest privileges of my life. Buckle up, Padre, because the storm is coming.

I also want to thank Father Ben for his courage in standing up for the truths of God and for his friendship.

I want to say to my dear friend and partner in the Kingdom, Deacon Ralph. I treasure every time God has put us on the battlefield to fight in His Name and for His Divine Will. I am so thankful for you and your advice!

And most importantly I want to thank the Trinity who are solely responsible for the book's content. Thank YOU for all I was...am...and will be. My only desire in life is to make YOU proud..may only YOUR WILL be done in my life...not mine.

And finally to the Blessed Virgin Mary, Our Mother and Queen. You have been the greatest teacher of my life and I would never have known Jesus so deeply if you hadn't taught me. I love you, MAMA!

God Bless You all,
Catherine Anne

CONTACT INFO- booksbycanne@aol.com

Made in the USA
Middletown, DE
25 May 2021

40421264R00146